KNOWER
OF THE
FIELD

PHALGUN PRATIVADI

World Castle Publishing, LLC
Pensacola, Florida
Copyright © 2025 Phalgun Prativadi
Hardback ISBN: 9798313794631
Paperback ISBN: 9798891263635
eBook ISBN: 9798891263642
First Edition World Castle Publishing, LLC, April 14, 2025
http://www.worldcastlepublishing.com

Cover: Cover Designs by Karen
Editor: Karen Fuller

PART ONE
BEING AND BECOMING

CHAPTER ONE

As Arya Krish sat and faced the new incoming class of physicians at the Institute, his eyes looked past them. His mind was somewhere else. Sunshine streamed in through the tall windows to his left, illuminating the large room with long beams of light, and glistened over the polished oak floors. The physicians sat at their individual wooden desks wearing white coats, and their arms rested on their desks, palms down. Fact was, they could have sat any way they wanted. They all happened to choose to sit the same way.

After all, we are the sum of our choices. He sat and stared past the physicians, thinking back to the countless times he'd said that to others—friends, family, colleagues, patients. He tried to remember the last time somebody said it to him and thought of his father, who'd told him that all the time when he was alive. Krish sighed and looked down. He also wore his white coat, and his hands rested on the desk. Under them was an envelope, already opened. He had a choice now, too. At 36 years old, a culmination of choices led to this one—a choice that would affect so much, even the dozen physicians who faced him. Their day-to-day lives might not change noticeably, and they would all remain oblivious, like brilliant pawns. It would certainly affect him, however, and send him on a trajectory toward a confrontation with the very people with whom he would form an alliance. All he had to do was sign the papers in the envelope.

The physicians sat silently, patiently waiting for him to address them. Krish's hand quivered as he opened the envelope and picked up the pen. *We are the sum of our choices*, he thought again. *It is the process of being and becoming*. He signed the papers, put them back in the envelope swiftly, and stood. The physicians remained still and watched intently. Arya noticed a beam of sunshine that fell over his desk as his tall frame fell in the bright light, and made his white coat almost glow.

"Welcome to Beacon Medical Institute," he said. Krish's smile was genuine. After all, he had hand-picked them. "Completing a five-year premedical and medical combination program at the top of your respective classes makes you the young cream of an elite crop and sets you all apart from the rest who completed similar programs. They will all undoubtedly have exemplary careers, as brilliant as they are and wherever they may be. But you are here instead of them because you shine brighter in our eyes. You have already demonstrated a service to humanity that is above and beyond the tepid empathy and compassion that prevails in society. For that, I salute you, and I invite you to join a dedicated effort to wield real power for the greater good."

Krish knew that these young physicians understood exactly what he was talking about as they looked at him in visible awe. He knew the words energized every single one of them and stirred the bright core of potential and capability he referenced. These traits did shine brighter in these select few. Actually, Krish had said the exact same words to others before them, but that didn't matter at this moment. They didn't know that, and his words affected them like rare and refreshing fruit. He had told a few others the same words in identical moments; they were true then, and they were true in that moment. The pedigree was few and proud.

He picked up the envelope and continued to scan the faces behind the desks. A moment of stillness and silence filled the sunlit room. The windows were tall and wide and had anyone turned toward them, they would have seen an impressive view.

The Institute's architecture was most certainly inspired by the surrounding landmarks and commanded the visual reverence that validated its location near the monuments and historic buildings. Arya Krish abruptly turned and walked toward the door. He paused for a moment and looked back at the physicians, who were waiting for him to continue, before leaving the room and closing the door behind him.

As he stood in the large hallway, he was aware of the man to his right, further down the hallway, hidden in the shadows between the beams of sunlight. Though Krish continued to look straight, he knew the man in the black suit. In fact, Krish had become accustomed to his presence as of late. Turning to his right, Krish watched the man go through a door on the other side of the hall. He knew that the man was waiting for Krish to deliver the envelope to him. However, Krish would return it in person to someone else.

Krish walked down the other hallway toward the board room. He trusted some people in the Institute, to an extent, and could turn to them for help if needed. But he had unconditional loyalty from only one person. He was going to meet Jay Asher.

His mind wandered as he walked down the sprawling hallway. The hall to the board room was illuminated by the bright sunshine that streamed in from the tall panoramic windows. These windows rose all the way to the 40-foot-tall ceilings. The large framed photographs and paintings on the vast inside wall were otherwise reminiscent of a grand walkway in a Victorian castle. Krish was at a significant crossroads as he reflected on the circumstances and the history that led to his tension.

Beacon Medical Institute occupied an exclusive part of the historic Foggy Bottom area of Washington, DC. It started as a small but highly sophisticated private medical practice of five physicians, all pioneers in several fields of biomedical science. Three of them, including Krish's father, were posthumously awarded the Nobel Prize in Medicine for what it was worth. They had developed the first commercially viable use of biosynthetic human tissue transplantation. With their discovery, organs were cultured in labs but were tailor-made for their recipients. This virtually eliminated transplant rejection and saved countless lives. They discovered, designed, and, after starting the private practice, implemented this technology successfully, cost-effectively, and independently for the first time. Through the work of the brightest minds of a generation, it became rare for people in the United States to die because they could not get a transplant. The impact had ripple effects at many levels on a national scale. Beacon's philanthropy, through its subsequent great wealth, eventually made it an internationally renowned institute.

The original five physicians started their practice with the combined wealth they had accumulated while working for the A1 Group. That organization had paid its foreign scientists exceedingly luxurious salaries for their brilliance. A1 Group also took their life's work, their individual freedom, and, in some cases, their lives. Arya Krish was in college when his father first told him, "We are all the sum of our choices." Later, Krish realized that everything was revealed to him in that conversation.

A1 Group began to fall around that time. Soon after, his father died in a car crash. Two of the other original five physicians were in the car also and shared the same fate. Shortly after that, the A1 Group fell apart, and the practice was established. A1 Group crumbled. But as it turned out, it was only a prototype of the next incarnation. The new practice soared to unimaginable heights and, in the future, became an iconic American institution with global reach and impact far beyond organ transplantation. His father's remaining original colleagues had continued their work after the others died, and by the time Arya Krish took up the reigns, Beacon Medical Institute was a global entity.

Eventually, it accumulated resources that allowed it to expand its influence beyond medicine, through humanitarian service on an international scale that gave Beacon admittedly unanticipated power and influence in media, technology, and politics. All of it came at a price, however.

Krish almost walked past the board room before he snapped out of his ruminations. He felt for the envelope in his pocket, opened the large oak doors, and walked into the board room. The bustling sounds from the hallway faded into silence as the door closed behind him. He turned and scanned the other end of the large room, where Jay Asher stood and looked out the window. Jay wore a navy blue pinstripe suit, and his broad shoulders swayed slightly. His face was contemplative, with pursed lips and slightly furrowed eyebrows.

Krish remained on the other side of the room but walked to the window near Asher and looked outside. No one else was in the room, and their voices echoed as they spoke.

"There's this idea," Asher said, "that if a vastly more advanced society were to discover a primitive society oblivious to their existence, the advanced society should not interfere in any way with the natural existence and fate of that primitive society. That would include, for example, some catastrophic event such as a natural disaster or epidemic that the advanced society would be capable of preventing."

"I've seen enough re-runs to know what the prime directive concept is," Krish said.

"Yes." Asher nodded slightly, almost in approval and praise, as if Krish had said something profound. "I think that's a pretty shady concept. Don't you?"

Krish smiled. "It makes me raise an eyebrow, I admit."

Asher snorted out a laugh and turned toward Krish. "So, what's going on?"

Krish walked toward the long wooden table that stretched

across the room and sat at the head of it. Asher remained standing where he was. "We've been friends since middle school, Jay, and the only reason I continue to involve you in all this is you're like a brother —"

"Skip the preamble. I'm pretty sure it's too late, anyhow," Asher said.

In the silence and anticipation that followed, Krish tried to focus on his intent and plan as he marshaled his thoughts. "We were already friends for eight or nine years, huh, when my dad died?" Krish asked.

Asher's face became solemn. He walked over to the table and sat next to Krish. "Yeah, that happened at the start of junior year in college, right? You guys had just gotten back from visiting India," Asher said.

"Yeah. We went on that pilgrimage to the Himalayas."

"Yes, the Himalayas. You've told me this before. Recently, in fact."

"It's 'himaaa-la-ya', not 'him-a-laay-ya'."

"Yes, you've told me that before, too."

"Then you already know it's a Sanskrit word, and the meaning changes if you pronounce it differently. It means 'abode of snow' if you say it right, and 'destruction of snow' otherwise," Krish said, slightly irritated.

"Alright, take it easy, OK?" Asher looked at him sternly. "What's the matter with you? You've been preoccupied for weeks now, talking about the same weird stuff. Tell me what's going on."

Arya Krish handed the envelope to Asher. He sat silently as Asher removed the pages and scanned them. Asher perused the papers more and more intently, then put them on the table without saying anything.

"You know my father worked for A1 Group," Krish said. "That's where he and his colleagues began and advanced their work on gene manipulation and biosynthesis. They were on such a tight leash that the A1 Group secretly implanted them with some sort of chip and monitored their every movement, even at home. When the A1 Group fell, my dad and his colleagues took back the work stolen from them and continued it on their own, forming the original practice. Well, I've recently discovered that those A1 Group guys, the ones who didn't go to prison, resurrected the company. Now it's called Alpha Corp."

"So, Alpha Corp is a spinoff of A1 Group?"

"One of the co-founders of A1 Group is the Director at Alpha Corp."

"Well, I remember your father worked for the A1 Group and all the news and whatnot when they were brought down. From what you're describing, they seem to have been quite sinister."

"They killed my father and two of his friends."

Asher had watched Krish intently the entire time. He sat back and rubbed his eyes. "You know, it's been a long time since you've brought that up," he said. "I never understood; it seems outlandish, in fact. I thought it was part of your grieving process, but you hadn't mentioned the other stuff until now."

"Alpha Corp picked up where A1 Group left off. They may not blatantly oppress or murder, at least as far as we know, but they have blood on their hands."

"And what is this contract supposed to accomplish?" Asher asked. He held up the papers. "Beacon is formally merging with Alpha Corp?"

"It gets us into the lion's den."

"But this is nothing new. Alpha Corp is a healthcare industry juggernaut. They have their hand in everything in the healthcare sector and beyond. We've been dealing with them for a long time in the work we do. I don't have to remind you of the run-ins we've had with them."

"We are entangled with them on many levels. I don't deny it as a means to an end," Krish said. "But this contract would merge us essentially, get us inside."

"To what end?" Asher asked. Arya Krish stood and started to pace. "You say they have blood on their hands. Where does that leave us? Without them, Beacon wouldn't be what it is now."

"I realize that. I've been asking myself that for a long time now. What does it make us?" Krish said.

Krish knew better than anyone the Institute's reliance on Alpha Corp's resources, especially early on for the drugs that sustained the first-generation bio-organs *in vivo*. In fact, they had a symbiotic relationship with an entity that embodied the exact opposite of what Beacon Medical Institute represented. But that relationship allowed Beacon to accomplish things beyond a scope they could have hoped for otherwise. Meanwhile, Alpha Corp became a monster that took a stranglehold of the healthcare industry and, consequently, the well-being of the people at large.

"In the real world, you must get your hands dirty sometimes to get things done, including noble things. I don't see how signing a contract balances that scale. You say it's a way into the lion's den? You're also giving them a seat at our table. This sounds like another means to an end. So, I ask again, to what end? Because this seems to be more of a personal vendetta than social justice."

Arya Krish walked to the other side of the room. He stood where Asher had been when he had first entered and looked out the window. Asher stood and walked over to him.

"Maybe it's about both," Krish said.

"Well, it sounds like you plan on slaying a monster."

"Do you have to become a monster to slay a monster?"

"The wise have always said you must know your enemy to defeat them.

"Maybe knowing is becoming."

"Takes one to know one, perhaps."

"Well, I wonder what we've become up to this point," Krish said. He picked up the papers Asher left on the table and walked toward the door. "Maybe we're already there."

"Well, let me know what needs to be done. We will make it happen."

Krish stopped but kept his back turned to Jay Asher. "When the time comes, my friend, you can count on it," Krish said as he left. As he walked on the skywalk toward the Research and Development lab, his mind was four years in the past, shortly after his 32nd birthday.

CHAPTER TWO

Four years in the past. Arya Krish sat up, straightened his seat, and leaned toward the window. His white polo shirt and gray cotton cargo pants had survived the flight in good condition, but his flip-flops were off, lost somewhere in the crevices near his seat. It was still at least an hour before sunrise, and the city lights twinkled below. As the plane descended, he watched the few cars on the streets and the headlights that were shining down the immediate road ahead of them. From this distance, it was amusing to see how little of the road they illuminated. It reminded him of ants scurrying in an ant farm.

After the plane taxied to the terminal and the signal was given, he watched while everyone rushed to get up and gather their luggage. As always, a few didn't bother to wait for the signal, and as always, their initiative bore no reward. They waited to be herded out like everyone else. He casually scanned the faces. Some showed travel fatigue, while others appeared remarkably fresh. After groping under his seat, he found his flip-flops, put them on, and stood to join the creeping line. He quickly got his backpack from the compartment above.

Even though the loading dock between the plane and terminal gate was enclosed, he felt the humid air as he stepped off and the smell that, if nothing else, let him know he was in some other part of the world. These were familiar sensations every time he landed in Bengaluru, India.

By the time he made it outside after customs, the pre-dawn twilight had crept over the horizon. As he stepped out, the humid breeze caught hold, and as it left, he felt the dense air and heard nightingales nearby and off in the distance. Tight rows of taxi cabs were lined up just outside. Next to them, a few cars came and went, some with headlights still on, as people met their arriving parties, greeted them fondly, and socialized a little before heading toward the parked cars.

Krish stood for a while outside the airport as he remembered the many prior occasions he'd arrived in a similar fashion. He had fond memories of his family being received the same way by his relatives. While Krish was growing up, this was a frequent summer destination, yet it all somehow felt new and unsettling to him in that moment.

His driver recognized him and ran over. After taking his luggage cart, the driver quickly pushed it toward a black sedan and loaded it as Krish walked toward the back passenger door. The driver stopped what he was doing and opened the door for him. Krish sat and opened the travel wallet he wore across his chest. He took out some cash, put it in his pocket, and zipped the wallet back up. The driver sat in front and started the car. "To the house, sir?" he asked, in the local Kannada language.

"Yes, for a couple of hours. Then to VC Farm," said Arya Krish, also in Kannada. He rolled the window down, felt the breeze on his face, and looked out at the world, taking it all in with his senses as they drove along. As they merged onto the overpass, the sun was over the horizon, and he saw the outskirts of the city clear to the horizon, with mega-cranes scattered over the landscape, resting next to half-built, high-rise apartment complexes like sleeping dinosaurs. As they later passed through the main streets of the inner city, he caught glimpses of life beginning its day. Vendors opened their doors. Some swept in front of their store or house. Roadside breakfast stands slowly gathered a crowd of people who stood as they ate or sipped coffee. The occasional bullock cart was interspersed among the growing volume of cars, buses, motorcycles, auto-rickshaws, and bicycles.

His eyes remained transfixed on the world as he passed by it, and he scanned the faces during traffic lights. Some locked eyes with him in that fleeting moment, making him feel as if they tried to tell him something for an instant. As they entered the residential areas, the streets grew quieter. Children in school uniforms walked in small groups, and the car passed by a few vendors on bicycles, calling out their merchandise in an almost lyrical fashion as the car approached the last house on the road. He got out and looked up at the three-story, manor-like home. The driver unloaded the suitcases and brought them up to the house while Krish unlocked the front door. The house had been prepared for his arrival. The tarp that had covered the furniture was folded and placed in the corner of the large foyer. He passed through into the large hall, with stone floors and ceilings that rose 25 feet. He looked up at the portraits that hung high above of his grandparents and his late parents. Fresh wreaths of flowers hung on them.

Upstairs, the driver passed through the hallway balcony with the suitcases. As he went up the staircase, Krish stopped in the hallway and looked down at the portraits and the large living room below. The driver came out of the bedroom. Krish handed him a generous tip and asked him to wait outside while he got cleaned up and changed. He came down about an hour later wearing a blue dress shirt and gray pants. As he stepped outside, he put on sunglasses, and the driver opened the door for him as he climbed into the sedan. Krish slept during much of the three-hour journey to VC Farm.

The midday sun bore down intensely as they followed the dirt roads and entered the small village. The car stopped next to the construction site of the school. Krish got out of the car, watched it drive away, and looked toward the construction site. A large crew was at work, and he watched the construction vehicles come and go. He looked down both sides of the road at the dozen or so concrete huts lining it. Each thatched roof hut was essentially one room with a kitchen in the corner, from what he remembered of the first time he was here, more than 15 years ago. A few large trees were between the huts, and the surrounding landscape was farmland with a single main road passing through in the distance. The breeze kicked up dust, slightly obscuring the few passers-by and wandering animals.

Eventually, the project manager emerged from the site and approached him. "Hello, Dr. Krish. It's very nice to see you again."

"Good afternoon, Praveen. It's good to see you, too. I'm glad I was finally able to make it on site."

"Yes. It seems we've been in constant long-distance communication, but it cannot replace a meeting in person."

Arya Krish smiled. "But I'm disappointed about the dirt roads, Praveen." He looked around and gestured down the road. "We talked about this. It should have been paved weeks ago, right?"

"It stalled again, Dr. Krish, after the main road was paved. Local authorities are still sitting on approvals."

"All they have to do is sign off on it. We're bearing the entire cost, including the government labor. What's the delay?"

"I'm pretty sure they're holding out for more of a share, sir." Praveen sounded sheepish.

Krish looked up at the sky in exasperation. "We've already paid their 'fees.' What more do they want?"

"As I've described before, Dr. Krish, these local government administrators are expecting more black money from you," Praveen said.

A certain nonchalance in his tone irritated Krish. It wasn't any fault of his, but Praveen seemed all too comfortable with the idea of local government officials shamelessly demanding money under the table from a purely humanitarian project. Rather, Praveen seemed resigned to the normalcy of it. Krish took a few steps toward the new school and looked around. This was the third time he had come here, and apart from this construction site, it didn't seem to have changed much. He felt he was on some mid-20th century movie set.

"The first time I came here was with my family when I was a teenager," he said. "My mother wanted to show me where she spent a part of her childhood. We met with some of the locals, and they invited us into their homes. We showed up from America looking like people out of this world, and they took us in like family. They shed tears with my mother as she recalled her experiences as a child there. She expressed a solemn pride in her humble origins, and they felt proud that one of their own had come back to reflect and pay respect. My father vowed to the elders that he would bring opportunities to everyone here and improve their quality of life while preserving their identity and tradition. That stayed in my memory, and it's been three years since I came back and met you for the first time to plan this development project." Krish turned around and looked at Praveen. "It's taking far too long. What are our options?"

"If you don't pay them, Dr. Krish, I'm concerned they simply won't act."

Krish walked toward him. "What are our alternatives? Can we convince them somehow? Do we turn to some other authorities?"

Praveen shook his head. "I have not brought it up to you yet, Dr. Krish, but I would suggest hiring some help."

"What, like lawyers? We've got plenty of those."

"No, sir. I'm talking about people who will use a brand of leverage to pressure the building authority officer to approve our plans."

Krish became silent, put his hands in his pockets, and slowly walked past Praveen down the road a distance. Praveen was suggesting they hire some muscle to lean on the local government officer. Arya Krish was uncomfortable enough dealing with these so-called fees and blatant bribery on the mainstream level. This would be venturing into a more sinister realm. He thought it a silly prospect and couldn't help but wonder, to what end? He had what he thought to be a straightforward vision. Beacon had the resources, which in most cases meant the money, to make it happen. All they needed was the necessary people to help or get out of the way. He expected people to approach him with hands held out; he regarded that as the price of doing business. But now he had to choose whether to become something else, and it somehow felt like he was descending to a level beneath his vision and intent.

Praveen watched Krish pace back and forth. Squinting hard in the glaring sun, Praveen's middle-aged features were apparent around his eyes and chin. His skin was dark and leathery, and he wore a tattered, short-sleeve, button-tee and old dull gray pants. Praveen had great admiration for young Dr. Krish's sincerity and enthusiasm. He'd never seen anyone work so hard without a single fiber of selfishness or ulterior motive.

Praveen remembered the first time they met. Arya Krish had seemed much younger then, and he'd exuded an energy and confidence that was contagious to those around him. Praveen recalled his bright eyes and sharp wit. He was instantly likable, always smiling, and made people want to help him. That drove the progress and success of the earlier projects. Krish initially seemed to be much more involved in developing the smaller local villages, bringing infrastructure—water, sanitation, electricity, schools, roads, and medical clinics. These few projects Praveen had been involved with were having a regional effect. It was more than charity. It was humanitarian aid on a scale that Praveen had never witnessed before. However, that meant the inevitable contact with far-reaching tentacles of bureaucracy and corruption. Praveen's life experience left him apathetic and complicit, content with it as the only available means to an end, namely his sustenance and livelihood. The daily grind had numbed his conscience, made it a luxury he couldn't afford anyway. Praveen was an intelligent and perceptive man, and he recognized the choice wrestling with Dr. Krish. He saw it on Krish's face as the dilemma turned over in his mind.

"Dr. Krish, in order to live in the jungle among the beasts, you either need a thick hide and horns to survive in their midst or fangs and claws to fight them with."

"I want to meet the building authority," Krish said. He turned around and walked back quickly. He took out his cell phone to alert the driver.

They drove through the rural country before they reached the nearby small town. Quickly, the quiet landscape was replaced by the bustle of the crowded streets. Krish observed the visual spectacle of a town that was growing too fast to keep up with itself. He remembered describing India to Asher as a land of contradictions and extremes juxtaposed; sprawling bungalows down the road from huts and tents, tall shopping malls next to local shack vendors, ancient temples next to fast-food chains. Horns blared as luxury cars drove alongside bullock carts and bicycles, and a cow stood in front of the glass-enclosed electronics store. It was different back home in the States; the extremes of social inequality were quite conveniently segregated from one another.

They passed the town square and pulled up in front of an old office building that housed the local government offices. Clouds had swept in as he got out of the car and walked inside. It was dark in the lobby, as little light made it through the dirty windows. Ceiling fans were spinning overhead, and no one else was around other than a woman at the reception desk. As Krish approached, she didn't bother to look up from her magazine.

"I'm looking for the District Building Authority office," Krish said.

"Third floor," she said, still looking down.

Krish stared at her for a moment, then walked toward the ancient elevator.

"Elevator broken," the woman said behind him.

He looked back at her in mild contempt, then turned toward the stairs. Krish walked up and passed through a doorway, then stood for a moment in front of a large room with rows of desks and cubicles. Phones rang, and people chatted, but no one took any notice of him. He walked past them down the middle aisle toward the back, where he saw a door labeled 'Commissioner.' He knocked once and opened the door without waiting. It was a small office with a musty odor.

Small piles of papers and file folders were scattered on the floor and on the single desk facing him. Dim light came through the windows behind the desk, casting a shadow over the man behind it. He sat and stared at Krish while chewing his lunch with his mouth open. He had a round face with a shameless, greasy comb-over, beady, tired eyes, and a thick mustache. He wore several gold rings, a gold watch, and a necklace. The initial look of surprise turned to a petulant scowl as Krish walked in and stood before him.

"Who are you? I don't have any appointments now," the man said.

Krish glanced down at the name plaque on his desk. "Mr. Murthy, my name is Arya Krish. I represent Beacon Medical Institute from the U.S., and I'm here about the VC Farm development project." He didn't bother to extend his hand toward Murthy.

"You'll have to come back with an appointment," Murthy said dismissively and resumed eating.

Krish stared at Murthy with a subtle look of disgust. He felt he was watching a pig at the trough. "Well, I'm only in the country a short while. We've filed all the appropriate applications and paid all the fees. I wanted to clarify what else you need from us to proceed."

Murthy shook his head as he bent over his food. "I think I made it pretty clear to your project manager what is pending. Of course, I'm aware of your development project, Mr. Krish. There's millions of dollars in it. I'd be happy to do my part and help you. All I ask is that I be fairly compensated for my participation."

Krish leaned forward, took Murthy's plate from him, and set it aside. Murthy looked up at him in astonishment initially, then anger.

"I need you to look at me when you're talking to me," Krish said as he rested his fists on the desk. "I'm not asking for your help, Mr. Murthy. I'm expecting you to simply do your job."

There was a moment of silence as they looked at each other, one sizing up the other. Murthy slowly leaned back in his chair, smiled slightly, and rested his folded hands on his protuberant belly.

"What is really your problem with me, Mr. Krish?"

"My problem is that you're deliberately impeding my attempt to help a community in an attempt to extort more money from me."

Murthy sat silently for a moment. He gestured toward the chair next to Krish. "Mr. Krish, may I tell you a little about myself?"

Arya Krish sighed and slowly stood up straight, went over to the chair, and sat down reluctantly.

Murthy swiveled his chair slightly to face him. "You must think you know all you need to know about me, Mr. Krish. I must seem like any other corrupt bureaucrat you've come across in the big cities, soliciting bribes to fund his gluttonous lifestyle. But as you can see," he said, gesturing to his surroundings, "I am not a rich man, certainly not remotely compared to you. Yes, I am fortunate enough to own a small home on a small lot. It has two bedrooms for me, my wife, our three children, and my mother to share. Admittedly, we are not entrenched in depraved poverty, the kind you've seen during your visits here, overwhelming your conscience and compelling you to exert yourself as you do. But I am not like those fat cats in Mysore or Bengaluru either, the ones you seem to equate me to. As you can see, my town is a couple of decades behind. I am grateful for my position in the district government. At least it gives my children a chance at a better life, perhaps somewhere else, such as the United States, where you are from."

Krish's face had unknowingly softened while Murthy spoke. "Mr. Murthy, I hear what you're saying. But frankly, I do not think it justifies hindering my efforts to help others. You need more money to support your family? There are other methods and means, more ethical and legitimate."

Murthy got up from his seat and walked over to the window. He peered through the dirty glass at the streets below. "You are wrong about that, Mr. Krish. I asked your project manager for $25,000. Did he bother to tell you that? I can't imagine it was the amount that stirred such disapproval on your part. The principle, then? I have no other means of obtaining that kind of money short of robbery. Think about it, Mr. Krish. That is more than a year's salary for me, but it is a drop in the bucket for someone like you. You've probably spent at least that much on your travel arrangements alone."

"So this is charity, not bribery?"

"The lines between the two blur, Mr. Krish. The ends justify the means sometimes. You seem to have a clear distinction in your mind between myself and those at VC Farm you wish to rescue. I merely point out that I am not all that different from them."

"They are not opposing me in order to gain something for themselves."

Murthy turned, walked toward Arya Krish, and sat on the corner of the desk. "I do not wish to oppose you, Mr. Krish. In fact, I admire what you are doing. But yes, I am looking out for myself and my family. And when I have some leverage on a person like you, I will look to use it for my family's sake. I do not think I am harming anyone by doing so."

Krish rose from his chair and walked over to the window himself. He looked out and pondered Murthy's comments. He couldn't help but sympathize to an extent with Murthy's intentions. Providing for one's family was a strong and noble motivator, but he wondered if it did, in fact, justify the way Murthy's actions affected others. He thought of VC Farm and his interaction with the locals all those years ago. It would be easy enough to give Murthy what he wanted and regard it as helping this man and his family. And yet, a deep-seated resentment was brewing for the choice Murthy left him and the position he put him in.

Arya Krish turned and started toward the door. "Mr. Murthy, while I understand your motives, I hope you choose to do the right thing."

"I hope you make the right choice, too, Mr. Krish, for me, my family, and for the people of VC Farm."

A flash of anger passed through Krish as he opened the door. "We all live with the choices we make," he said. Without looking back, he closed the door behind him as he left.

As they drove back home, Krish stared out the window, looking past the scenery. He was imagining the daily life of Murthy and his family in their modest home with two bedrooms. It certainly seemed to be a strenuous life the way Murthy described it. But Krish continued to come back to his main grievance. He was being extorted by Murthy, as he had said, plain and simple. As he thought about that man, using his family as a sales pitch to justify his bribe solicitation, he felt his blood boil. A stone-cold look came over his face. He recalled Murthy's obnoxious behavior, the gold rings squeezing his fat stubby fingers, and was repulsed. He took out his cell phone and called Praveen.

"Praveen, do what it takes to get those permits and push the project forward. I do not want anyone harmed, though," he said and hung up.

It rained almost constantly the following two days. Sunshine eventually returned, the humidity lifted, and it was an exceedingly pleasant day as Arya Krish went to visit one of the medical clinics set up at another smaller village on the outskirts of Bengaluru. A refreshing breeze blew, and the main street of the village was bustling with activity as he walked toward the medical clinic, which was part of the development project for this village, completed about six months prior. He sauntered along the sidewalk in high spirits, stopped on the way at a few vendors, and enjoyed coffee at a local outdoor café. As he sipped, he sat and looked out at the day in the life of this village, which one year ago resembled a miniature version of VC Farm. Krish spearheaded the developmental projects, which brought sanitation, paved roads connecting it to the nearby highway, a new school, and a small medical clinic. The commerce and local small businesses followed suit on their own. It had been more than a year since he had been there. He had spent three months here at that time, personally managing the project, and now he marveled at the progress and change. Across the street from him, people were busy doing business with the local vendors. He watched the man behind the counter at the bakery scrambling to keep up with the demanding crowd. The road was full, mainly of two-wheelers and a few bullock carts. A few scant cars and auto-rickshaws were interspersed, and the noise of the traffic filled the air.

Arya Krish finished his coffee, paid the check, and proceeded to the medical clinic. It was a humble, two-story concrete building that housed a walk-in clinic, a pharmacy, and some office space on the second floor. Part of the upper floor served as living quarters for the clinicians, who were mainly locals trained by Beacon staff to carry on simple daily operations. He had also enlisted the help of some local physicians to help maintain and run the clinic, compensating them generously. The lobby was small and had a reception desk in the middle, with exam rooms on either side and a waiting area behind it. The faint sterile smell of antiseptic greeted Krish, and he was shown upstairs to a small conference room. He waited alone there for the manager on duty to come with the other staff to meet with him.

The room was sparsely furnished with a small conference table and a few chairs. It didn't seem like it was used much other than for storing some medical equipment. He walked over to the window and looked out at the street below. Krish noticed a black van in the distance, farther down the main road. It stood out among the other vehicles, and he observed it keenly as it approached the clinic. It pulled up to the entrance and stopped. Krish immediately noticed the Alpha Corp decal on the side panel. As he curiously watched the driver get out and come around to the side door, the manager came into the room. He came up beside Krish and looked out the window.

"Who is that?" Krish asked.

"A representative from a company called Alpha Corp, sir."

"Yes, I know what Alpha Corp is. They're quite large in the US. But what are they doing here?"

"They've come to meet with you, sir. They contacted us about a week ago and inquired about your plans to visit here. I assumed you were expecting them."

Krish gave the manager a look of surmise, then watched the driver open the side door. A tall, distinguished-looking, white man with dark silver hair emerged from the van. He wore a black suit. The visitor stood for a moment on the sidewalk and looked both ways, then glanced up at the building. Krish could not tell if he saw them, but it almost seemed as if the man looked right at him. The man said something to the driver and walked inside.

Arya Krish looked around the room. "Show me to your office and bring him there after having him wait downstairs for a few minutes," he said.

They walked down the hall to the manager's small office. It had the appearance of a small study, well kept, with a wide, tall bookshelf on the side wall. Krish sat behind the large desk and waited. He was admittedly caught off guard by this unexpected visitor, and he couldn't help but wonder if that was the intent. His direct dealings with Alpha Corp were peripheral and intermittent up until that point. In fact, he didn't know much more about them beyond the public record. They were already quite well established in the healthcare and pharmaceutical industries and had collaborated with Beacon Medical Institute in the US on past transplant protocols and some clinical trials. Arya Krish was keeping up in particular with the recent news of Alpha Corp's involvement with the CDC regarding new clinical guidelines for additional vaccinations that Alpha Corp had recently developed. Krish found their growing influence and involvement dubious, and his suspicions carried over now as he sat staring at the door, waiting for the man to enter. A few moments later, the manager opened the door and showed the man in, then closed the door as he left. Krish sat silently, looking at the tall man in the black suit.

"Dr. Krish, my name is Jason Rook. I'm an executive liaison with Alpha Corp," he said. He walked over to the desk and extended his hand.

Arya Krish stood and shook it. "Nice to meet you, Mr.

Rook, please have a seat. I admit I'm rather surprised to find Alpha Corp in this neck of the woods."

"Well, I'm very glad to meet you, Dr. Krish, and honored," Rook said. He smiled and sat in the chair facing the desk. "Yes, I can understand your surprise. Frankly, I wasn't expecting to actually meet you like this. We learned you were going to be here and took a chance."

Krish found Rook's evasiveness transparent and relayed it in his tone. "Well then, what exactly brings you here, Mr. Rook?" he asked as he sat down.

"In fact, we have a corporate office in Bengaluru, Dr. Krish. Recently established. India has been an appealing business prospect to us for a while. I must say I admire the work you've done here as of late. I've been sent on behalf of Alpha Corp to propose a collaboration that would be mutually beneficial. We can be a resource to you. For example, we could provide reliable pharmaceuticals to your medical clinics and hospitals that you've sponsored in the city."

Arya Krish eyed Jason Rook keenly. "So you want to supply medicines to our clinics and affiliated hospitals. And what is it you are seeking in return?"

"Well, as I said, we are looking to establish a presence here, Dr. Krish. Having an ally like you would certainly benefit us in our efforts. We hope you'll help us plug into the healthcare sector in Bengaluru."

"I think you might be overestimating my sphere of influence here, Mr. Rook. I am a visitor here, doing some humanitarian service. In fact, it's largely a private enterprise."

"I think you underestimate your sphere of influence, Dr. Krish. While your work here is born of personal aspirations, you have the business connections as a result of your projects. You have the backing of your Beacon Medical Institute, not to mention your father's work in establishing tertiary hospitals in Bengaluru.

That gives your family name a lot of pull around here."

Krish leaned forward slightly with a solemn look. "What do you know of my father's work, Mr. Rook?"

Rook's tone became slightly defensive. "He was a Nobel Laureate, after all, Dr. Krish," he said. "His work is a matter of public record. Obviously, there's the legacy he and his compatriots left behind back home. I know that he brought some of that legacy to a few of the larger hospitals here, helping advance them to the world-class centers they are now reputed to be. You are doing the same social service on an even larger scale, it seems."

"That is kind of you to say, Mr. Rook, but I'm not sure how I can help Alpha Corp. I am not formally involved with those hospitals or in the health care industry here at all, for that matter."

"Nevertheless, you have connections here that we simply do not, and your personal endorsement would go a long way for us."

Krish leaned back and sat silently. They were asking him to vouch for them essentially while promising in return the pharmaceutical resources he was struggling for in the local sector. They knew what he needed, what would appeal to him. He swiveled the chair toward the window behind him. *Another means to an end,* he thought.

"Well, Mr. Rook, your proposal is certainly worth considering. But I cannot say more than that at the moment. I need to think about it for a bit," he said.

"I expected as much, Dr. Krish. I'm just glad I got to meet you in person and plant the seed, so to speak," Mr. Rook stood. Krish stood as well and shook his hand.

"Someone will show you out, I'm sure."

"Thank you for your time. We'll be in touch," Rook said. He left and closed the door behind him.

Arya Krish sat again and looked out the window. He

watched Rook get into the van and drive off.

Within a few days, Krish received a call from the clinic manager stating that a shipment of medicines and supplies had arrived, courtesy of Alpha Corp. He considered it good news and was relieved because he struggled to find a reliable medical supplier at a reasonable price. Still, he had mixed feelings about the unexpected news. It essentially forced his hand. He could turn away the supplies or comply with Rook's proposal. As anticipated, he received phone calls the following days from the chief medical officers of the large medical centers in Bengaluru that confirmed his endorsement of Alpha Corp's solicitations. With the benefit now in mind that his clinics would have for the locals, Krish gave Alpha Corp what they wanted.

On his last day before flying back home, Arya Krish went back to VC Farm. It was drizzling by the time he arrived in the early afternoon, and the smell of wet earth filled the air as he got out of the car near the school site. Praveen waited for him inside the single large building that would be the new school. It was two stories tall and was surrounded by a large compound. The exterior was still unfinished, as was the interior. However, the roof was complete, and it offered shelter for them from the light rain. A small crew worked that day on the interior plumbing and electrical wiring. Krish walked up to Praveen and shook his hand.

"How are you, Praveen? It's looking good in here. The classrooms seem large enough, I think."

"Yes sir, we're definitely making progress here. I'm happy to say we'll be moving ahead with the road paving and the streetlights as well." Praveen showed him the permits.

Krish took them in hand and browsed them briefly. He handed them back and eyed Praveen curiously. "So, Murthy was finally agreeable?"

"No. His replacement was more reasonable, however."

Krish couldn't contain his surprise. "Replacement? What

happened to Murthy?"

"He resigned, Dr. Krish. And from what I know, he packed up everything and left."

"What? Why? Is this our doing? Tell me exactly what happened, Praveen."

"You said do what it takes, Dr. Krish. The people we consulted made it clear to him that he had to do what we asked or suffer the consequences."

"I also said specifically that no one was to be harmed!"

"I assure you no one was, Dr. Krish."

"Were you there, Praveen? Who were these people? What did they do exactly?"

Praveen became nervous seeing Krish behave that way. He had never seen him lose composure. "Sir, I don't know exactly. I try not to ask too many questions."

Krish paced nervously. His conversation with Murthy played back in his mind, and he thought of Murthy's wife, three children, and mother. "I have to know what happened."

"I do not advise confronting these sorts of people, Dr. Krish. They were a means to an end, that's all."

Krish stopped and stared at Praveen as he said those words. *A means to an end.* He sweated profusely, and his heart raced. "Where does Murthy live, Praveen? I have to find him now," he said in a hurried tone.

As he walked out into the rain toward the car, he signaled Praveen to follow him. They got in and drove toward town. After a while, they turned off the main road and drove down side roads for a while through sparse residential neighborhoods before they finally arrived at Murthy's residence.

Krish nearly leapt out of the car before it came to a stop. He walked briskly to the small front gate and stopped. It was just as he had pictured it, just as Murthy described: a small, gray, single-level concrete house with small windows behind steel frames. Krish passed through the front gate into the small lot, barely enough to fit a car and a small garden. No car was visible, however. He stood still and breathed heavily. Praveen stayed back near the car.

The drizzle turned into a downpour as Krish stood helplessly and looked at the vandalized house. All of the windows were broken, and the door was dented heavily. Random household items, small pieces of furniture, and a few clothes were strewn about the front steps. Krish slowly walked up to the front door and tried to open it, but it was locked. He went to the window and peered inside. The house was empty. He made out a small main room and a kitchen in the corner. Two doors at the far end of the house presumably led to the bedrooms.

Drenched at that point, he turned and looked toward Praveen and the car. Praveen stood still in the rain as well and watched him intently. Krish caught a glimpse of a small tricycle next to the front gate. The tricycle was smashed and contorted, and a deflated soccer ball was next to it. He thought of the children and choked on a surge of emotion as he walked back to the car and got inside without saying a word. Praveen looked once more at the house, then got in as well.

They did not speak on the ride back. Krish dropped Praveen off and remained silent during the drive back to his house. He stared out the window the entire time, and his mind was in a dull, thoughtless stupor.

That night, Krish arrived at the airport in the same daze. The people he interacted with seemed far away, with voices muffled and distant. He couldn't even recall how he got on the plane. As he sat in his seat, he watched the other passengers board. Krish watched the economy-class passengers walk through the first-class cabin as they glanced around. He remembered again and again Murthy's brief description of his life, a life turned upside down with one phone call. Twenty-five thousand dollars.

A drop in the bucket, he remembered Murthy saying. Krish tried to remind himself that it was the principle, though, that led him to make the choice. He could not bring himself to allow Murthy to leverage him, to back him into a corner like that.

He recalled Praveen's comment about living in the jungle among the beasts. For the first time, he felt his blood run cold in his veins, and a hard look came over his face. He looked at the other first-class passengers. Some sat with legs crossed and sipped wine or champagne, while others read or tapped away at their electronics. He somehow perceived a smug look on those strangers' faces at that moment and found them revolting. At the same time, he recoiled with self-loathing for being among them. A dull numbness washed over him like he was draped with a heavy cloak. He leaned back and closed his eyes.

CHAPTER THREE

Three years passed. Soon to be 35, Arya Krish thought that he felt older than he should as he sat at his desk at the Institute, browsing reports related to his various humanitarian projects. He was deep in thought about the last couple of years. He periodically received those reports from Praveen, who was now his executive manager of all regional projects. By any measure, the success of his humanitarian enterprises exceeded his hopes. He had duplicated the success of VC Farm at other locations, and the impact earned him local celebrity status, as well as media attention, in Bengaluru and in the US.

Krish's white coat hung on the side coat rack, and his slumped posture surely wrinkled his expensive suit. He stared blankly at the computer screen when Jay Asher walked into his office.

"So, they're still letting you work here, huh?" Asher smiled broadly.

Arya Krish snapped out of his daze and quickly got up to greet him. "Welcome home, my friend," he said. Krish smiled and hugged Asher, then stepped back and looked him up and down as he admired his military class-A dress uniform. Decorations and medals were immaculately displayed over his left chest. "So, what now? Should I salute you?"

"Well, they did make me a Lt. Colonel."

"Oh, wow. Too bad I still outrank you then!"

They laughed as Krish went back to his desk and sat down. Asher walked over to the window next to it and stood looking out at the view of D.C.

"I'm glad you're back safe and sound," Krish said.

"Thankfully, I wasn't directly in harm's way, though I did venture close to the front lines on occasion," Asher's tone was somber. "I'm just a surgeon who humbly tried to help out his fellow man. Those combat troops are the tip of the spear."

"Regardless, I'm proud of you, brother. Now you get to help me out around here."

"Doesn't look like you need much help, man," Asher said as he looked around. "Congratulations on becoming Director and CEO at such a tender age. It was merely a formality, I suppose. You seemed to have been at the helm for some time now. I've seen you and Beacon more in the news lately."

"I want you working here with me, as Chief Operations Officer," Arya Krish said suddenly.

Asher turned toward Krish for a moment, and Krish watched him as he remained silent for a while. Krish could tell Asher was considering the request, but his mind was distracted and wandering. The strained look in Asher's piercing hazel eyes was familiar to Krish. He saw it on his own face lately. The sunlight cast a long shadow behind Asher as he stood tall and still, his hands in his pockets. Asher slowly looked down at his decorations, then walked over and sat across from Krish.

"I'm tired, Arya," Asher said. "I'm disappointed in myself for feeling so burnt out already. I had anticipated the wear and tear before signing up, but it was more than I expected in so many ways. And now my bones feel heavy, and I must struggle to concentrate. It makes me wonder what I'm capable of at this point."

Krish leaned forward, rested his folded hands on his desk, and looked at Asher intently. He remembered the similar words his father used to describe the stifling circumstances he had endured at the A1 Group when his father was in his late 20s. "Do you feel it was worth it? What you were doing over there?"

"What do you mean?"

"I mean, you obviously helped others, saved lives, and treated injuries. But the cause itself, the reason you guys were all there, was it worth what you saw and went through?"

"Depends on what cause you're referencing. I would say everyone there had an individual cause that sustained them, more so than anything political or in the interests of national security. I believe most were patriots and honored their duty to country. But by far, family and home were closest to their hearts and on their minds in the darkest hours."

"Well, sure. Their family and home life are a slice of the larger whole and the greater good that defines their patriotism as well."

"Yeah. Well, while you're over there, you can't help wonder whether what's happening there matters at all over here."

"You seem to have seen your share over there," Krish said meekly.

Asher shrugged. "I'm a military trauma surgeon. So yeah, I saw what combat did to others up close and personal, and I tried to help. When you're there, you're in the moment, and only your immediate surroundings matter. I'm proud I helped those guys in whatever way I could."

"Well, that was your personal cause then: service to your fellow soldiers. That was your call of duty. What you became as a result, what you've had to bring back with you—does it seem worth it?"

"I'm not sure what you mean by worth it. But yes, it does for the time being. But those other guys must go on living with the physical and mental scars. I think of bearing witness to what they went through, what they were put through, by the guys in suits over here," Asher said. He waved his hand toward the outside. "When I think of that, I feel relatively unscathed by comparison."

He looked down.

Krish got up and paced slowly between his desk and the window. "I would never compare my experience with yours, but I wonder about these things. I, too, feel like I've been fighting wholeheartedly for a vision. And as a result, I also feel I've lost part of myself." He paused at the window.

Asher looked up at him curiously. "What do you mean?"

"The humanitarian aid projects here and abroad. A while ago, I accepted the costs of accomplishing the magnitude I envisioned, beyond financial."

"Let me guess. You got your hands a little dirty and rubbed shoulders with the uglier elements? Had to push some people out of the way to get what you needed done? So what's the problem?" Asher asked. He stood and walked over to his friend.

Krish was silent for a moment. For the first time in a while, he thought back to Murthy and the mangled tricycle in front of the abandoned house. A strained look came into his eyes as Asher watched him and waited. "I've had trouble with the contradictions of some of my actions, driven by perceived ends I felt justified whatever means were necessary." Arya Krish paused to marshal his thoughts. "Tensions and circumstances surrounded me that compelled me to retaliate with the same corrupt force as my opposition, and only later consider the ripple effects. It's made me think back to the first time I felt my blood boil and the first time I felt it run cold. I felt myself change, and as if I could not live in my own skin. That feeling passed soon enough. That is what perturbs me the most."

As Asher listened, a certain look of amusement crept into his expression. He'd done this for as long as Asher had known him. Asher patted him on the shoulder, smiled slightly, and turned toward the door without replying. Krish looked at him, wanting to continue the conversation, but as he watched Asher walk toward the door, he was resigned to leaving it there. Asher stopped and turned to him.

"I've seen the work you've done. It's gotten public attention and praise. Sure, nobody likes to mention the shady side of it all, but I don't think you should be losing any sleep. Look, it's simple, really. In your mind, you put all the good you've done, all the change in the lives of all those people, and weigh it against the collateral damage and the conflicting but necessary things you've had to do. Without thinking about it much, it becomes obvious which side wins out. That's your equation."

A knock sounded on the door, and Krish called for them to come in. A young, attractive woman opened the door, wearing a gray pantsuit that followed all her appropriate curves, with a light blue shirt. She had dark brown hair and green eyes and wore a tasteful matching pearl necklace and earrings. The woman stood and smiled in the doorway while Asher turned and glanced at Krish with a goofy smile that quickly swept over his face. She looked at Asher with admiration.

"I'm sorry to interrupt, Dr. Krish," she said as she turned to him.

"No worries," Krish said. He walked toward them. "This is Lt. Colonel Jay Asher, MD." Krish dramatically gestured at Asher. "Dr. Asher, this is Dr. Abigale Bishop. She'll be replacing me as Chair of Infectious Diseases."

Bishop turned toward Asher and shook his hand. "Thank you for your service! I've heard about you quite a bit since starting here. I understand we may get to see more of you around?"

"Only believe the good stuff you hear," Asher said. He winked and continued toward the door. Bishop came into the room to let Asher through, and they smiled at each other as they passed. Asher paused and turned back.

"I plan to be around," he said as he glanced again at Krish. "I need to clean the desert sand out of my ears, so to speak. I certainly see more incentive now to hurry back." Asher smiled, then turned and walked out.

Bishop smiled as she watched Asher leave, then she turned toward Arya Krish. He walked back to his chair and sat down.

"Dr. Krish, I wanted to check and see if you still wanted to round today with the house staff. Or if you prefer I do it?"

"No. It's fine, Dr. Bishop. I can round. I know the census pretty well."

"OK, no problem. Talk to you later," she said, and she left. Krish sat alone in silence.

***

He stood in front of the closed door in a circle with two Infectious Diseases (ID) fellows and listened intently. One of the ID fellows presented the patient's history and physical information to him. Aas was the trend in society at large, these physicians-in-training usually conformed to a single arbitrary but consistent and effective mode of operation. They all wore bright white coats. Lately, it seemed to him that they all looked and sounded the same. None of their individuality came through in their clothing, behavior, or interactions. Other house staff, nurses, visitors, and others walked past them. The hallway was busy as teams from different specialties also made rounds on the floors and convened in a similar fashion or went in and out of the rooms.

Krish listed to the ID fellow. "This is a 28-year-old male, type one diabetic with failed pancreatic and renal transplants, with a long-standing history of intravenous drug use. He has hepatitis C and failed treatment five years ago. HIV test this admission was negative. He has had several hospitalizations this year for methicillin-resistant Staphylococcus aureus, or MRSA, skin abscesses on his arms. He was admitted two weeks ago after being found unresponsive in his bedroom, secondary to a heroin overdose. He was intubated in the field and admitted to the ICU.

His course is significant for septic shock secondary to MRSA endocarditis, septic emboli to the brain, spleen, and kidneys, acute respiratory distress syndrome, renal failure now requiring dialysis, splenic abscesses, cerebrovascular accident, now status post-tracheostomy and percutaneous endoscopic gastrostomy tube. He has been unresponsive and vent-dependent. His blood cultures have been negative for five days now. He remains on IV vancomycin with every hemodialysis, with therapeutic levels. Plan is for at least a six-week course." The fellow paused and looked up at Arya Krish in an anticipating manner as if waiting for him to comment.

Krish looked back at him. He leaned forward slightly, kept his hands behind his back, and remained silent with slightly pursed lips. The fellow cleared his throat nervously and looked back down at his papers.

"You know when I was in training." Arya Krish paused, and the ID fellows snapped their attention to him immediately. "The director of the ICU on rounds expected us to present the overnight ICU admissions without any notes. According to him, we admitted the patients and took care of them all night, so we should know them off the top of our heads. I personally don't see anything wrong with having something in your hand to glance at to keep things organized. But in retrospect, I do appreciate my attending's point and feel I benefited from the exercise."

The fellow shuffled his papers and rocked back and forth on his feet.

Krish continued. "I only bring that up as an anecdote to highlight the idea of training yourself at this stage in your career to have your patients organized in your head in a way that makes sense for you and allows you to communicate and inform. I think that down the road, when you're an attending, you'll reflect on your training and appreciate the exercise, as I do. OK, so we've been following this guy almost since admission. Nothing has changed much from our perspective. He'll get his antibiotics for the appropriate duration. But with the anoxic brain injury and multi-organ dysfunction, obviously, the family has been wrestling with the idea of withdrawing care. He's failed attempts to wean off the ventilator. He's awake but otherwise unresponsive. This is how he'll remain while he is alive." Krish paused and scanned their faces. He could tell they had empathy, but at the same time, he detected a casual regard toward the situation. They were desensitized to it by now.

"So, his father's in there, I presume?"

"Yes, Dr. Krish."

"OK." Krish moved toward the door. The fellows stepped in line behind him to follow. He knew they were frustrated at having to spend time with this patient and his father, as busy as they were. They were not changing anything in their plan of care. The ICU team and internal medicine service would address the goals of care. He stopped and glanced back at them. "Why don't you guys break off and finish seeing the remaining consults? I'll let you know when we'll meet again."

"OK. Thanks, Dr. Krish," they said in unison and hurried off.

Krish stood still for a moment, then faced the door, knocked, and entered. He looked over at the patient and noted the pale, cachectic face, the eyes rolled back in his head, and the tracheostomy attached to the ventilator. A blanket covered his body. Krish shifted his glance over to the patient's father, who stood at the foot of the bed and looked at his son. His arms were crossed over his chest. A light shone over the patient from the head of the bed, and a window from the far end of the room let in the daylight. It was an overcast day, and as the clouds moved swiftly across the sky, the ambience in the room dimmed and brightened. Everything else was still for a moment as Krish walked up to the father, stood next to him, and also looked at the patient. They stood for a moment without speaking as the monitors and IV drips beeped monotonously in the background.

"You think he's feeling any pain, doc?" the father asked. He was a short man with a large belly, gray hair, and a mustache. He looked like a young Santa Clause as a civilian during the off-season. His eyes were bloodshot, and dried tears had left streaks down his face, which showed a few fine wrinkles. He looked straight ahead as he spoke.

Krish glanced at the vital signs on the screen, the ventilator settings, and IV drips. He also looked straight ahead as he spoke. "He doesn't seem to be in distress. But frankly, it's difficult to tell, Mr. Roman. His heart rate isn't fast, and the vent is breathing for him, for the most part. He isn't sedated, but he's on continuous IV pain meds."

The father nodded. He glanced over and said, "Rest of your group not here today?"

"No, I cut them loose. They're busy enough," he said. After a short pause, he continued. "Mr. Roman, I'm one of the infection doctors. You might remember."

"Yes, I remember you, doc. You tell me that every time."

"I know, it's a habit. You've seen a lot of doctors along the way."

"Yeah, a lot of doctors come and go. I admit I have trouble keeping track."

"So, we've discussed before your son's condition and prospects of recovery. I wonder what your thoughts are now."

"I've talked to the ICU doctor. We're taking him off life support." He choked back his emotion.

Krish nodded solemnly. They remained silent for a moment. "I think that's the right thing to do, Mr. Roman."

"Well, he wouldn't want to be kept alive like this, be a vegetable. I don't want him like this." The father sobbed quietly. He walked over to the head of the bed and put his hand on his son's forehead. Krish walked to the head of the bed and stood on the other side. "You know, his mother died 10 years ago this Sunday. He was 18. He was never the same after that," the father said.

Krish looked up at him.

"You've been a bad boy, Nick," the father said. He leaned in and kissed his son on the forehead. "You say hi to Mom, give her a kiss for me."

Krish continued to watch the patient's father respectfully. He tried to imagine what this man was going through, having already lost his wife and now losing his son like this. And the patient himself, his choices and lifestyle, forged in large part by events beyond his control. They had their consequences and paved the path to this moment. He had seen this before, had patients this young succumb on other occasions, and he had tried to console the parents. However, now that he had a baby boy himself, Krish felt he was somehow unqualified until then to really console parents on the loss of their child.

But this case had piqued his interest for other reasons. This young man had received pancreatic and kidney transplants five years ago at Beacon Medical. However, because his maintenance meds stopped being covered by his insurance, he fell off them, and both transplants failed. At that time, the organ synthesis technology required more medications to sustain the synthetic organs *in vivo*, and the drugs were more expensive.

Obviously, this factored into paving his path. In Krish's mind, that meant Alpha Corp factored into it. They controlled the medicine and the insurance coverage for this patient and decided he was not worth covering. Krish suspected it had a lot to do with the patient's lifestyle and the social resources it consumed. Lately, Krish had followed similar stories and instances where Alpha Corp wielded a troubling power over the access and scope for health care. Certainly, for decades the insurance companies had slowly taken over the health care system. As a result, they had dangerous power over an individual's access to resources, including doctors, hospitals, nursing facilities, technology, and medications. Ultimately, the insurance company decided what happened to the patient. It was an insidious takeover that corrupted the politicians in their favor and desensitized the public to their blatant power grab. Now, it was normal to decline a certain treatment, facility, or medicine because the insurance company decided it wasn't worth the price. But at the same time, the insurance company also influenced how much the damn thing cost!

"I feel for you, Mr. Roman. Please let me know if I can be of any help. I'll leave you be." The father looked at him and nodded. Arya Krish nodded back, then quietly left the room.

He spent the rest of the day in his office reviewing reports, records, and press releases pertaining to Alpha Corp. He had learned more and more lately about their various dealings in the health industry and political realms. It was remarkable, really. Over the last decade, Alpha Corp had acquired local health systems up and down the East Coast. These included an insurance company, a pharmaceutical company, and one of the leading research and development institutes. Lately, they had become big players as lobbyists in the political realm close to home in DC. Most people were more familiar with their feel-good television advertisements. Many of their ads propagated an integrated healthcare entity. In fact, Alpha Corp had quite suavely gained regional control of the major arms of health care: hospitals, insurance, and pharmaceuticals. While there was some public debate and even outcry initially, as insurance companies gained more and more power and took the decision-making away from doctors and patients, over time, it died down and became mute. People became numb to the insidious usurpation. The sort of apathetic conformity that seemed to pervade the social conscience at large facilitated the advancement of companies like Alpha Corp in their power-hungry ambitions.

It was approaching midnight by the time Krish shut down his computer and got up to leave. He turned the light off as he left his office and closed the door. The administrative and academic buildings on that end of the campus were empty at that time of night. As Krish stood in the hallway, he paused when he heard a door close down the other hallway. He walked toward the sound, and as he turned the corner, he caught a glimpse of a man walking away from him toward the exit on the other end of the hallway. Krish quickly stepped back out of sight and peeked around the corner, and watched a tall man in a dark suit walk hurriedly and pass through the exit. Krish quickly turned back toward his office and went out a different exit down the side stairs.

Krish stepped outside into the narrow alley from the side door, and the pavement was still wet from a rainfall. The streetlights shone down from above like spotlights as he passed in and out of light and shadow. He walked swiftly down the alley and through the side street. His feet could barely be heard on the wet asphalt as they glided low over the ground. Krish came to the end of the small street and paused. He stood in the shadows as he peered around the building down the street and watched the man walk over to a black sedan parked under a streetlight. As he approached the car, the light caught his face. Krish recognized Jason Rook. He watched with a stern yet puzzled look on his face as Rook glanced up and down the street quickly before he got into his car and drove away.

The following morning, Arya Krish and Jay Asher sat in his office. Krish described his first meeting with Jason Rook and his sighting the previous night.

"So, up until last night, you hadn't seen this Jason Rook since meeting him in India like three years ago?" Asher asked.

"No. I spoke to him over the phone briefly a couple of

times over the last year or so. It was mostly about some of the things Alpha Corp was involved with in some of my projects."

"So what the hell was he doing here? How did he even get inside the building?"

"I don't have answers yet, man, but I intend to find out. And I may need your help."

"OK, where do we start?"

"Well, you asked the right questions. We need to find out how he got in and what he was doing."

"You should be able to access security logs, right?"

"Yeah, I checked those. It doesn't look like he used any employee ID access. I'm guessing that he somehow overrode the electronic access independently."

"Where exactly did you see him?"

"Honestly, I could have sworn he came out of Abigale Bishop's office just before I saw him based on where he was in that hallway."

"Bishop? The pretty one from yesterday?"

"Yeah."

"Hmm." Asher stood and paced slowly. "So whatever business he had, it was presumably in her office. Guy like that has a clear objective coming in. What do we know about this Bishop?"

Krish leaned back in his chair, folded his hands under his chin, and shrugged.

"All we really know is her professional history and what's on her record," he said. "Trained and worked in the Tri-State area. She was Chair of Medicine at a teaching hospital in Connecticut before signing with us. That hospital was acquired by Alpha Corp and merged into their regional health network over there about six months prior to her leaving."

Asher stopped and turned toward Krish. "Well, you mentioned that rather casually. Begs the question, doesn't it? She may still be connected with them."

"I don't know, man. She seemed pretty clean-cut," Krish said. "We did vet her before hiring, for what it's worth. Like I said, she left within six months of them coming into the picture." Krish stood up and walked over to the window. "What're you thinking, some sort of corporate espionage?"

"I think that goes without saying, doesn't it? Fact is, this guy from Alpha Corp was in your building, and I don't think he wanted to be seen."

"I realize that. But now we're implying that Bishop is collaborating? And what, that makes her some kind of a double agent? It seems a little far-fetched."

"Aren't you the one who's been investigating Alpha Corp in your free time? From what little you've told me, you're compiling quite a rap sheet outlining their corruptive enterprise at large. Honestly, I'm not all that surprised. But it does seem a little extreme for someone to physically break in like that. They're after things we keep offline, on-site. Keep in mind, Beacon has a cutting-edge R&D department and big contracts with Alpha Corp competitors."

Arya Krish sighed. "We're also collaborating with Alpha to a large extent. Maybe more than anyone else at this point. Somehow, I've become more and more entangled with them." He walked back to his desk and leaned over it with his fists. "So, what to do from here?"

Asher walked over to the other side of the desk. "I suppose we're left waiting and watching. At least we know something is up. You might want to keep a closer eye on Bishop, maybe even think about confronting her about all this."

"I'll try to talk to her casually later today," Krish said.

Abigale Bishop was nowhere to be seen that day. In fact, she did not show up for the following week. After the second week of no contact, Arya Krish sent someone to her home to inquire. Her Georgetown apartment was empty. They never heard from her again.

***

Krish sat in his car and watched activities at the large, rectangular building. This was his second day to observe the shiny, mirrored-glass, modern façade in a sprawling business complex in one of the affluent suburbs outside DC. He'd parked about a block away and across the street and watched as people came and went. His mind churned, as it did the previous day, as he remembered the incidents surrounding his VC Farm project. Praveen's words about living in the jungle among the other beasts echoed frequently during his ruminations.

As he waited and watched, he couldn't help but wonder what he was doing. After the Jason Rook sighting and Bishop's disappearance, he'd felt compelled to do something to investigate. Bishop had taken over his old position, so she had not been at the Institute for very long. Her office was examined, including her computer. When the IT department tried to access it, the offline computer had already been wiped clean without any record of a data transfer. No missing person report had been filed with the police. Her biographical information on file, including next of kin, was carefully fabricated on further inspection. He had reached a dead end and took it upon himself to find a lead. Deep in thought, his attention was diverted until a loud tapping rattled the window. It startled him back to his surroundings. He turned to his left and couldn't conceal his shock at seeing Jason Rook's face in the driver's side window. Krish paused and gathered himself before lowering the window halfway.

Rook looked at him with an amused expression. "Is this your first stakeout, Dr. Krish, or are you here to enjoy the scenery?"

Arya Krish remained silent. He slowly reached for the door handle and opened it. Rook stood up straight and moved aside to let him out. Krish got out, closed the door, and stood silently, looking at him. Rook wore his usual fitted black suit, white shirt, and black tie. He looked the same as he did the first time they met in India. Krish also wore a designer, tailor-made suit.

They eyed each other for a moment before Rook walked toward the building without saying anything. Krish hesitated for a moment, then followed him. As they neared it, Krish looked up at the tall, glass building. It towered 20 stories up and glared in the spring sunshine. They walked through a sprawling courtyard, past well-trimmed trees and benches where others sat. Krish noted that everyone was dressed the same, with men in black suits and women in black dress suits. Farther away were other buildings, but the immediate area seemed distinct from the rest of the complex.

Neither spoke as Krish and Rook entered the building's vast lobby. It was modern and sleekly arranged, with sitting areas, computer stations, and a small café opposite the entrance. The ceiling must have been 50 feet high. Echoing footsteps and quiet chatter could be heard as they went to a quiet corner and sat across from each other. Rook watched intently as Krish looked around for a moment, taking it all in with unconcealed curiosity.

"Quite different in its architecture than your Beacon Medical Institute, Dr. Krish. Of course, given your location, it makes sense to be consistent with the classical surroundings, if you know what I mean," Rook said. Krish stopped looking around and focused on him but remained silent. "This is a satellite location for Alpha Corp. As you know, our headquarters is in New York."

Krish did not speak. Rook remained quiet for a while as well. He leaned back with his legs crossed and brushed some lint off his jacket–or at least pretended to.

"Well, I guess you're going to make me ask, Dr. Krish.

What exactly are you doing here anyway?"

Krish did not answer right away as he calculated his response. "I happened to see you at Beacon Medical Institute, Mr. Rook. About three weeks ago. I was there when you emerged from Abigale Bishop's office, and I watched you leave and drive away. That is why I am here."

Rook's brow furrowed as if he was puzzled by Krish's remark. He brought his folded hands near his face and rested his chin on them in a thoughtful manner. It seemed he was also calculating his responses carefully.

"I'll admit to your claims, Dr. Krish. But frankly, it still doesn't explain what you were doing sitting in your car in front of this building. I'm not even sure you know what you were doing, to be honest."

"Quite simply, Mr. Rook, I was waiting to spot you, or perhaps Dr. Bishop, and seek out answers."

"Well, I can't speak to the whereabouts of Dr. Bishop, but here we are, Dr. Krish. Fire away."

"What were you doing in my building?"

Rook shrugged. "Call it reconnaissance. Gathering information."

Krish found it difficult to tolerate Rook's audacity. "What you did was blatantly illegal, Mr. Rook, yet you readily admit to it."

"Well, if that was your main concern, I imagine you would have gone to the police, Dr. Krish. Why didn't you? I suppose you knew it wouldn't amount to much, anyway. A half-hearted inquiry perhaps, with no leads worth pursuing in the end."

"What were you doing in my building exactly? What happened to Dr. Bishop? Why was her computer wiped clean?"

Jason Rook did not answer right away. He could sense the tension emanating from Arya Krish, and he waited, letting it fester. When he spoke, it was in the tone of a teacher explaining long division to a child. "Dr. Krish, all I can say is we're not out to harm you, your Institute, or your mission. In fact, personally, I have a great deal of admiration for you. I've seen your interviews on the news networks. You and Beacon Medical Institute have gained great public favor, and your brilliance is undeniable. I'd like to think I am an educated man, even a wise man, and I find the opportunity of an honest dialogue with you very exciting."

Krish sighed softly in an exasperated manner, which conveyed to Rook that his flattery was hollow and dubious.

"I'm being quite sincere, Dr. Krish," Rook said, picking up on the vibe. "I wouldn't insult you by being pretentious. I am trying to be as forthcoming and straightforward as possible. Your star is rising. It has been for some time now. Your sphere of influence, so to speak, has expanded into a realm that I think you may be unprepared to navigate."

Rook paused, anticipating a response. Krish remained silent, but he was piqued by Rook's comments. They struck a chord with his own reflections, and he wanted to allow Rook to continue along the same train of thought. After a moment, Rook brought his hands down. He turned and looked out the window as he continued.

"Perhaps Alpha Corp would not be too happy to hear me talking to you like this. Then again, it's no secret really, is it? You've heard of Big Oil, Big Pharma, and the aura that surrounds them regarding politics, money, power...and corruption. But that public impression doesn't really scratch the surface. There isn't much that is out of bounds when jostling for real power. The ends most certainly justify — or warrant is perhaps the better word — the means."

"What does all this have to do with me, my Institute, and my mission, as you put it?" Krish replied, and Rook quickly turned his face back toward him.

"Like I said, you have become a relevant player in the

healthcare industry, particularly in R&D. I guess what I'm saying is, don't be surprised if the likes of Alpha Corp take an interest and keep an eye on you."

"Keeping an eye is one thing. Breaking into my building and stealing information is another."

"Again, Dr. Krish, don't be so surprised. Believe it or not, it happens all the time. Information is a valuable currency, Dr. Krish. It can wield power beyond money." Rook leaned in with a sincere expression. "Look, all I'm trying to do is clue you in to how it is at this level. I say again, we mean you no harm. As you know, we have a collaboration that you have benefited greatly from, you have to admit, as have we. So, in that way, your continued success is in our best interests as well."

Krish read between the lines, and Rook knew it. It was a conversation between two intelligent men, and behind the encouraging words and show of respect was a simple statement. Or warning.

"So until there is a conflict of interest, I have nothing to worry about, and I can rest assured that your company's probing, and whatever else they may do, is otherwise benign?" Krish said sarcastically.

Jason Rook smiled. His admiration of Krish on a personal level was perhaps genuine. At the same time, Rook was also an agent, a veteran soldier to his own cause. He stood abruptly and buttoned his jacket. Arya Krish stood quickly as well.

"Well, I guess we have an understanding, Dr. Krish. You'll have to excuse me now. Feel free to hang around as long as you like," Rook said dismissively. He shook Krish's hand and walked away. Krish watched him leave. After standing alone for a moment in dissatisfaction, he left.

On the drive home, Krish was lost in thought. He remembered patient Nick Roman and Nick's father. Admittedly, Krish struggled to find empathy for a patient like that, someone whose self-destructive choices led him down an inevitable path. Still, medically speaking, at least, he was a recent snapshot of real people put out to pasture by a faceless corporation. Krish then reflected on Jason Rook and was conflicted over his words. He sensed a sincerity and even reverence. Yet, in the end, he was left with nothing more than consolation and fair warning. He was being regarded as a sheep at the mercy of the wolves like Alpha Corp. In response, a hardened resolve began to manifest in him. Once again, he felt the blood run hot and cold in his veins. His nostrils flared as a hard look came over his eyes. He would keep his guard up and bide his time, for now. Rook was right about one thing. Krish needed their collaboration to sustain his objectives. It made him think ahead to his trip to India in the next few months.

CHAPTER FOUR

Praveen sat with a calm look on his face. He wore a nice, fitted suit, but admittedly, it may have looked somewhat odd on him. He was clean-cut, but his features still bore the wear of the elements. He watched patiently as the man sitting across the desk from him read the documents Praveen had handed him. The office was quiet, except for the hum of the overhead fan and the sound of pages flipping.

The man was middle-aged, with sharp features and a thick, well-groomed moustache. He had an angry and concerned look on his face. After a few minutes he stopped, flung the papers on the desk, and looked up. Praveen looked back at him with an unchanged expression.

"What exactly is this, some sort of blackmail attempt? Am I supposed to cower and do whatever you demand of me next?"

"We do not want or expect you to cower, Chief Minister Gowda. But yes, we do have demands of you, and it would be in your best interest to favor ours," Praveen replied in a calm, almost consoling tone.

"Or else what? You'll make these documents and photos public in an attempt to defame me or get me in trouble with the law?"

Praveen slowly moved his chair closer to the desk, leaned in, and gathered the papers. "Look. Mr. Gowda, sir, we do not want to be enemies. In fact, we prefer the opposite. I've clearly defined what we want. No one can deny our honorable intentions. The legislation we want you to push through will give tax exemptions and other benefits to the orphanages and charities we are backing and open doors for them to truly benefit those they are trying to help. Especially the children, Mr. Gowda. My employer is particularly intent on removing any red tape or bureaucratic obstacles affecting their aid and progress. Initially, that is all we reached out to you for, if you remember. But like many others we've come across, you seemed more focused on what we can do for you in return instead. Suffice it to say, we don't have much tolerance for that. It represents the very corruption and political immorality we oppose."

Chief Minister Gowda sat silently for a moment as Praveen took the papers and put them back in the envelope.

"Your employer. Of course. I've heard of Dr. Arya Krish from the US. Typical American attitude, coming here and thinking he can throw his weight around, get his way however he wishes."

Praveen gave him a hard look. "You've heard of him, no doubt, from the news coverage, which means you know the public sentiment toward him at large. He's a social reformer, philanthropist, and humanist, Mr. Gowda, the likes of which someone like you is unlikely to comprehend."

"And does the public know how he goes about his business?" Gowda asked. He gestured toward the envelope as Praveen put it inside his inner jacket pocket. "I wonder how they'd feel about that."

Praveen smiled and stood. "I say again, Mr. Gowda, your own self-interests would best be served by aligning yourself with us rather than opposing us. We'll be in touch if we don't hear from you in a timely manner." He turned and left.

Praveen emerged from the government capitol building in downtown Bengaluru and walked briskly across its large, well-kept courtyard. It was a sunny day and warm, as usual. Praveen passed between the scattered sprinklers as they watered the lawns. He approached a shiny black limousine with chrome trim that was parked under the shade of a large tree. Praveen opened the back door, sat inside, and looked across at Arya Krish, who sat and silently looked out the closed, tinted window at the passers-by. Praveen waited for him to speak.

Krish was silent for a while. His eyes were narrow, with a far-off look. "How'd it go?" he asked.

"About as expected, Dr. Krish. The usual posturing, but I think he'll come around. I'll follow it up in about a week if you think that's OK."

Krish nodded and still looked out the window. "Thanks, Praveen. I'll leave it to you. I think I'll go by the orphanage before I head home."

"OK. Should I come with you?"

"No, that's OK. I'll go on my own. We'll talk again before I travel back to the US."

"Yes, Dr. Krish." Praveen got out of the limousine.

Krish sat alone. He sighed with visible fatigue. As he looked out at the world it seemed surreal to him, far away, a facsimile. Krish no longer sought out a connection as he peered through the tinted window. The detachment made him more effective, cold, and calculative. At moments like this, however, he sought out the humanity he tried to preserve and nurture. That's why he had to go to the orphanage that day and strained to remember his visits with his parents. He wanted to recall the raw impressions and emotions that bubbled at the surface of his conscience as a young adult as he interacted with those unfortunate and remarkable children. He leaned back and rubbed his eyes slowly, then lowered the privacy glass and instructed the driver to proceed to the orphanage.

The former private home was in a suburb outside the city. Krish had bought it and renovated it into an orphanage that housed 25 girls ages eight to fifteen. It was run by a dedicated staff, some of whom had been residents when they were children. All of the former and current orphan residents were rescued from the streets. Krish had made it a first-rate facility, with living quarters for the staff, dormitory-style accommodations for the children, a few small classrooms, an outside play area, and 24/7 security. He set up educational trusts for all of them and provided primary schooling and medical care.

Krish spent the rest of the day there. He talked with the staff, visited with the children, and even sat in during their classes and listened to them sing. Krish scanned their faces and observed their interactions with each other and the staff. Some of the children didn't smile. It was obvious their young spirits had been crushed early, never allowed to blossom. Others, especially the older ones, showed remarkable resilience. They were actively involved in caring for the younger ones. All they really had was each other. Krish let his heart pour out and allowed himself to be overcome with empathy and humility. It was a cathartic experience, and he felt they were his salvation as much as he was theirs.

Monsoon season was soon to come, but sunshine remained in the forecast for several days. It was the day before he traveled back home, and, as planned, he visited the VC Farm for the first time in almost three years. As his car drove down the main road toward the school, Krish looked around through the closed, tinted window. With mixed feelings, he took in the stark contrast of the town from the last time he saw it. He observed brand-name signs and shops that had replaced the local vendors and farmer markets. As they passed through the busy streets, most of the locals were dressed in Western clothes now. They talked on cell phones and drove modern cars. Krish had brought to this village sanitation and other utilities, paved roads, streetlights, a formal police presence, and a modern school. But this modernization came with excesses and conformity and maybe robbed this place of its own identity. He couldn't imagine any of these strangers offering him the hospitality or intimate human interaction he'd experienced during his first visit as a teenager with his family all those years ago.

They pulled up to the school, and the driver let Krish out of the car. He got out, looked up at the school, and walked inside the compound. At the main entrance stood a woman in a simple sari. She looked similar in age to him but was almost ten years older. She had a pleasant face with bright, alert eyes, high cheekbones, and a sharp nose. She smiled as Krish approached and greeted him with the traditional Namaste gesture. Krish reciprocated.

"Good afternoon, Dr. Krish. So nice to finally meet you in person," she said.

"I'm very happy to see you, Dr. Varma," he said. He smiled, as he had looked forward to meeting her for a while. She was a native of VC Farm and was self-made. Varma earned her education in Bengaluru through sheer merit. She completed her Ph.D. in education and was elected the district representative in the state legislature. These credentials made her essentially the de facto mayor of VC.

"You may not believe this, but it seems my mother met you and your family many years ago when you visited here. She met you in her neighbor's house, where you stayed that day."

"Oh, wow. I didn't realize that," Krish said with genuine surprise and emotion. They walked upstairs and sat on a terrace that looked out onto the main street toward the town square. They bantered for a while over coffee before the conversation turned toward topics of more gravity.

"So, what do you think of VC these days, Dr. Krish?"

"Well, it's come a long way, to say the least," he said carefully. "I'm very curious about how you regard everything that has happened here, Dr. Varma, being a native of this place."

Dr. Varma paused and looked out over the town. "Overall, I'm very happy to see the development and modernization that has come here. I feel the overall quality of life has improved dramatically. Of course, seeing my hometown change almost beyond recognition was difficult in a way, but I think that is a natural sentiment."

Krish nodded but remained silent.

"You should be very proud, Dr. Krish. In my opinion, the people of VC Farm owe their livelihood to you. Your personal efforts, as well as the backing of your Beacon Medical Institute and your partners, have truly changed the landscape around here."

A puzzled look came over Krish's face. "Partners?"

"Yes," she said. She turned to face him. "Alpha Corp has been involved with the medical clinic, obviously. And over the last year or so, Alpha has been actively recruiting in this town for their pharmaceutical manufacturing plant outside Bengaluru and their research projects in the US. They've mentioned their collaboration with your Institute. I've been meaning to ask you more about that, Dr. Krish. They recruited several graduating students here for their education and research program in the US."

Krish's face became cast over and clammy. He struggled initially to get his words out. "Wait, what are you talking about, Dr. Varma? What has Alpha Corp been doing here?"

Dr. Varma had a curious look on her face. "I assumed you were involved one way or another, based on their description. Although they were admittedly vague and suspicious, frankly. I was able to meet once with someone in person from their company, and that was almost a year ago."

"I don't know anything about their dealings other than the medicines they've been supplying to the clinic here," Krish said. "Tell me more about what else they're doing, please."

"Dr. Krish, are you OK? You seem quite perturbed." Dr. Varma leaned toward him in concern.

Krish realized his reaction and quickly composed himself. "No, I'm fine, just surprised to hear what you're telling me. Despite what they might have told you, I have not been involved in anything else they're doing."

"Oh, interesting. They certainly seemed to give that impression in their communications. So, as you know, they supplied medicines. Shortly thereafter, they started recruiting employees for the pharm plant they built about two years ago. But it's only more recently that they actively sought out graduating students to take abroad. They approached their candidates directly and offered some sort of academic scholarship, even stipends for their family members. They kept me out of the loop somewhat. I became more curious in recent days after hearing from people here that they had lost touch with family members who had accepted Alpha's offer and left for the US."

Arya Krish leaned forward and looked wide-eyed at Dr. Varma as she spoke. He was breathing fast and sweating profusely. He tried to concentrate on what she was telling him, but his mind was flooded with speculation and thoughts of his recent encounters with Alpha Corp and all the circumstances that surrounded his father's experiences. Krish suddenly stood and paced nervously, forgetting his surroundings. He had made his way to the far end of the terrace, standing with one hand on his hip, the other tapping lightly on his chin in a pensive manner.

Dr. Varma stopped talking, stood, and walked over to him. "Dr. Krish, what's wrong? What's going on? Do you know something?"

Krish came out of his daze a little. He turned to Dr. Varma and looked her in the eye for a moment without saying anything.

"Actually, no, Dr. Varma, I don't know anything other than what you have just told me. But I am going to find out. I need you to give me as much information as you can about these people that they recruited, as well as any past communications you have had with Alpha Corp. I don't blame those guys for being concerned for their family members, especially if they haven't heard from them. That is unusual indeed. But I'm sure they're fine, Dr. Varma. I'll try to do what I can to track them down."

"That's fine, Dr. Krish, I'm sure they'd appreciate that," she said casually and smiled. Krish smiled back nervously, and they went back downstairs. He gathered as much information as he could before he left VC Farm and prepared for his return to the US.

***

Arya Krish strolled alongside the Reflecting Pool, just past the World War II Memorial, as he headed toward the Lincoln Memorial. A few thin clouds passed through the sky, and it was a comfortable summer day in Washington, DC. He had worked tirelessly the last several weeks since his return, immersed in the daily operations of the Institute. Krish had intensified his local social efforts as well and was returning from meetings with legislators on Capitol Hill. It was small-time lobbying, comparatively, but he sought out any advantage to advance his agenda, particularly in local public education. All the while, however, his mind turned over the information he had learned through his own investigation, as well as from Dr. Varma during his recent visit. He recalled some of the things his father told him about his remarkable experiences with the A1 Group. For the moment, Krish didn't consider even a remote connection, but it certainly fueled his speculation. He was resolved to find out more by any means necessary.

He sat on the steps of the Lincoln Memorial and watched the passers-by. Part of him wanted to leave well enough alone. He felt he might jeopardize what he had built up to this point if he probed further and created a confrontation with Alpha Corp. Then again, how could he remain silent and not pursue? Much was still unknown to him, but the information he did have obligated him to act on it.

"So, you're wearing your military uniform to get the extra attention?" Krish asked Asher as he approached.

Asher shook his head. "I've been sitting in on committee meetings with these clowns. What a futile exercise that's been. Half of the people who make the decisions and policies that affect the VA and active military personnel have never served. I look at some of the faces and wonder if they have ever had a deep thought or genuine feeling about any of it."

Krish frowned and nodded. "Most of the leaders of this country, including the Commander in Chief, have no military experience, direct or indirect."

Asher shrugged as he looked out on the National Mall. "Well, I don't know that it should be compulsory. Abraham Lincoln wasn't a military man, and he led the nation through a civil war." He gestured behind him. "But the old send the young to fight their wars. Meanwhile, people wave their little American flags in the parades, then go home and let reality TV wash over them. They're content that they've expressed their patriotism without ever bearing any real burden or bothering to gain insight themselves about what is going on and what the soldiers go through after they come home. People think they're doing their part by watching the latest Hollywood war movie or visiting one of these memorials. Only a tiny percent of the population who directly bear the burden have any clue. Let me tell you, man, I've felt the warm blood pour over my fingers as I pressed on the bleeding artery of a 19- or 20-year-old kid and looked in his fading eyes as he stammered for his mommy before succumbing to his wounds. When I listen to these people at these committee meetings or hearings drone on, I want to grab them by the collar and shove their faces into that scene. Force them to confront the reality they conveniently distance themselves from, yet have the audacity to rule over."

Krish observed Asher blink away the welled-up tears and turn his head away. Krish looked back straight ahead and reflected on his own sentiments toward those he had encountered in the past.

"Society at large tends to let the suffering and hardships of others pass them by," Krish said. "It's much easier that way."

Asher looked at Krish with a furrowed brow and a slight frown. "You sounded like you were scheming something when you called earlier."

Krish didn't reply right away, and they both sat silently for a while. Some of the people around looked at them as they walked by. Perhaps they recognized Arya Krish, or Asher's outfit caught their attention. Krish debated for a moment how to broach the topic.

"I haven't forgotten that Jason Rook violated Beacon," he said. He looked straight ahead, out over the Mall.

Asher nodded. "I haven't either, my friend. How did all that play out?"

"I confronted him about it. He admitted to it and basically said put up and shut up. Obviously, we are not about to do that."

"So he admitted to it, huh? Would've been nice to catch that on tape."

Krish shook his head. "Yeah. Well, I'm not exactly experienced in this sort of thing. Besides, they're not afraid of the law or of any other consequence, for that matter. That's the clear impression I got."

They stood and walked toward the Washington Monument but remained silent.

Krish marshaled his thoughts. "After the audacity of their actions toward us, I'm not interested in running to the law, frankly." He looked around as they walked casually, and to any observer, they may as well have been talking about the local sports teams' prospects. "The more I find out, the more my morbid curiosity about them has turned into a smoldering resentment. It was easy enough to compile their various shady enterprises in one sense. Like the influence on new vaccine guidelines so they'd include their latest products, regardless of the public health necessity. Or the manufacture and distribution of drugs abroad that failed FDA approval here in the US. And the opioid peddling, let alone the daily hijacking of the health care system at large with drug overpricing, insurance gouging, all of it. But after my last trip to India, I've come to think they're up to something even more sinister. They seem to be recruiting vulnerable foreign candidates and bringing them here. But some of them aren't heard from again, according to their families. I wonder how Beacon and whatever they were seeking when they broke in factor into it all."

Krish paused and looked at Asher, waiting patiently for a response.

"Well, you've brought up several things here," Asher said. He turned to Krish. They stopped walking and stood near the World War II Memorial. "Those former things you mentioned? While I share in your disapproval, those things are not overtly something I think we can prosecute them for, legally or otherwise. And the latter? It's rather vague, my friend, and you seem to be speculating on minimal information."

Krish sighed as he looked on at the Memorial. "It's hard to explain, man. But I think back to what my dad went through in his life and feel like I'm being summoned to confront Alpha Corp. It got personal after what Jason Rook did. I want to hit them back."

"Wait a minute," Asher said, with a wave of his hand. "What do you mean, with your father? What's he got to do with any of this?"

"Nothing. Never mind," Krish said.

Asher eyed him keenly as if trying to read his mind. "Well,

what is it you have in mind? You want to hit them back, rattle their cage a little, huh? OK, so what are you going to do, break into their building and steal something of theirs?"

Krish shook his head. "Not exactly."

"OK. Good, because that's not as straightforward as you might think. You should know guys like Alpha Corp, with everything they deal in, they take their security pretty seriously. Some of these big corporations have small private militaries, and I'm sure Alpha Corp is strapped. That Jason Rook guy is probably ex-military himself, and he's one among many on their payroll. In my opinion, if you want to play their game, you'd be putting yourself in harm's way."

"Then we need to explore potential resources on our side. I know you have connections along those military lines. What do you think? Anything there we can tap into?"

Asher thought for a moment without answering. It was obvious he was not taking the conversation lightly. Krish knew he was willing to do whatever was asked if the circumstances called for it.

"Yes," Asher said. He nodded slightly in a contemplative manner. "I think we can consult some people. Sounds like we want a certain brand of information, something Alpha Corp is protecting and doesn't want to get out."

"Yeah, something we can leverage, put them back on their heels a little. Information is power. I think if we can crack their shell, we'll find something they would fear."

"If we pursue this, it will most certainly escalate. They will find out, most likely, and retaliate. We'd be venturing deeper into the macabre. Is that something you're prepared to do?"

"Honestly, I don't know. It's often that way, isn't it? Circumstances manifest without preparing you for what they demand of you. Instead, you find yourself rising or falling to the occasion. I don't know if this is the right thing to do, if it is wise or even sane, for that matter. All I feel is the tension, something that will not go away by simply ignoring or going about my usual business."

Asher put his hand on Krish's shoulder. Krish felt the emotion bubbling from within and showed it on his face. "OK, I'll see what we can come up with. It'll take some time. But trust me, we're jumping in with both feet."

Krish nodded with a stern look of resolve.

For a while, things remained status quo. It had been a few weeks, in fact, since that conversation with Asher, and Krish had deferred to him to get back with an update. In the meantime, it was business as usual at Beacon Medical Institute. Krish remained intensely involved with clinical medicine. Just as he did with the orphanage and the children there, he sought out the human interactions that revealed the nuances of the human condition. It was like turning a shiny gem and watching it catch the light in different ways.

He arrived at the outpatient clinic and went straight to the patient room, knocked, and opened the door. Krish stood in the doorway and looked at the man standing over the female patient, who was still on the transport gurney.

"I'm sorry to keep you waiting, sir," Krish said. "I'll be with you shortly. I want to take a minute to carefully review the records that were sent over. Please bear with me."

The man nodded, and Krish closed the door and went to his office. After a while, he knew about the patient and returned. He knocked on the door and entered. As he did so, he saw the husband bent over his wife, massaging her arms and saying something to her in a soft voice. Krish stood back quietly for a moment. Then, the man turned toward him and shook his hand.

"Hello, doctor. How are you?"

"I'm fine, Mr. Fisher. Nice to meet you," Krish replied with a smile. The man was in his early 60s and appeared quite fit and healthy. He wore a gray t-shirt and jeans. His short dark gray hair was combed neatly, and he had a mustache. Behind his glasses were large, soulful, tired blue eyes, like a bulldog. Krish walked to the other side of the gurney and looked at the patient. Her eyes were open with an alert gaze and tracked him occasionally. She had a slight grimace, and a tracheostomy stuck out of her neck.

"Well, sir," Krish said, "I looked over everything that was sent to us. From my understanding, your wife doesn't speak and is able to move her arms slightly but cannot move her legs. That has pretty much been the case since her stroke?"

Mr. Fisher nodded and looked at his wife's face. "Yeah. She gained some movement in her arms. But so far, that's it."

"And it's been almost a year now since it happened?"

"Yup. It'll be a year on the 26th."

"She was otherwise healthy, it seemed, before it happened."

Mr. Fisher had a far-off look on his face as he looked up at Krish. "We had both just retired and looked forward to our retired life together," he said. He nodded slightly, and his lips were pressed together.

His statement struck Krish to the core, and he quickly choked back his emotions. He was able to throw his mind into Mr. Fisher's world. It was a typical story where a husband and wife spent the previous 35 years of their lives for the better and looked ahead to a leisurely life together. But their lives were turned upside down by a singular, random event. With his experience as a doctor, Krish could envision this couple's daily lives together, but now in the nursing home. Mrs. Fisher was paralyzed and non-verbal but cognitively intact and completely aware. Her husband was devout and tenaciously tended to his wife with every fiber of his being. It was clear that his life would be consumed with her medical care as long as she was alive. *How does that make Mrs. Fisher feel?* Krish wondered. *Did she feel she was dragging him down? Did she want to continue like this? What were the husband's expectations?*

He examined her thoroughly while Mr. Fisher stood back respectfully and waited. Krish placed his stethoscope over the back of his neck and turned toward Fisher. "Well, sir, I think her sacral wound is infected. That's what's causing her elevated white cell count and low-grade fever. I do not think it's the trach site or a respiratory infection. Actually, I smelled the wound as soon as I entered the room."

Fisher shook his head. "They kept saying it was her trach and that she had bronchitis. I admit I haven't seen the wound. I couldn't bring myself to see it. I don't know if they paid any attention to it, either."

"Well, that's why they referred you to us, to help out. I suggest a few weeks of IV antibiotics and a plastic surgeon to help us out, as well. I know him from the hospital. He's excellent," Krish said.

His demeanor inspired confidence in Fisher. Krish's reputation certainly preceded him as well. Fisher walked over to his wife and stroked her face with his hand. "Whatever you say, doctor. I feel so much better about things since coming here. As soon as you poked your head in and said you were going to take a minute to look over her records, I knew we came to the right place."

Krish walked over and stood next to him. Mrs. Fisher lay with her eyes open now and was able to hear everything that was said.

"What have they told you regarding her neurological status, Mr. Fisher? That is obviously her defining issue."

"She's going to have a repeat MRI at the one-year mark. They basically said where she is at that point is likely where she'll stay," Mr. Fisher said.

Arya Krish nodded.

"They keep working with her at the nursing home. I gotta

say, doc, some days she surprises all of them with her progress. She'll suddenly lift her arm up and point, with all of us watching. Other days, though, she's not as engaged and takes a huge step backward. I can see it in her eyes. She gets tired."

"I don't know what your expectations are, Mr. Fisher, but I feel I have to bring up the prospect that your wife's recovery may not change much beyond this point. I wonder, for your sake and hers, have you thought about that much at all?"

Mr. Fisher turned toward Krish. "I know what happened to her was bad and permanent. But I admit that part of me is holding out for a miracle, doc. Sometimes, I look in her eyes, and I feel she's going to surprise us all yet again." He looked back at his wife. "Maybe I'm old and stupid," he said as they made eye contact.

Krish didn't know what to say, so he remained silent. They both stood quietly for a moment.

"You believe in miracles, doc?"

Krish thought for a moment. "I believe some miracles are possible, and some miracles are impossible."

Fisher sighed and didn't respond. Krish looked at him and watched the expression on his face for a moment. He debated whether or not to continue the difficult conversation. He believed he helped Fisher by getting him to think about their future and his wife's mortality.

"Mr. Fisher, I think it is important from a practical standpoint to think about some possible circumstances that may come up in the future. I've seen this situation many times and seen patients and their families go through this before. And I feel compelled to share my insight with you in the hopes that it may spare you difficulty down the road. For example, I think you must be clear about what you would want done if your wife's heart stopped beating. Would you want them to crack her ribs doing chest compressions and shock her in an attempt to resuscitate her? If she was not able to breathe on her own, would you want her to be on a ventilator? These are fundamental questions to answer clearly because, God forbid, if that situation arises, things happen fast, and there isn't time to consider it. I advise you to think about what she would want in these situations and make it official in her medical record."

Fisher nodded. "You're not the first one to bring that up, doc. I've dodged the decision-making to this point. I can't bring myself to think about it."

"Well, your wife is in there, Mr. Fisher. She's listening to our conversation. She is cognitively intact and can communicate at least a little if she's shown any motor function. It seems you can talk to her about these things as husband and wife. She must have her own thoughts and ideas about her quality of life and yours. It seems to me it's something the two of you should share."

Fisher shook his head, and a look of despair came over his face. Krish decided not to pursue the topic further. He put his hand on Fisher's shoulder.

"Just some food for thought, Mr. Fisher. Like I said, for the moment, we'll focus on what's in front of us. We'll move ahead with the things I said earlier with the antibiotics and plastic surgery evaluation."

Mr. Fisher nodded and turned to Krish. They shook hands, and Mr. Fisher hugged him and thanked him. Krish left the room, went to his office, and closed the door. He slumped back into his chair and swiveled toward the window. He looked out at the view and sat alone for a while.

CHAPTER FIVE

It was a late autumn day, overcast, and everything was grayscale as a result. Yet the colorful leaves on the trees were all the more bright and vibrant. Arya Krish wore a dark blue suit as he sat quietly on one of the benches in the courtyard. He looked straight ahead, and his hands rested in his lap. Other than the few passers-by in their black and white suits, all seemed still, though an occasional crisp breeze rustled the leaves. Krish tuned out his surroundings and contemplated his course of action as he waited. He sat for a long time that day, and though he sensed Jason Rook's approach, he didn't react as Rook came over and sat next to him. For a moment, they both sat next to each other and silently looked straight ahead.

Finally, Rook spoke. "Well, Dr. Krish, should I consider this as your calling card from now on?"

"I take it you know why I'm here?"

"I connected the dots after I saw you sitting here. I admit, I didn't think you were capable of something like this. Or inclined, for that matter. It's not an easy task, breaching our secure information." Rook paused. "Let us be clear. That is why you're here. It was your doing, right?"

Krish continued to look ahead, and he didn't answer right away. He took out a flash drive and handed it to Rook.

"I figured you guys would know something happened and what was compromised. Yes, it was us, and here's the proof. Well, now I know what you were after that night in our building."

Rook looked at Krish and scoffed. "What is it you think you know, Dr. Krish?" he asked with a smirk.

Krish's tone and expression remained grave. "You went after our R&D. This is how you guys operate, huh? Don't have the innovation yourself, so you gotta steal it from others? Fortunately, it doesn't look like you got very far. You seem to know about the Panacea Project, particularly after that, it looked like. Well, we've come to know some things, too. The politician accounts, the slush funds. They're all interesting enough. But I'm curious about those nameless employee accounts and addresses. I suspect they have something to do with the foreigners Alpha Corp recruits and brings over, like the ones from Bengaluru. What can you tell me about that, Mr. Rook?"

"I assume that is a rhetorical question, Dr. Krish. You can't seriously be expecting any sort of answer."

Jason Rook stood, looked down at Arya Krish, and slowly started walking. Krish stood and followed him almost reluctantly. They walked in silence for a while, farther away from the building and the people. After a while, Jason Rook stopped and turned toward Krish.

"I'm still not sure what you're doing, Dr. Krish. Are you trying to prove something? I suppose you know better than going to the cops. What is it you want, exactly?"

"All I can say is, knowing what I know, I cannot sit idly by. We are men of action, Mr. Rook, you and I. You can expect me to continue to pursue this."

"Knowing what you know, huh? First of all, it doesn't seem like you know much at all. Second, I find it interesting that you are taking the moral high ground here. You deny your hands are dirty as well? Has anyone questioned your methods in some of the things you do, as noble as you claim them to be?" Rook got up close in Krish's face and gave him a hard look.

Krish remained calm, though his breathing became fast and shallow. Rook suddenly grabbed Krish by the collar. Krish tried to shake loose, but Rook's grip was like a vise. He held

Rook's wrists as they stared each other down.

"I want you to seriously consider the consequences of your actions, Dr. Krish, so listen closely. I'm saying this for your own good. There's an underground layer in our industry that you should leave alone. You don't belong in that realm, OK? Whatever insight or experience you think you have with the darker elements doesn't qualify you, believe me."

Rook let him go and stood back. Krish straightened his jacket, then stood quietly with his hands in his pockets. His face was unperturbed, and he had a hard look of resolve. Rook remained silent and calm as well. His respect for Krish likely remained genuine, for what it was worth.

"Look, Dr. Krish. You have your vast enterprise, with all the good it is doing for society here and abroad. Given how much our two entities collaborate and intertwine, it would not be in your best interests to escalate this. It can become very dangerous." Rook flashed the handgun in his left shoulder holster. Krish glanced at it and looked back at Rook without much reaction.

"Just think about it, Dr. Krish. We'll leave things at that for the time being. I'll be seeing you around, though. You can count on it." Rook buttoned his suit jacket and gave a nod to Krish, then turned and walked away.

After Krish made his way back to his car and sat by himself, he let his guard down, and the emotions surged forth. Rook's intimidation was not without effect. In spite of all his deliberation, Krish was impulsive in his choice to confront Alpha Corp. Rook had snapped into focus what was at stake collaterally. Krish remembered his wife and son and thought of all he had accomplished and had yet to accomplish. He couldn't deny Rook's point about his irrevocable ties with Alpha Corp. He was more unsettled with the lack of control he felt over the entire situation. Part of him contemplated abandoning his pursuit and dedicating himself entirely to his personal vision, but he knew it would make him feel like a hypocrite to remain silent and idle.

The following day, Krish was in the R&D section of Beacon Medical Institute. The vast underground lab was the size of a large warehouse. It was well-lit, with various stations, benches, and technology catering to the cutting-edge work done there. It had been almost a year since he had been down there and about as long since he had last followed up on the Panacea Project. He was there now to meet Vincent Halliday, the head of R&D. Krish turned as he heard the main door open and saw Halliday walk toward him. Dr. Halliday walked rather swiftly for a man his size. He was a bald black man, standing 6'5", with a short, thick neck and large, broad shoulders. It was easy to tell he was a college linebacker in his day. He had a round face with large, intelligent eyes, a sharp nose, and a beard that outlined his strong square jawline. Krish was a lean 6'2", but he always felt dwarfed in Halliday's presence.

"Dr. Krish! To what do I owe the honor?" Halliday boomed.

"It's good to see you, Dr. Halliday," Krish said. He smiled. "Just wanted to make sure you weren't getting cabin fever down here."

Halliday guffawed heartily. Krish laughed as well as they shook hands. They bantered back and forth for a while before Krish broached the topic of interest.

"Actually, Dr. Halliday, I want to inquire about the Panacea Project. I admit I have not kept up with your reports. Honestly, they were quite technical."

Halliday nodded and walked toward one of the computer stations as Arya Krish followed.

The Panacea Project was launched more than a year ago. It explored the prospects of carbon-based nanotechnology, including custom synthesized substrates, even nanorobotics, on the biochemical scale that might potentially serve any number of functions. Those functions might include cellular surgery and antimicrobials against multidrug-resistant organisms that could, in theory, be custom-made to a particular culture. Other functions might include cancer immunotherapy, autoimmune neutralization, and gene manipulation and augmentation. The concept was to essentially synthesize custom molecules using new gene technology to affect human physiology at the cellular, molecular, and, possibly, atomic level. If it came to fruition, it would open the doors to making the incurable curable. Thus, the name.

"Well, I think it's best to kind of walk through the different arms of development currently underway," Halliday said as he logged into his computer and pulled up the relevant files and data. Krish watched intently.

"So, maybe of most interest to you would be the antimicrobial application," Halliday said. "Basically, we're exploring two modes of customizable antimicrobial effect toward a target microorganism, whether it be bacteria, fungi, or virus. Any particular bacteria cultured can be analyzed for specific antigens, both intracellular and extracellular, and we would try to synthesize an active substrate, either a carbon-based nano-robot or an organic biochemical. In my opinion, the bio-organic may be more feasible in the short term, though the carbon-based nano-robot technology would likely be more durable and reproducible on a larger scale. But the problem with the latter is it likely cannot be reliably implemented without tedious *in vivo* studies."

"Well, Dr. Halliday, your opinion is all that matters on this subject," Krish said. He had hand-picked Vincent Halliday for his brilliance in pioneering the field.

"Thank you, Dr. Krish, that's very kind. I'm honored to be a part of it. I truly feel that when this comes into being, in whatever form, it will be a milestone in human history. Kind of like when penicillin ushered in the age of modern medicine.

Of course, the potential applications of this technology go well beyond infectious diseases."

"So, what is the barrier to developing the nanotechnology?"

Halliday shrugged and went into silent thought for a moment. "Basically, there would be no way to be consistent in producing viable and functional molecules without experimenting on humans. Animal, even primate models, would not sufficiently mimic the HLA variabilities that would be essential to account for preventing immune rejection or interference. In fact, the problem applies to both the bio-organic and carbon-nanotech models, to an extent, but there are other technical limitations to bio-organic synthesis."

Arya Krish's eyes were wide as he listened to Halliday. His mind left the conversation and connected the dots with all he had investigated and encountered with Alpha Corp. *What if Alpha Corp is advancing their own development efforts with human experimentation?* This thought exploded in Krish's mind, and he must have had a strange look on his face.

Halliday looked at Krish inquisitively. "Dr. Krish, are you OK?"

Krish refocused and looked at Halliday. "Yes. Of course, Dr. Halliday," he said. Krish nodded slowly. "I remember now that I have another appointment. I'll definitely come back and pick this up with you again if that's alright with you?"

"Whatever you like, Dr. Krish. I'm available."

They shook hands, and Krish rushed out of the lab toward his office. He sat in front of his computer and scrolled through Alpha Corp data. He paused and reviewed the addresses in the database linked with cryptic labels, such as Subject C45. The zip codes were for the surrounding suburbs, for the most part. But Krish did not recognize all of them. The addresses and subject labels were grouped in folders named HLA, followed by a number. Krish leaned back in his chair, turned away from the computer, and looked out the window. He stood and walked over to look outdoors. Down the street below, he saw Jason Rook's sedan parked at the curb, as it had been the last several days. Rook stood beside it with his hands folded over his belt line. He reminded Krish of a Secret Service agent. Krish had accepted this new surveillance from Alpha Corp, not knowing what else to make of it. His mind went back to their last encounter and Rook's exhibition of physicality and side-arm. Krish watched with a calculating look on his face as he contemplated his choices. He did not feel it would be worthwhile to go to the authorities in any capacity. Krish knew he really had nothing beyond circumstantial evidence, and he felt they would be powerless anyway against such an adversary. He was being called into action and felt this was something he had to see through personally. Krish went back to his computer, printed a hard copy of all the files for safekeeping, grabbed a few sheets with the addresses, and left.

***

It was late as Krish drove along the winding backroads in a suburb about 40 minutes outside of DC. A dense fog hovered as he passed through suburban residential neighborhoods and eventually drove on narrow rural roads with no other lights other than his headlights illuminating the immediate road in front of him. He relied mainly on his GPS to show him the address location. The fog lifted as he passed through a wooded area into a clearing and made out a few small farmhouses. The GPS alerted him that he had reached his destination, and Krish slowed down to a crawl. He saw a gravel driveway with a mailbox that looked fairly new. The house number matched the address he wanted. Krish slowly pulled up near the driveway and stopped, then turned off the engine. He looked toward the house but only saw a dim porch light. After a moment of hesitation, he reconsidered his intentions. He was there to confirm his suspicions that Alpha Corp was recruiting, coercing, or outwardly abducting human test subjects, probably both abroad and domestically. Although spurred to act, perhaps impulsively, he sat for a moment and contemplated his next move. Finally, he reached for the door.

Suddenly, a bright pair of headlights came on about 20 feet down the road, startling and blinding him. Krish put his hand up in front of his face and squinted at the lights. He saw a figure open the driver's side door and get out. Krish watched the silhouette walk toward the car and stand in front of it. While he couldn't make out a face, he knew from the tall, lean shadow that it was Jason Rook. Krish quickly got out of his car, closed the door, and walked in front of it. He saw Rook clearer now. Only insects could be heard, and no other noises were in the vicinity. Arya Krish juggled mixed emotions of surprise, anxiety, and exasperation. When he spoke, however, it was in a calm, confident voice.

"Boy, you really are everywhere, aren't you?" Krish shook his head.

"I'm not sure what you're looking for here, Dr. Krish, but I wouldn't bother."

"Just thought I'd go for a drive in the country, actually. You know, get away from it all."

Jason Rook nodded and acknowledged the sarcasm. "I ask that you come with me, Dr. Krish. Someone would like to meet you."

Krish looked toward the house. "Who, the guy who lives here?"

"No, my boss, actually. The Director."

"Well, it's late. Maybe we can arrange for an appointment some other time."

"He won't be available again, Dr. Krish. I think you'll want to meet him." Jason Rook walked toward Krish, "After all, he was your father's boss once as well."

Krish's expression remained calm, but immediately, his

heart raced, and he broke out in a sweat. His initial reaction was skepticism. Perhaps Rook lied to get him to come along. But on reconsideration, that didn't make sense. It didn't align with their attitude and mode of operation. They didn't have to resort to something like that to get their way.

"What did you say?" asked Krish.

"Yes, that's right. While we're good at keeping secrets, I must admit I'm surprised you didn't know. He's the only executive remaining from the former A1 Group. But perhaps it would be better to hear it from him. Do you agree?"

Arya Krish's mind raced. Dimly, he nodded and was shown to Rook's sedan. He sat alone in the back while Rook drove. The windows were tinted, as well as the privacy barrier between the front and back of the car. Krish could not tell where they were going. Krish sat quietly and looked out the window, even though he couldn't see anything. His mind was elsewhere as he tried to recall everything his father had said about his experience as a young scientist at the A1 Group. His father had told him about meetings with the Directors. He'd shared accounts of their stifling control tactics, from the implanted monitoring devices to the ubiquitous cameras, the fabricated correspondences with his father's family, and the deaths of his other colleagues.

All of it was now relevant in a new light. All of it, however, was also eclipsed by Krish's long-lived suspicion of foul play surrounding his father's death. Unfortunately, it remained only suspicion, based on his conversations with his father leading up to the crash and the prescience his father exhibited in his comments regarding the A1 Group's ruthlessness. Now, after 15 years, Krish contemplated the newly revealed link between the past and present, like beads on a string. After about 30 minutes, he sensed the car slowed. He came back to the present. The anticipation of coming face-to-face with his father's former boss and his current adversary was electrifying. His mind swam in speculation of the unknown, and he became focused on getting answers.

A steady drizzle was visible in the single light above the door as the car pulled up. Jason Rook let Krish out of the car. He got out and looked around with curiosity. Other than the single light over the door of the building, it was pitch dark. Krish saw dark red brick around the steel door but made out little else about his surroundings. Rook came around and led them to the door. They paused for a moment before being buzzed it.

Beyond the door was a long, narrow hallway. It had bare, white concrete walls and floor, and it was well-lit from the tall ceiling. They walked down the hallway in silence to the elevator door at the end. No button was pressed. But after a moment, the door opened on its own, and they got inside. The elevator itself was elegant, like what might be seen at a luxury hotel, with mirrors on the walls. Krish glanced at Rook through the mirror as they stood next to each other, both with their hands in their pockets. The elevator door opened, and Krish was led into a small room where a security guard stood next to a detector, like the kind in airports.

"I'll ask you to empty your pockets, Dr. Krish. This man will search you afterward," Rook said.

Krish gave Rook a suspicious look, then placed his belongings in the tray. He passed through the detector and was patted down by the guard. The guard nodded to Rook.

"Proceed through the doors, Dr. Krish. You will get your stuff back when you leave."

He looked back at Rook, who remained where he was near the elevator. The guard opened the door and signaled to Krish to proceed inside. Krish turned and went inside. It was a very large oval-shaped office suite with tall ceilings from which modern-style lights hung. It was sparsely furnished for such a vast room. A fire roared in the large Victorian-style fireplace.

Next to it was a modern wet bar. On the other side of the room were large television and computer screens. And in the middle, at the far end of the room, was a large executive desk. In front of it stood a man who seemed to be a colleague of Rook, similar in appearance and demeanor. Behind the desk, somewhat in the shadows, stood a stout man in a gray suit. He looked out a thin, tall, rectangular window, the only one in the room.

"You can go now," said the man behind the desk.

Krish flinched, then watched the other man leave and close the door behind him.

"Winter's coming early," the man said in a coarse but articulate voice. He still looked out the window. Krish remained silent. After a moment, the man emerged from the shadow near the window and stood in front of the desk. His hands were in his pockets as he looked at Krish. His skin was ashen and aged, like old stone, and reminded Krish of a gargoyle. His face was expressionless, other than a subtle perpetual frown.

Krish took a couple of steps forward. "Who are you?" he asked.

The man shrugged. "My name doesn't matter, Dr. Krish. I am the head of Alpha Corp. That is all you need to know."

Krish nodded slowly. "So, what am I doing here?"

The man sat in his chair and gestured toward the chair in front of the desk. Krish's expression remained frustrated, but he went over and sat across from him.

"I think that is a question we'll have to answer together, Dr. Krish. But I would rephrase it. What is it you want? Perhaps if we clarify that, we can understand our relationship a little better."

The man's tone was authoritative and commanded attention. He rested his elbows on the chair's armrests with his hands up near his face. His countenance remained unchanged throughout, and his eyes were fixed on Krish with a stone-cold gaze.

Arya Krish remained silent. To his surprise, he did not have a ready answer to the man's seemingly simple question. *What was it he wanted?* So many answers rushed to the surface. He had his philanthropy and humanitarian vision, his life's work. His scientific pursuits were important, and they were tied into the former. The conspiracies surrounding Alpha Corp, of which he had scratched the surface, no doubt caused irritation to the man who sat in front of him. Finally, the haunting and unresolved death of his father deserved time and attention. In his mind, they were all tied together — beads on a string.

"I would guess you have many answers to that question," the man said. "In short, you want it all, don't you? It's all so complicated. Everything is connected, inescapably, affecting one another. That is the nature of the universe at large, I suppose, isn't it? And human nature as well — to want everything, I mean. I admit I'm guilty of that, Dr. Krish."

"Human nature is mutable, shaped by the unique human ability to choose," Krish replied, almost reciting it. He felt he was falling behind in a verbal chess match.

"Absolutely. Everything you need to know about a man can be derived from the choices he makes." The man paused and stared at Krish for a moment. "And now we apply that principle to you, Dr. Krish, in an attempt to answer my question."

The man leaned back a little. He swiveled slightly back and forth, and while nothing in his demeanor changed, Krish perceived he was amusing himself with this dialogue.

"You are a man who makes choices with solely the end goal in mind. All your choices are driven by that. You are willing to suspend some principles in the process. You recalibrated your moral compass, as it were, as a result. I think you know what I'm talking about. The bribery, the blackmail, the intimidation, extortion — all the means you've employed, oddly enough in

India far more than here at home, to meet your ends. Means that are justified in your mind on the merits of all that altruism and humanity that shine through and glare out the compromises made along the way."

"And your point is what, sir?" Krish asked. "You're not the first to point this out to me. I've come across many claiming to be more similar to me than I realize or give them credit for because they, too, seek their own noble ends and justify their actions through them. Doesn't everyone do what you are describing on one scale or another? The ends justify the means. It is a time-old adage, one that has been defended and refuted since its genesis. I see no point in debating it with you now."

The man shook his head disapprovingly. "I am not interested in debating with you, Dr. Krish. I say again, I am making an articulated effort to answer the question that is the premise of our meeting. What is it you want? You have not told me yourself, so I go through this exercise. But I do confess I am rather enjoying and taking advantage of this opportunity, Dr. Krish. It is not often I get to pick the brain of a genius. Believe me, I am not trying to flatter you in any way. But I'm sure you know that anyway. Those people you describe who claimed they had something in common with you? They had no business comparing themselves with their puny self-centered greed that they tried to pass off as noble ambition, I'm sure."

Krish paid close attention to every word he said. But he shifted in his chair impatiently.

"But I go back to the choices you've made to bring your vision forward. They are certainly telling, aren't they? To a man of your insight, I am sure the consequences have not escaped you regarding your tactics and their effect on real people you saw as obstacles in your path. And yet you continued. And as a result, you have altered the path of literally millions and subsequent generations in entire geographic regions. It seems clear to me now what it is you want. So your humanitarian enterprise is most important. We have participated to some extent in it, but we can do much more. As a partner, we can open all the doors. You would simply have to point. Think of it, Dr. Krish. Your scope to affect social change expands exponentially in that case. How do you feel about that?"

I feel like I'm being asked by the devil to sell my soul, Arya Krish wanted to say, but he refrained and remained silent for a moment. Part of him found the proposal appealing. He thought of the prospects and envisioned something almost on the scale of nation-building. He knew the man could make it happen, and just imagining that kind of power and the good it could do was intoxicating. But so much else was on his mind.

"Well, sir," he said guardedly, "it certainly sounds enticing on the surface. But forgive me for being skeptical. I can't help but wonder, what is it you seek in return? What's the catch?"

The man nodded and acknowledged the anticipated response from Arya Krish.

"Quite simple, Dr. Krish. I expect you to reciprocate in cooperation and collaboration. Your amateur probing and investigation into our operations have become a nuisance. That will cease. The research and development at Beacon Medical Institute will merge with ours and as a result, I anticipate significantly accelerating its progress. Those are the broad strokes, Dr. Krish, but I think you get the idea."

The man swiftly reached into a drawer. He pulled out a sealed envelope and placed it on the desk.

"It will be a formal partnership between our institutions, with each retaining its autonomy." He pushed the envelope across the desk. "This will be the contract between us. Take your time in reviewing and revising it if you wish. In fact, until it satisfies our mutual interests."

Krish looked down at the envelope, then back up at the

man. He leaned forward. But instead of picking up the envelope, he stood. The man watched him casually. Krish slowly walked toward the monitors at the other end of the room, which were off. The man remained where he was.

"What is the alternative?" Krish asked. He kept his back toward the man.

"Again, it would be driven by choice. If you choose to continue along the current lines, then we will make sure your projects come to a screeching stop. Make no mistake, Dr. Krish. I will make it my mission to undo everything you have built," the man said coldly.

Krish turned and faced the man sitting at the desk.

"Your words do not exactly inspire any sort of confidence or trust that would engender the kind of so-called partnership you're proposing. Sounds more like demands and threats."

"I prefer to be blunt in these matters so there will be no misunderstanding."

"Well, then. Allow me to be equally blunt. If we are to be enemies, it would be a mutual destruction, I can assure you. I can do plenty of damage on my own."

"Let us not escalate our rhetoric any further, Dr. Krish. I think we are losing sight of the point of this conversation. It comes back to what it is you want. You will have to choose what is more important to you. I will say this, your apparent idea of gathering some evidence and submitting it to the authorities or to public scrutiny will bear no consequence in either case. Litigation is impotent, and public awareness is an oxymoron. In the times we live in, the masses are dull, asleep, dimly aware of little else other than their sports teams' playoff hopes and what happened on the last episode of whatever hit TV show they watched. As in so many points in history, under such circumstances, those in the power grab operate with impunity. The public will remain silent, like the marionette that suddenly looks up and sees the strings and hands playing above. Unable to bear the strain of trying to comprehend any of it, the marionette contentedly goes back to being the puppet it deserves to be. Your energy and efforts would be better directed toward your true life's work."

Krish remained silent as his mind turned over every option. He had to concede the man's point. The social and humanitarian work and all that happens with Beacon Medical Institute had to be preserved. He had to find another way to defeat Alpha Corp. Especially now, knowing the identity of this man. Krish's resolve hardened. He walked back over to the desk and sat down.

"There is one other thing to discuss before I consider your offer," he said.

"What is that?"

"I understand my father worked for you at the A1 Group."

"Yes, that is correct," the man replied quickly.

"My father told me everything that happened there. He shared what he experienced. I want to hear from you exactly what happened to them."

"Your father died in a car crash with two of his colleagues, if I'm not mistaken. I'm afraid I don't know much more than that."

"I say again," Arya Krish said in a low, unwavering voice, "I know exactly what was going on in the A1 Group. Others died while working there, other scientists. It was pretty clear to my father that you, the A1 Group, killed them."

The man stared at Krish with the same expressionless look. "Well, your father testified before the grand jury to that and many other things, Dr. Krish. That was when you were a kid. It led to some corporate criminal charges and the dissolution of the A1Group. But, as you know, there were no murder indictments. Your father died almost ten years after all that. I'm not sure where you see the connection."

The man stood, slowly walked back over to the thin

window, and looked outside. A slight scowl crept onto Krish's face as he watched him.

"I don't feel I have to hide anything from you, Dr. Krish. Your father made some powerful enemies, and that kind of bad blood can spawn the most sinister actions, I suppose." The man turned and locked eyes with Krish. "If I were you, I would draw a lesson from your father's tragedy."

Arya Krish felt a surge of anger that almost drove him to pounce on the man and choke the life out of him. It took all his self-control to show no reaction to the man's words. Krish took deep breaths as he stood and took the envelope in his hand. The man watched him do so, then turned away and looked out the window again. Nothing else was said. Krish turned and walked out of the room.

The winter came early. In fact, it was uneventful, at least in regard to him and Alpha Corp. But all was not dormant. He visited India again but did not attend to his work there. Instead, he toured the ancient temples with his wife and son, as he had done with his family when he was younger. He looked up at the towering stone that bore the burden of history on its façade and connected with the cool, grainy feel of it on his hands and beneath his feet. At times, he closed his eyes and felt as if his surroundings tried to communicate with him through his senses. In those ancient spiritual surroundings, he truly felt a part of something larger. It freed him temporarily from the tensions that surrounded him and, with that separation, made them seem transient and trivial.

It never left his mind, though.

All the while, Krish ruminated and devised plans and methods to confront and expose Alpha Corp. It started on the drive back that night after meeting the man, as he sat silently, alone in the back of the sedan, behind the tinted windows. For the first time, thoughts of mortal revenge simmered against the man he met, the man Krish held responsible for his father's death. He took satisfaction in allowing his mind to dwell on them.

CHAPTER SIX

As Arya Krish sat and faced the new incoming class of physicians at the Institute, his eyes looked past them. His mind was somewhere else. Sunshine streamed in through the tall windows to his left, and this illuminated the large room with long beams of light and glistened over the polished oak floors. He was 36 years old, and a culmination of choices led to this moment. He realized he was breathing too fast and took a moment to consider his decision one more time in the context of the larger plan he had set in motion. Eventually, he signed the papers, addressed the physicians, and left.

He met with Asher and showed him the envelope Steinhart had given him for the first time. Krish revealed part of the plan to him, but not everything. Not yet. He needed a few more crucial things to fall into place first. Eventually, he would reach out to Asher as his only means to the final endgame if Asher agreed to help him. Krish would ask a lot of him when the time came. For the moment, he proceeded toward the R&D lab to meet Vincent Halliday.

As he entered, Krish found the lab empty of its usual staff. In fact, most of the lights were off, and all the stations were powered down, except in the far corner. He looked down toward that last station, which was brightly lit from above, and headed toward it. As he approached, he saw Halliday bent over the station, working intently. Halliday did not notice him right away. It wasn't until Krish stood next to him that he looked up suddenly, slightly startled.

"Oh! Dr. Krish. Sorry, I was just finishing up here,"

Halliday said.

"No problem, Dr. Halliday," Krish said. He smiled and looked down at the lab bench as Dr. Halliday leaned in again and resumed his work. Halliday looked through his magnified eyepiece as he attached wires into a small circuit board in a black plastic casing about the size of a flash drive. Krish observed Halliday's alert and focused eyes guide his large, steady hands as he finished connecting the device to the laptop.

"We're almost done, just need to program it," Halliday said. He removed his work glasses and turned his attention to the laptop. After a little typing and a few clicks, he paused for a moment while the computer worked. They both stood silently and stared at the computer, like watching a pot of water boil. After a minute or so, Halliday carefully removed the wires from the device and replaced the top casing over the circuit. He took the device in his hand and examined it briefly. He handed it to Krish, who held it between his thumb and forefinger and brought it near his face.

"So. This is it, huh?" Krish asked.

"Yup. Kept it small and nondescript, as you specified."

"How does it work exactly?"

"Well, it's meant to look like a flash drive, complete with USB. You can plug it into a computer to transfer data and charge it. It's got a small battery, maybe a couple hours life."

"How far can it sense?" Krish asked in a business-like tone.

Halliday pondered for a moment. "I would say a good 20 or 25 feet," he said. "Based on the brand and model information you provided, I've programmed it to interrogate the pacemaker remotely and store its specifications. It will ping the same receiver in the pacemaker that is used to program it remotely by the manufacturer. Sort of like Bluetooth technology."

"Will it make any difference if a wall is in between?"

"I doubt it," Halliday replied.

Krish nodded and remained silent for a moment. He put the device in his pocket and looked at Halliday keenly. "Just to be clear now, the information it will download will allow me to send commands to the pacemaker?"

"Well, it'll give you the information needed to do so about the specific pacemaker. But you'd need access to the transmitter the manufacturer uses. They usually have their own satellite networks, if I'm not mistaken."

Krish was silent again as he looked at Halliday. He perceived Halliday's sincerity and desire to fulfill what was requested of him. Krish felt fortunate he was able to turn to Halliday for help.

"Listen, Dr. Halliday, I know I've been vague about all of this and have asked your absolute confidence without giving you much information about what's going on. I want you to know I truly appreciate your help despite being kept in the dark."

"It's absolutely no problem, Dr. Krish." Halliday shook his head. "I'm happy to help you any way I can, whatever it may be. I used the discretion you requested. As you can see, I empty out the lab when I work on this. The fact that you personally asked for this is enough for me."

Krish was moved by his loyalty. He shook Halliday's hand and smiled. "Thank you again, Dr. Halliday. Hopefully, I won't trouble you again with some random side project."

Halliday smiled back. "Any time, Dr. Krish."

Arya Krish returned to his office and slumped down into his chair. He took the device out of his pocket, looked at it for a moment, then leaned back and stared up at the ceiling. The usual bright, alert look in his eyes slowly faded as his thoughts receded into an increasingly dark space in his mind. He felt his blood slow in his veins, and a weight settled over his body as if a thick cloak was draped over him. Thoughts of vengeance, justice, nostalgia, and morality swirled about in a turbulent rumination.

They had become more than thoughts now. They had manifested into action.

As he held the device in hand, the device that was part of the means to his ultimate revenge, he perceived a new giddiness and excitement at the prospect of fulfilling a vendetta that he had carried with him for so long. At the same time, he felt the pangs of his conscience, which could not deny the moral ramifications that far surpassed his prior compromises and justifications. It made him feel cold and heavy, like stone.

He slowly sat up straight in his chair, closed his eyes, and took slow, measured breaths. While he focused on his breathing, he consciously relaxed the muscles of his face, neck, shoulders, and the rest of his body. As he did so, he felt the tension release and the weight lift. With his eyes still closed, his mind's eye focused on a point in the dark void. He let thoughts pass through his mind as they came initially, then slowly focused them toward memories of his experiences at various ancient temples and other historic sites that had left deep impressions on him. Behind his closed eyes, he focused his mind on a single point and imagined a steady light, like a planet in the night sky. His thoughts quieted, and stillness was in the silence as his mind became calm and steady, like a pouring stream of oil. Arya Krish opened his eyes slowly and had a calm, collected look on his face.

He turned his attention to his computer and plugged the device into one of the ports. Krish scrolled through the database acquired from the Alpha Corp hack and quickly found the section he needed. He'd gone through most of the data several times already, so he was familiar with the organization of the file directories. Krish scanned the directory of Alpha Corp employees until he came to the personnel file of interest. He stopped and leaned forward slightly. Information about this person was scattered. Most information was under a nameless account with only an employee number, like the others that had the addresses linked to them. This one had no address, though. That's what had caught his attention initially. He cross-referenced with the rest of the data acquired and compiled it into one profile with the name of the man he met that night, the one who presented him with the envelope.

Vladimir Steinhart.

Among the history for Steinhart was his medical profile, and Krish went back to it to confirm the Halliday device had been programmed to the correct pacemaker model and serial number. Krish closed the profile and paused, then looked again at the other employee numbers with only an address attached to them. For a while, he sat still in that chair, alone in his office, and contemplated his plan at large. Finally, he glanced at the envelope on the desk, the one he had carried with him all day. He picked it up and left.

***

Krish sat alone in a small family conference room in Beacon's Medical Center and waited for the others to arrive. The room was utilitarian and brightly lit, with a simple conference table with office chairs, a whiteboard on the wall, and a computer on wheels. He agreed to attend this meeting with the ICU attending physician and the family of a patient who had requested his consultation. The situation was a familiar example of a long-standing grievance in the healthcare system. A 90-year-old man with end-stage Alzheimer's dementia was permanently unresponsive. He was bedbound with a tracheostomy and a feeding tube, and he was rotting away in a nursing home. The patient was frequently admitted to the hospital after nearly attaining the sweet release of death. He would go back on a ventilator and would be stabilized long enough to go back to the nursing home, then do it all over again in a few weeks. The patient's only remaining family, namely his obstinate son, wanted it so. He was his father's healthcare proxy and chose to have him hooked back up to the ventilator, poked and prodded with needles and tubes, and pumped full of medicines that prolonged the man's death rather than his life.

This was not the first such meeting with the family and an ICU physician. Prior attempts to reason with the son were futile. However, this was the first time Krish met them, and it was at the request of the ICU physician.

After a short while, a soft knock was on the door. The ICU physician opened it and let the son enter before following him in. Krish sat at the head of the table, and the other two sat on either side of him. The son recognized Krish and shook his hand respectfully. The son was probably in his 60s, with short, dark gray hair and bushy eyebrows. He wore a white dress shirt with dark pinstripes and dark pants. He had a condescending look in his eyes. To Krish, he had the air of a man who demanded the respect of others around him rather than commanding it.

The ICU physician spoke first. He summarized the patient's status and explained to the son everything that was being addressed and treated. The patient remained ventilator-dependent and did not seem to be able to wean off any time soon. Essentially, the ICU physician told the son that his father was deteriorating and actively dying. Medical interventions were increasingly futile.

"Your father remains on medicines to support his blood pressure. It's putting a strain on his heart and decreasing blood flow to his extremities. At this point, we are doing more harm than good, in my opinion," he said.

Krish looked at the patient's son and noted the disapproving look on his face. It made Krish resent the man. It seemed he blamed everyone else for what was happening to his father. A growing air of frustration was in the room, shared by all three of them. Arya Krish listened while the ICU physician answered the son's questions. After a pause in the conversation,

Krish spoke for the first time.

"Mr. Blythe, Dr. Carter asked me to come and offer my opinion on your father's condition and situation," he said. Blythe listened intently. Krish's reputation preceded him. "It is just one man's opinion," Krish said. "But I can give you my insight as food for thought. I believe your intentions are in the best interests of your father. But, having experienced this kind of situation many times with other patients and families, I've observed that sometimes the family members wind up doing more harm than good. Again, in my opinion. They harm their loved one, albeit with noble intents, as I mentioned."

Blythe, the patient's son, nodded with interest while Krish spoke in a calm manner but remained silent.

"If your father survives and leaves this hospital, Mr. Blythe, chances are high he'll come back within two weeks, given how frail he is. At best, he goes back to the nursing home demented and nonfunctional, which is how he was before this hospitalization. How would you describe his quality of life before this hospitalization?"

The son thought for a moment. "Poor."

"I can't help but wonder what we hope to accomplish, then. Given his quality of life at best, I do not think we are doing him any favors by keeping him attached to machines and pumping toxic medicines into him, Mr. Blythe."

Krish waited for the son to respond. Dr. Carter looked at the son as well, but he had a checked-out expression on his face. A heavy silence filled the room.

"So you're saying we should take him off the machines and kill him?" the son asked. He shook his head.

"I wouldn't say that, Mr. Blythe. I'm suggesting we focus on him being comfortable and pain-free and let him die. There's an important distinction here. I agree that withdrawing care is much more difficult than withholding. That is why we often bring up the issue before escalation, as physicians have done on prior occasions with you, I'm sure. But it is important to continue to address it, Mr. Blythe. I come at this from a physician's perspective and attitude, admittedly, but for what it's worth, having experienced this on several occasions, I can't help but reflect on it from a personal standpoint as well. In contemplating our mortality and the mortality of our loved ones, I've asked myself what I would do in your position. Both my parents died fairly early, but I can say that if this was my 90-year-old father, I would make him comfortable and let him die with dignity, surrounded by his loved ones, as we would all like for ourselves," Krish said.

Sincerity and wisdom were in his tone and countenance. Carter nodded concurringly. Blythe leaned back in his chair and rubbed his eyes, either in exasperation or epiphany. They talked for a little while longer, mainly answering a few more questions about the patient's condition and prognosis. Eventually, nothing more could be said, and everyone rose. Blythe shook hands with the two physicians and was on his way out the door. Before he left, he turned back and told them he would talk to his family about withdrawing care.

"Well, it might have finally sunk in," Carter said after Blythe left. "I appreciate your willingness to take time to talk to him. It was a big help. I don't understand how they can be so oblivious to what they're doing to their loved ones. That poor old guy is getting tortured by modern medicine, and his family either doesn't get it or doesn't care."

"Well, for what it's worth, it seemed like he has his father's best interests at heart. But we've seen all sorts, as you know, Dr. Carter. Who knows the lifetime of history between father and son here?"

"Yeah. Ignorance, daddy issues, or maybe they want to keep cashing his Social Security checks. Who knows," Carter said with frustration. "There's gotta be a better way. I wanted to avoid convening an ethics committee and going down that bureaucratic route. For whatever reason, it can't be in the physician's capacity to decide when medical intervention is futile and unethical because that would be a death panel, according to the Philistines."

Krish sighed and smiled. "And what would we call what just happened here? I don't see the distinction," he said.

Dr. Carter snorted. He shook Krish's hand, left, and closed the door behind him.

Krish sat alone in the room. After a moment, another knock came, and the door opened. Krish looked up at Jason Rook as he stealthily came into the room and closed the door quietly. Krish looked at him as one might look at a clumsy, undesirable roommate who had just returned home. Rook stood near the door in the Secret Service pose.

"Mr. Rook, to what do I owe the pleasure?"

"My employer is requesting the finalized contract, Dr. Krish."

Krish nodded without replying. They stared at each other in silence for a moment, with expressionless faces.

"I intend to deliver it directly to Vladimir Steinhart," Krish said.

Rook couldn't conceal a flash of surprise at the mention of the name. He shifted subtly as he stood without responding for a moment. "We'll be by to escort you tonight," he said. He left quickly.

Krish sat in his office late that night. The room was dark except for the computer screen shining on his thoughtful expression. He spent several hours carefully reviewing the rest of the hacked data. After shutting down the computer, he left his office with the envelope and Halliday device, which he attached to his keychain. The hallways were only dimly lit as he passed through light and shadow and left through a side exit. It was a pleasant, early spring night, cloudless, with no moon.

He came out into the alley. Lights from above illuminated it like spotlights. As Krish looked to his left, he saw a dark sedan about 50 feet away under one of the streetlights. He didn't want it waiting at his home, so he deliberately met the car at the Institute. He walked over to the sedan and let himself in the backseat. Once again, the windows were tinted black, and the privacy divider was up between the back and front of the car.

Krish sat with his hand in his pocket and clutched his keychain. He thought about the size of the office, the elevator room outside of it, the security guard in that room, and the one that was in the office. He thought about Jason Rook and the prior meetings with him. Presumably, Rook drove, like last time. Krish looked at the tinted divider, then leaned forward and knocked on it. No answer. He waited for a moment, then knocked again and leaned back in his seat. It seemed like a long time before the divider lowered. Krish quickly looked out the windshield and saw nothing more than the headlights illuminating the immediate road in front of them. Jason Rook looked straight ahead as he drove.

After a while, Arya Krish spoke. "So, it is still you," he said. Rook gave no response. "You know, I was thinking back to our first meeting in India. Little did I know you'd be the guy I would see lurking around every corner for the past year. I wonder what'll happen now. If this goes through, I might be considered one of your bosses afterward. How do you feel about that, Mr. Rook?" Krish had an amused look on his face.

Rook looked straight ahead in silence before he replied. "I don't feel one way or another about it, Dr. Krish. I'd try to be an effective employee, as always." He paused for a moment. "I've expressed my sincere admiration toward you on prior occasions and have made it clear it's nothing personal."

Krish nodded. "Yes, you have. And now that you mention

that, I realize you remind me a lot of a friend of mine in India. His name is Praveen. Oh, right. I assume you already know him. He's one of the most loyal guys I've got. It's a hard thing to come by, true loyalty. In my opinion, it must spawn from a distinct tie that binds, some bond between the two. I've sometimes wondered what that would be from his part. We're not family or old friends. I do know he believes in our cause. He's seen the fruits of our labor and was a believer from the beginning. I know that's part of it, but not sure if there's something else."

"I imagine you've become friends on a personal level as well over time," Rook said.

"Yes, I would say so. I agree that would play a part as well. I've helped his family out and would go out of my way to do so again. But in the beginning, it must have been the same commitment to an ideal that made us kindred spirits, so to speak."

They silently watched the winding road in front of them.

"You have anything like that with Alpha Corp, Mr. Rook? What is your tie that binds? A man of your intelligence likely demands more than a salary for his loyalty. Even behind the objective dutifulness you project, you must have some powerful motivator. Even a soldier's commitment to duty is backed by a principle of personal loyalty and patriotism."

"You don't know who I am or what I've done, Dr. Krish. I'm not sure you'd remain so interested, either, if I told you. We'll be there soon."

The divider rose and separated them again. Krish was alone with his thoughts for the remainder of the drive. Soon, they pulled to a stop, and Rook let him out. He stepped out and looked around at the familiar door, dark brick, and single overhead light, surrounded in darkness. It started to rain again. He made his way down the well-lit white hallway, walked behind Rook, and waited for the elevator. Stepping out of it upstairs, he looked around at the small security room. Rook motioned toward the table and detector. Krish walked over calmly and took out his keys, wallet, and phone. He placed them on the table and went through the detector.

"You'll get your stuff back when you leave," Rook said. He nodded toward the door.

Krish glanced back at Rook and the keychain, then turned forward and opened the door. He stepped inside and let the door close behind him. The scene was unchanged, except no fire was in the fireplace. Steinhart stood by the single tall, narrow window at the far corner of the room and looked outside. The other man stood in front of the desk between them in the Secret Service pose.

"You may go, Mr. Knight," Steinhart said without looking.

Knight glanced at him, then made his way to the door. Krish stepped aside and let Knight pass, then looked down to his right at a chair near the door and sat down. He watched Steinhart for a while without saying anything.

Steinhart remained where he stood and looked out the window. Finally, he looked at Krish. "Spring seems to be finally settling in. April showers and the whole bit," Steinhart said. Krish remained silent.

"You might briefly remember Mr. Knight from our last meeting. Marcus Knight, a good man. Loyal. It's hard to come by loyalty these days. Maybe it was always hard to come by," he said and shrugged.

Steinhart turned and walked toward his desk. Seeing Krish sitting at the far end of the room, he came around, stood in front of the desk, and leaned back against it. His hands were in his pockets. He was about 20 feet from where Krish sat. He wore an expensive gray suit with a dark shirt and a blood-red tie. His gargoyle face had the same slight scowl, and the way the light caught his features exaggerated his deep facial creases, like fissures on a jagged mountain face.

Krish looked at him initially, then glanced around the

room. He sat with his legs crossed and his arms up on the high, broad armrests. He looked like he relaxed in a soaker tub. A pleased expression was on his face as if he had just moved into a nice house. He looked back at Steinhart and met his stare.

"Well, it took you long enough to get back to us, Dr. Krish," Steinhart said grudgingly. They would have to speak loudly in the large room.

"Well, I had to make a lot of changes to the agreement, Vladimir Steinhart."

Steinhart's countenance remained unchanged, but Krish perceived a glint in his eye that may have betrayed a flash of surprise and anxiety.

"What sort of changes?"

Krish shrugged. "Ones that hopefully engender some trust and loyalty between us, or at least obligate it."

"How very noble, Dr. Krish," Steinhart said. Even though his expression never changed, his words and the way he spoke were candid. His last sentiment was lathered in sarcasm. "I don't sense much of that hostility and skepticism so evident from our first meeting. What's changed in you then, Dr. Krish?"

"I've embraced your appeal to my primary desire and purpose. You very shrewdly deduced what it was I want most, if you remember. You were right. And now, I plan to use and unleash the full arsenal of Alpha Corp for my own purposes. You advertised opening all the doors. So be it. But remind me again, Mr. Steinhart, what was it exactly that you wanted in this agreement? You were going after our R&D and, of course, its crown jewel, the Panacea Project. I believe I know your intent with it, Mr. Steinhart. If I'm not mistaken, you intend to conduct human trials. Where do you find the subjects?" Krish asked bluntly.

Steinhart crossed his arms. "Your questions may be answered soon, Dr. Krish, if you truly have brought a signed agreement. You'll have all the information you want and all the means you need. You've already demonstrated the means by which you're willing to attain your ends. I'm sure you'll find our partnership all the more effective. And while your curiosity may or may not be fueled by some misperception of a supposed moral superiority, I am sure your self-aware conscience reminds itself of the increasingly blurring lines of distinction between you and I as a result of your own choices and actions. I say that because I get the feeling you think of me as some sort of villain and look down on me."

Krish was silent for a moment. "Well." He reached in his jacket pocket for the envelope and changed the subject, "I hope you find the changes I've proposed agreeable. It essentially creates transparency and full access between you and I. And I've suggested exclusive authority to the two of us, with mutual consent mandatory for any major operations and actions of both Alpha Corp and Beacon Medical Institute. A merger. I'm thinking that'll be the appropriate circumstances that will engender trust and loyalty between us."

Krish stood and held the envelope up near his chest and gently tapped on it with one finger as he looked at Steinhart, who remained silent.

"Ah, yes, loyalty," Steinhart grunted.

Krish stood quietly, looked at him, then extended the envelope outward. Steinhart remained by his desk with his arms crossed and had a contemptuous look on his unchanged countenance. Krish gave a stern look back as Steinhart eventually walked over to him and took the envelope. It was the closest Arya Krish had stood to him, and they locked eyes like two prize fighters. Steinhart slowly extended his hand, and Krish shook it distantly.

Steinhart turned around and walked toward his desk. "You'll hear from me in a timely manner, Dr. Krish, I assure you."

Krish said nothing and left. He couldn't bear the presence of that man much longer. While he stood and looked at Steinhart, flashes of his father sparked the impulse to leap on top of Steinhart and strangle the life out of him. It was fleeting, of course, but a part of him indulged in it. In the next room, he grabbed his belongings quickly and stood in the elevator with Knight at his side. Krish looked straight ahead with an angry, determined look. His steps were fast and broad down the white hallway and out into the waiting sedan. As he sat slumped in the back seat, his mind wallowed in the tepid pool of distaste, contempt, and malice he had accumulated toward Steinhart since he found him and met him.

Krish looked down at the Halliday device he had detached from his keychain. Despite Steinhart's insinuations regarding Krish's practice of the ends justifying the means, there was moral clarity for him. However, if he went through with his intended plan and saw it through to the end, then the lines would be all the more blurred, if not erased. There would be no turning back.

He was dropped off at the Institute past midnight, and he stayed behind as the sedan drove off before proceeding to his office. In the dark, the computer screen shone on his face as he sat with anticipation. He plugged in the device and waited for the verdict. After a moment, a look of satisfaction and relief came over his face as he realized the device had successfully interrogated the pacemaker. A wry smile slowly crept in while he removed the device and shut down the computer. The room went dark as Krish leaned back in his chair.

CHAPTER SEVEN

As Arya Krish opened the door to the conference room, he heard his own voice on the television inside. He stepped in and saw Jay Asher sitting alone at the middle of the large oak conference table. Asher's back was turned, and he faced the large flat screen on the far wall. Despite the thin, overcast, bright daylight streamed in through the tall windows, lending ambience to the large board room. Asher wore a blue suit and reclined in a large office chair. An entertained smile was on his face as he listened intently. Arya Krish wore a black suit and remained standing near the door as he watched the contemporary news talk show host interview him.

"So, Dr. Krish, here are a few statistics about Beacon Medical Institute I'll share with the audience," the host said. He was a young-looking, middle-aged man with slicked-back silver hair and wore a trendy suit and tie. His show was very popular among young adults because he made current events accessible and interesting to them.

"…Top ten in net worth among private corporations in the United States," he continued. "Most net profit amount spent on charity and social or humanitarian services here and abroad among private companies. Forty percent of the Institute's profit is directed toward philanthropy, both in the United States and abroad. The majority of the rest goes toward the research and development department, which holds most of the patents in the field over the last 10 years. And at the helm is you, as the majority owner, along with two of the remaining original founders still alive. They choose to remain silent partners. Is that correct?"

"Yes, that's accurate. But I remain close to them and often seek out their advice." Krish smiled pleasantly and appeared very relaxed as he sat across from the host's desk. A mug of coffee was in front of him.

"So, Dr. Krish," the host said. A playful smile was on his face. "It has not escaped our observation that you have been hitting the TV circuit with the news networks and other talk shows. When a man of your stature seeks media attention, it signifies something. Particularly you, who has always preferred to maintain a low personal profile. So it begs the question, sir, what are you up to? I can only assume it's related to the recent merger deal we've all heard about by now between Beacon and Alpha Corp."

"As a matter of fact, one is tied to the other. You mentioned our investment in our R&D program, which goes back to the very beginnings of the Institute. Original innovation and pioneering brought about Beacon Medical Institute. And now is a very important time as we aggressively advance a project of ours that will culminate in a paradigm shift in modern medicine, just as the original organ synthesis technology did. We call it the Panacea Project."

The host turned to the audience in a comedic fashion. "Panacea, Greek for 'all curing,' for those who don't know," he said.

"That's right," Krish said. He nodded. "With the capabilities Alpha Corp brings to the table, I'm hoping to accelerate our progress. I think in the midst of this large merger, I've reflected more so than before on the purpose and legacy of Beacon Medical Institute. I want it to be a social reformer and, in the process, contribute as much as it can to humanity. I think it also dawned on me, finally, that I have the unique privilege of having access to commercial media, such as yourself, frankly."

The host smiled and nodded as he listened. It seemed to

Krish, at that moment sitting with him, that he was enthusiastic and fully engaged in what Krish said.

"So, is this more of a PR maneuver and solely that, if it's the case?" the host asked.

"No. Quite the contrary, actually. I've seen it as a distinct advantage politicians wield in their covetous relationship with the press. Commercial media is a means to access the social conscience and start social dialogues. And it remains distinctive from the realm of social media, where certainly the same is possible."

"The two realms, as you put it, overlap, in fact," the host said in a matter-of-fact manner. He leaned forward in his seat. "Alright, we'll invite the rest of our panel and continue our discussion after this." He extended his hand toward Arya Krish.

Asher hit the mute button on the remote and left the TV on. Krish slowly made his way to the table while they watched the screen quietly. He sat and continued to look toward the TV. Asher did the same, still with a smile on his face. The oak table between them glistened in the silver daylight, and their voices echoed as they spoke.

"So, just between us, you've decided to run for office, haven't you? Congressman? Dare I say, President?" Asher asked.

Krish shook his head. "No. Like I said to that guy, I'm not interested in being a politician. I want to be the strings and hands playing above the puppets."

Asher looked at him and nodded.

"Well, I am catching glimpses of your master plan and am ready to hear all about it. Because some things are missing," Asher said with a friendly touch of rancor.

"Oh, I'll be asking you to be quite directly involved from this point forward. Irrevocably, in fact." Krish turned and looked at Asher. Asher watched him and remained silent.

"I admit, brother," Krish said, "I've imagined versions

of this conversation countless times in my head over the past months. It's like how they taught us in Little League to visualize yourself at bat. Despite all that deliberation, I don't seem to know how or where to begin."

"Well, keep talking. You'll find your way."

Krish was silent and thoughtful for a moment. "*There is a tide in the affairs of men. When taken at the flood, that tide leads on to fortune.* I read that somewhere, I just remembered it now for some reason. Fitting for the moment and struck me somehow." He smirked as he continued to look off toward the windows. Asher observed him and found his elusive, dry humor suspicious and irritating.

"Ironic that you cite those words. Shakespeare. Julius Caesar, Act IV, Scene Three, I think. Brutus and Cassius are discussing late-stage Roman civil war strategy."

Arya Krish was dumbfounded by Asher's response. He didn't know what to say. "A window of opportunity showed me one possible fulfillment of my purpose," he said eventually. "It was when I met Vladimir Steinhart."

"Vladimir Steinhart? Never heard of him."

"Remember when I first showed you the envelope and the final agreement? I told you then that one of the directors of the former A1 Group headed Alpha Corp. I met that man. His name is Vladimir Steinhart."

Asher became more serious as Krish spoke. He had a solemn look on his face, and he remained silent, allowing Krish to pause and continue.

"During that meeting, I basically confronted him about my suspicions, to put it lightly, regarding the circumstances surrounding the deaths of my father and his friends. I tell you, Asher, it was an unusually precise and premeditated conversation on both parts. Nothing was said haphazardly. I know from what he said that all my suspicions are, in fact, true. That moment was a catalyst that sent me on an unexpected trajectory. It's been a gradual transformation, and I don't know how to describe it."

"Well, there's no statute of limitations on murder. If there's some sort of lead you have, we can pry it open," Asher said.

Krish was again silent for a moment before replying. "Steinhart was fearless, cold. He regarded government power as an acquired asset, something under his payroll, something to wield at his own will. Just having that conversation with him somehow gave me a glimpse of what's behind the curtain. I told you before that I intend to destroy Alpha Corp. That is no longer the case. I intend to destroy Steinhart and take over Alpha Corp."

Asher leaned back and looked at Arya Krish incredulously. "So, you're going to cut off the head of the monster and replace it with your own? How do you intend to destroy Steinhart?"

Krish took a moment to focus on his breathing. He felt the muscles in his neck and shoulders quickly relax. "Steinhart is pacemaker-dependent. State-of-the-art device transmits and receives data and commands remotely to and from the manufacturer and physician."

Krish paused for a moment and waited for Asher to speculate and respond. There was no reply. Asher sat quietly with a stern look.

"I asked Vincent Halliday to build a device that reads the pacemaker and downloads the information necessary to transmit commands to it." Krish met Asher's stare.

"So you plan on killing this man, Steinhart? Murdering him."

Krish shook his head with obvious frustration. "I knew you were going to say that! It is not murder," he said. "I know my father's story. Growing up, I learned about the journey that brought him to this country and his experiences during that time with his employer, the A1 Group. In the weeks before he died, after all the testifying and grand jury indictments, he basically sat me down and told me exactly how these corporations control it all. They won't let something like the law of the land interfere. They scoff at it and regard it as a nuisance. My father saw colleagues die under mysterious circumstances, and his own life was threatened. He told me the job was going to be finished, one way or another. They killed him, and no justice has been offered. I have no doubt that, in light of this agreement, they will come after me sooner or later. I say this is combat, not murder. It is the only justice now." Krish leaned forward, almost pleadingly.

"Combat." Asher nodded slowly. "You have a device that will remotely stop the pacemaker in this Steinhart, thereby killing him. And with this new partnership as a bridge, you'll take over everything?"

Krish sat up. "I don't have the device yet. Halliday's device only accessed the pacemaker specifications. I need your help to obtain a device that will use those specifications to de-activate the pacemaker remotely." He looked up.

Asher laughed. "How am I supposed to do that?"

"I know you have resources, OK? You can have this device built, there's no question. I did not want to involve anyone else, including Halliday, in this part of it."

"Man, when you said involve irrevocably, you weren't kidding. I'm not sure I can help you kill this man, Arya." Asher's face was an earnest look of concern. "A part of me is surprised you've gone through with it this far."

"Are you telling me you don't see my side of it at all?" Krish asked as he stood. "Steinhart is only the beginning. We can pick up the reins and direct power at the political and governmental levels toward our cause. We can shape policies to benefit society at large, be the tip of the spear for humanism, and usher in a renaissance. It's something that will continue to write history long after we're gone. You have to see the vision to be fully aware of what is at stake, what are the ends, and what are the means. I think about all the patients we see, random glimpses of everyday people entangled in a system that is designed and manipulated to benefit those hiding in the shadows, watching from above. The ripple effect trickles down to every patient room I've been in, with people unknowingly bound by the shackles. Everyone is a chess piece, including the politicians and all the way to the President, I'm sure. It's played by the people behind the money and the lobbyists, the guys with private militaries who employ the politicians. But we have a path to infiltrate them and become their equals."

"And you feel it is your destiny to take that path and be the savior of the people?"

Anger flashed across Krish's face. "Don't mock me, alright? I don't know what your point is in implying I'm some sort of egomaniac with delusions of grandeur. Each one of us is an agent of an ideal, measured only in the effect we can have on the world and others. I aspire to be an agent of a greater good, but life's lessons and the law of nature have made clear that we all need fangs and claws, the hunter's instinct in us, the eye of the tiger. There's a Sanskrit word for it, *shakti*. Power, strength. We wield it like fire, and our virtue is judged on the purpose and intent with which we wield it. Whether to burn and destroy or forge and create. Krish gave an exasperated wave of his hand. "Look. You're a smart guy. You can figure it out." He turned and walked toward the large, wide windows that spanned the far wall. Krish paced back and forth and occasionally stopped to look out at the view.

Asher remained silent and watched him for a while. He watched the subtle flares of expression on Krish's face as he brooded, and Asher recognized his conflict and tension. Krish was not the type to look back after a decision or course of action, and his deepest beliefs could be a blinding guiding light to his aspirations.

"Some food for thought," Asher said. "That kind of absolute power you look to usurp corrupts absolutely. The guys in the shadows, from Big Pharma, Big Oil, Big Banks, The Syndicate that truly shape things on a geopolitical scale? They have the power they sought so ravenously, and now their rabid avarice is all that's left of them. The bad blood you'll brew to get there slows in your veins and turns to stone. If you take the necessary path to that kind of power, the same will happen to you, and you'll be dragged down by its weight. Any noble intentions about what you would've done with it may not last that long or be relevant."

Krish stopped pacing when Asher spoke and listened intently, with a pensive look on his face. At that moment, he thought of his wife and three-year-old son and turned sober.

"Listen, I'm asking you explicitly. I need you to reach out to your resources and, based on the specifications I've obtained, have a simple transmitter constructed that can remotely send a command to the pacemaker to stop. Just think about it. Do not answer me now, and let's not speak of it further. Actually, I do have another request."

Asher smiled in disbelief. "Oh, that wasn't enough, huh?"

"Remember I told you a few months ago about the employee number with only addresses And my encounter with Dr. Varma in India? And the Panacea Project? All that stuff? Remember?"

"Right. The idea that Alpha Corp wanted to experiment on humans or something."

"Yeah, something along those lines. Well, I tried looking up one of those addresses, but Rook stopped me before I actually did it. We need to go back."

"We?"

"Yeah, us. Since this partnership with them has gone public, and maybe after seeing the media exposure bolster, they seem to have stopped surveilling me. Or reduced it, at least. Haven't seen much of Jason Rook recently."

"I would think they have those addresses under surveillance, though," Asher said.

"Yeah, I considered that. We may have to be discreet. But I need to see for myself, and so do you. We need to know what we have to fight for. Then you'll understand why I have to do this."

Asher sat thoughtfully for a moment. "OK, I'm in."

Krish stood near the windows with his hands in his pockets, and Asher sat at the table and faced him. Krish looked at Asher with resolve on his face, then turned and left without saying anything. Asher sat alone for a while. "There is a tide in the affairs of men, which, taken at the flood, leads on to fortune. Omitted, all the voyage of their life is bound in shallows and in miseries. On such a full sea are we now afloat, and we must take the current when it serves or lose our ventures," he recited under his breath.

***

The early summer night was draped in the pale light of a full moon with clear skies. In the rural suburbs, Arya Krish and Jay Asher sat in a car and looked out at the house about 40 yards down the road. Asher was in the driver's seat. He looked through the single eyepiece of a scope. Krish sat next to him and peered out the windshield in anticipation.

"Visibility is pretty good. I haven't seen anyone outside the house. A light turned on and then off upstairs, so it looks like there's at least one person inside." Asher handed the scope to Krish.

Krish glanced at the scope as he took it, then looked at Asher. "You look in your element on this little mission, my friend," he said, impressed. "I didn't think the army trained surgeons in reconnaissance."

"Marines, actually," Asher looked out at the house.

"I've had a little extra field training since I was spearheading the operation models for proxy front-line mobile surgical and triage units. Sometimes, you need to be able to handle enemy encounters. That's how I know most of my resources, as you put it."

"That's good." Krish looked through the scope. "Because, admittedly, I have no idea what I'm doing."

"You're a smart guy. You'll figure it out," Asher said with a smirk.

Krish smiled as he put the scope down. "All right, tough guy. What do you suggest from here?"

Asher thought for a moment. "It doesn't seem like the house is under guard, so I don't think we need to be overly covert. But I think we should approach from the side door and see if anyone answers."

Krish nodded. They stealthily got out of the car and walked into the woods in a parallel direction to the house. Twigs snapped beneath them softly amid the background noise of insects as they turned toward the house and headed for the tree line. They stopped at the tree line and looked at the clearing that surrounded the house. Everything was otherwise still, and they crossed the clearing toward the single French door at the back of the house. A white curtain blocked their view inside.

Asher knocked on the door. Initially, there was no answer to the second knock. Then the light inside turned on. They looked at each other, then at the door in anticipation. The doorknob rattled softly, and the door opened. A thin, young Chinese man met their gaze. He looked nervous, inquisitive, and frail, like he was on chemotherapy.

"Sir, do you know who I am?" Krish asked quickly.

The man studied him for a moment before a look of recognition came over his face. "I've seen you on TV. You're the doctor from Beacon Medical Institute," he said. He spoke English very well but with a thick and heavy accent.

"Can we come in and talk to you for a moment?" Krish asked.

The man paused, poked his head through the doorway, and peered past them into the night. He looked at them and nodded his head, then motioned them inside. They stepped into a small but modern and clean open-concept living space just off of the kitchen. Asher and Krish stood near the door and looked around curiously as the man went into the living room.

He turned back toward them and said, "Feel free to sit down."

They followed him in and sat in a pair of recliners facing a couch, where the man sat down. A sleek coffee table was between them, with some magazines on it, and a flat-screen TV was on the wall. The man looked at them with tired but alert eyes. He took slow, deep breaths and sat quietly as if he were waiting for them to speak.

"I'm Arya Krish, as you seem to know, and this is Jay Asher. What is your name, sir?"

The man didn't answer right away. "Kai Chowan."

"Mr. Chowan, do you work for Alpha Corp?" asked Krish.

"From what I've seen on the news, I think you would know the answer to that, Dr. Krish," Chowan replied, with a perceived look of disappointment.

"My understanding is that you do work for them. But as you know, our partnership is relatively new and recent. So I am trying to get directly oriented to the more, shall we say, clandestine projects Alpha Corp is running. Long before our partnership, Mr. Chowan."

"So you have met with the others as well?"

Arya Krish hesitated. "Not exactly," he said. "In fact, that is why we are here. I want to know how you've come to be here, Mr. Chowan. Tell us your story, please."

"Why me?" Chowan asked.

"It's pretty random," Asher said.

Chowan looked at Asher, surprised that he answered, then nodded. He marshaled his thoughts for a moment before speaking. "I am from a small town in southern China. I came to the US about six years ago with an academic scholarship and internship with Alpha Corp."

"How did you get that?" Krish asked.

"I was top of my class." Chowan shrugged. "One of their representatives came to my town and recruited me. It was an amazing opportunity, with my higher education plus a stipend that would allow my family to escape poverty. My siblings would have fully funded educations. I considered myself very fortunate."

"And how do you feel about it all now, Mr. Chowan, six years later?" Asher asked.

Chowan looked at him earnestly. "My family there remains well off, Mr. Asher. My siblings are completing post-graduate studies and will have prestigious careers. Because of that, I feel happy and fulfilled, sir."

"Please go on." Krish leaned forward.

"I completed my education and trained in their lab, worked on various projects. Then, a little more than a year ago, they approached me about enrolling in a clinical trial as a test subject. They offered nearly triple my benefits, which would essentially make my family wealthy back home. I accepted. Well, there was that, and they lifted some of the restrictions I worked under when I was a scientist in the lab. I moved here and have remained since."

"What is the clinical trial?" Krish asked.

"It's some new form of pharmacotherapy." Chowan shook his head. "It's hard to explain. They're trying to develop a synthetic infusion that contains carbon-based nanotechnology fashioned to any number of purposes, theoretically," Chowan said.

"Let me guess," Asher said. "Your trial involves antimicrobial applications because it is theoretically the most feasible."

Chowan gave him a puzzled look. "Yes, that's right. The synthetic molecules are relatively less complex, though much more so than conventional antibiotics. They still induce a host versus graft response. They're looking for the best way to collect the necessary HLA variability data to steer their production efforts. This was the solution."

"How many others are there like you?" Krish asked.

"It's a pretty diverse group. Several dozen, from the United States and different parts of the world. The ethnic diversity is the best sample. Most of us were previously scientists designing the trial."

"So, you volunteered to do this?" Asher asked.

Krish nodded. "Yeah. Are you here by your own choice, Mr. Chowan? The others as well?"

Mr. Chowan paused and thought for a moment. "I chose it as a means to an end. Alpha Corp definitely didn't tell me everything when they recruited me back home. The place I lived before this house, when I was a scientist, was under surveillance, including cameras in the house. You wind up signing much of your privacy over to them, but you can accomplish what you want. They hold up their end of the bargain."

These words echoed in his mind as Krish looked at Mr. Chowan with a bewildered expression.

Next to him, Asher hardly contained his laughter. "Chose? Their end of the bargain?" He smiled. "Tell me, Mr. Chowan, is there a retirement package in this bargain? Do you have any plans after you no longer work here? Have you seen your family since you've been here?"

"As a matter of fact, I have. They visited two years ago. I saw the strain lifted in my parents after they became financially independent. They looked younger than the last time I saw them. It is a result of what I am doing, and it is the cause. I am merely a soldier to my cause."

Asher shook his head in disbelief. They remained quiet for a while.

Mr. Chowan leaned forward. "You are very successful men, but I think you know enough about depravity to understand the pressures and desperation it exerts on you."

Krish and Asher looked at each other, speechless. Eventually, Krish stood and looked back at Chowan. Seeing him stand, Asher stood as well.

"You need to come with me, Mr. Chowan, said Krish. "As a result of the partnership between Beacon Medical Institute and Alpha Corp, I am co-director of this project, and we need to collaborate right away. This will not continue any longer."

Chowan had a curious look. He stood slowly and looked at both of them as he considered his options. Finally, he headed to the kitchen counter, took his wallet and keys in his hand, then walked toward the front door. Krish and Asher followed him outside into the pleasant night and led him to the car.

Dark, thin clouds had moved in. As they drove down the winding roads through the woods, rain splattered the windshield as a steady drizzle was illuminated in the headlights. They cleared the large woods and drove down the straight country roads. Chowan told them more about himself and the others. In the midst of their conversation, Asher glanced in the rear-view mirror as he drove. Headlights in the distance approached rapidly. Krish noticed and looked back over his shoulder. Chowan saw him and did the same.

The headlights came up on them fast, and the intent quickly became obvious. They braced as the other car rammed them from behind and nearly sent their car into a tailspin. Asher grasped the steering wheel tightly with both hands as he regained control of the car. The other car swerved swiftly to their right and accelerated to come up next to them. Asher watched through the passenger side mirror, and just as the other car approached the back passenger window, Asher tapped on the brakes and slowed down quickly. The other car suddenly passed them, and just as it did, Asher steered into the driver-side back corner bumper, fishtailing the other car and sending it into a tailspin. Asher took his foot off the gas pedal, and their car slowed as the other car lost control in front of them and flipped over, cartwheeling over a side ravine about 50 yards ahead of them. Asher applied the brakes, and their car came to a stop. Everyone sat for a while without saying anything, breathing hard and staring ahead of them at the steam and smoke rising from the ravine. The rain pelting the car was the only sound.

"Stay here, please, Mr. Chowan." Asher opened his door.

Asher and Krish got out of the car and jogged toward the ravine. They stopped and looked down over the sharp ravine about 30 feet below. Krish focused his eyes on the wreckage. The car had landed on its wheels, and the driver's door was torn off. The hood was missing as well, and smoke billowed in the dim, obscured moonlight. Krish saw a man in a black suit slumped back in the driver's seat. Krish squinted and peered through the rain and, after a moment, recognized the man as Marcus Knight, bloodied and unconscious. He saw Knight's agonal, shallow breathing become weaker and weaker. Krish's mind was swimming as he impulsively made a move toward the wreckage.

Asher quickly grabbed him and held him back. "No!" He restrained Krish.

"He's still alive!"

"He tried to kill us!" Asher said. He let Krish go and pushed him back a little.

Krish stood still and looked at him, breathing heavily.

"There's nothing we can do for him," Asher said. "We have to go. Now."

Krish looked back at the wreckage. He could no longer make out any breathing movements on Knight. He glanced up at the rain and the moon, thinly veiled behind the clouds, and he sighed in resignation and bewilderment. Then he turned and walked back toward the car.

Asher took one last look down the ravine as well, then turned and followed. As they stood at their doors, they faced each other. Asher looked up at Arya Krish. "Remember that thing you asked me for earlier?" he said.

Krish stopped, looked at him with anticipation, and saw a familiar cold look on his face.

"You'll have it."

CHAPTER EIGHT

At the crack of dawn, the first sunlight crept steadily over the horizon, poured into the new morning sky, and gilded the tall Alpha Corp building. Arya Krish sat alone on one of the benches in the courtyard and looked straight ahead of him. No one else was around, and the cacophony of chirping morning birds filled the air. He had a calm look on his face as he sat straight and took slow, deep breaths. They had left the ravine only a few hours ago, yet it seemed so much longer. He felt as if he had a lifetime of reflection and introspection since then. Asher's words when they left the scene the previous night made Krish's end game imminent, and he could not stop thinking about the prospects and repercussions.

Eventually, he noticed a man in his peripheral vision. The man wore a black suit and approached from the side. Krish continued to look forward as Jason Rook walked up and sat next to him on the bench. The sun had emerged from the distant tree line, and they sat silently for a moment, perhaps enjoying the exceedingly picturesque summer morning.

Krish was the first to speak. "Do you know what happened to Marcus Knight?" He did not look at Rook.

Rook did not answer right away. "I do not know anyone by that name," he said.

"Oh, good. So you won't miss him."

After a moment of silence, Krish took in a deep breath as if bored. "Tides seem to be shifting swiftly," he said. "Events are taking on an inexorable quality, and I'm seeing far downstream, recognizing the almost fateful outcome. As this partnership matures, there may wind up being power shifts. I go out of my way to come say this to you because I can tell you with some confidence that things would swing my way if that was the case. I haven't quite made up my mind about you. While you've already pointed out that I know practically nothing about you, I somehow feel you would be a valuable ally. So I go out of my way."

"I'm a dutiful man, Dr. Krish," Rook said. "I will be loyal to whoever employs me."

"You should know something. I intend to transform things beyond Alpha Corp, with the same vicious ambition Steinhart displays and using the same fangs and claws, only redirected toward very different, opposite ends. You're familiar with what I'm about. Right, Mr. Rook? And the work I do? This so-called partnership is only the beginning. I plan to use every means at my disposal. I don't suppose you would object. In fact, I think you would welcome such a change, assuming you had any sort of conscience attached to that dutifulness you boast of."

Rook gave no reply, but Arya Krish felt the tension that emanated from him. Krish remained silent as well for a while, to let it fester. He continued. "I'll give you the benefit of the doubt and assume there is, indeed, more than duty in your heart. I want to believe your moral compass, while rusted over, can still be restored. That leaves the ball in your court, Mr. Rook, as certain swift transitions take place at the highest level."

He looked at Rook, read his expression, and felt he was not tied to Steinhart the same way as Marcus Knight. They were of the same breed, but Steinhart did not own Rook. He could be made into a useful and effective asset with some retraining.

"I need a direct way to contact you, Mr. Rook, as I may be in need of your services at any moment." Krish looked at him. Rook turned and looked back at him, then reached inside his suit jacket. Krish watched his hand go past the shoulder holster and to the jacket pocket as he took out a card and handed it over. Krish took it, glanced at the phone number printed on it, then put it away. They sat for a moment in silence, then Jason Rook stood and walked away.

***

Later that afternoon, Arya Krish stood on the balcony of his DC mansion. He'd removed his suit jacket and tie and looked out at the view before he turned and sat down. It remained a sunny day and was pleasantly warm. He hadn't slept at all. In fact, he drove back to the ravine after he saw Rook, only to find it bare of any evidence of a crash. No skid marks were on the road, and no accident reports had been filed. Obviously, others were privy to the facts and events, and Krish speculated about the cover-up. Leela, his wife, came outside.

"Hello, sweetness," he said with a smile.

"He was too excited that you were home during the day. He didn't want to sleep." Leela sat next to him. She wore jeans and a t-shirt. Her wavy hair framed her pretty face and smile, which never seemed to fade, even in moments of gravity. Krish put his arm around her, and they looked out at the view.

"OK, so finish what you were telling me. You went to a scientist's house?" she asked.

Krish hesitated before he answered. "Yeah. I never got the chance to talk to anyone the first time I went there. So we meet this scientist, Kai Chowan, originally from China. We kept calling him Mr., but in fact he earned a PhD with help from Alpha Corp. He's now voluntarily a human test subject in the very study he helped design. He sees all of it, the intimate surveillance, lack of personal freedom, the exploitation, and everything else, as a small price to pay for the rewards. But he's ensured his family's prosperity and well-being. He sees it as an opportunity, a means to an end, and considers himself a soldier to his cause."

"Wow. So Alpha Corp is basically exploiting their

desperation and twisting it into a call of duty to provide for their families. And their experimental trial is all tied into the data they stole from the Panacea Project?"

"Yeah." Krish nodded.

"And now you're partnered up with this Steinhart guy." She shook her head.

"Yeah. Keep your enemies closer, as they say. My intent is to ultimately take him down and take over all of it. It's the only way to unmake everything they've created." Krish was deliberately vague. He had not mentioned anything about Marcus Knight and the crash, and he had not told her his true intent regarding Steinhart. He looked at her for a moment and hesitated again. "Do you remember I told you Steinhart used to be at A1 Group? In a way, I can't help but hold him responsible for what happened to my father. To all of us, really. Steinhart deserves to go down hard, you know. An eye for an eye. At this point, it feels like there's no other justice at times."

"An eye for an eye makes the whole world blind." She lifted her head up from his shoulder and looked up at him. Krish nodded. "Gandhi said that."She smiled.

Krish couldn't help but smile, too.

"You know," he said, "my final goal is to infiltrate the syndicate that wields all the power behind the curtain. I want to exert as much influence over it toward humanitarian and social service on a scale that can steer the course of society at large. It sounds farfetched and lofty when I say it out loud. I feel like I have to explain myself every time. But I've turned the whole thing over in my head again and again, and the real concern is losing a part of myself as a result when I finally achieve it. And a large part of that is you two. I worry about how this will affect all of us."

He paused and waited for her to respond. She had a thoughtful countenance and said nothing as if she waited for him to continue.

"The problem is," he said, "I don't know if what I consider very possible is, in fact, ludicrous or if I am truly in a position that only a few have ever been. I can't help but imagine the possibilities if I manipulated resources at that level, the level where Alpha Corp operates. It would catapult and complete what we've done at Beacon thus far. We'd introduce a new genetic age because of the Panacea Project."

"It might be risky," she said.

Krish looked at her. He kept hesitating, always on the verge of disclosing it all, the entire truth. But for her sake and safety, if nothing else, he would not.

"I wonder how far I should be willing to go for the cause," he said. "Certainly, noble intents can be misguided and even twisted into something different. Yet the willingness to sacrifice everything, including one's self, for a cause is a virtue, by any measure."

"It is ultimately the ideal, the cause as you put it, which validates the willingness, though. Not all martyrdom is virtuous."

"The virtue of the means is measured in the ideals of the ends, whatever the standard might be that the measure is based on." Krish nodded and went into a thoughtful silence.

"Sounds pretty arbitrary," she said with a puzzled look.

"Listen, I've been thinking," he said after a brief silence. "I want you guys to go to India. Right away, in fact. I think with this merger, and some of the things coming up with the Panacea Project, it'll spare you the high profile. I really want to keep you two away from the prying media's attention, and if I start getting aggressive with my plan for Alpha Corp, it will certainly escalate beyond that. Just for a while, you could lay low." He looked at her earnestly.

"Well, what about you?" she asked with a calm but serious look.

"I'll join you guys soon," he said, and gave her a kiss. They sat for a while on the balcony and talked of other things.

***

It was almost two weeks later, close to midnight. A few people passed by as they entered and left the airport terminal. Arya Krish stood outside the terminal and looked down at his hand. His mind was somewhere else. He didn't hear the cars and taxis and didn't take notice of the passers-by. Krish stared at the transmitter in his right hand. It was a simple, small, black box with a single red button and an LED light. It looked like a movie prop. But Asher had assured him it was long-range tested against the same model before programming it to the specifications Krish had provided from the Halliday device. There was no doubt that if he pressed that button, it would do what it was made to do.

As he looked down at his hand, he imagined the moment the button was pressed and the pacemaker received the command. Krish would not be there. He wouldn't have to look at Steinhart as life left his eyes. It made the deed that much easier and almost felt like cheating. It might be the only thing that allowed him to conceivably take Steinhart's life. Despite his convictions, he doubted he was capable of looking Steinhart in the eyes and killing him. And yet, he recalled the feeling he had in Steinhart's office, the fleeting impulse to pounce and strangle the life out of him. An odd dissatisfaction ran through his thoughts as he looked down. It was intertwined with the exhilarating anticipation of achieving the purest revenge and justice that he had been indulging in that seemed to remain unfulfilled.

Now, Krish had bitter reflections on the small and big choices leading to that planned and yet strangely anxious and befuddling moment. His mind's eye crafted the scene. Steinhart, either lying in bed asleep and never waking up or standing in that damn office of his, near the single tall, narrow window, looking out at whatever was there, either alone or possibly with Rook, having replaced Knight. Krish thought for a moment what Rook's reaction might be if he witnessed Steinhart's sudden collapse.

An electrifying sensation coursed through his body as the potential for the final action mounted in his entire being. His chest was numb, and the butterflies in his stomach nauseated him. He stared at the little red button below his thumb. His hand trembled, and he became aware of his rapid breathing. After a pause, he thought of his family, his parents, and everything his father told him. He remembered the exact moment he first heard of the car crash that killed his father and his friends. Krish concentrated on his breathing. A stone-cold look of resolve came over his face as the bad blood stirred up inside him. His hand was steady.

Somewhere in his head was the first atom, or whatever conceptual quanta of energy, that became something different as a direct result of his free will. Nothing else was introduced into the status quo that would result in any calculable thermodynamic event. And yet, those first atoms suddenly altered and emerged from the status quo as a first cause, which would lead to everything else. All the other atoms that comprised the ion channels in his neurons allowed charged ions to shift and created an impulse that would lead to a cascade down through the tip of his thumb and made it move toward the button. Who knows the true origins of that first cause, in that very first channel that somehow opened by what can only be described as a force of nature wielded by the conscience.

The LED light went on, which indicated the signal was sent and received. Arya Krish threw the transmitter in the trash as he entered the airport.

Krish had a surreal, foggy journey to Bengaluru, India. In the airports, he sat at the gate and stared at the others who sat near him. Some had their legs crossed as they tapped away at their devices. The rare ones who caught his gaze were doing something else, such as reading an actual book. But he paid no particular attention. His mind was a murky pool of cluttered thoughts. He pictured others among the strangers around him, like Praveen, Murthy, Roman, Fisher, and Blythe. He imagined them watching him as he was watching them. His surroundings felt muffled and distant, like being underwater or behind glass, and he was both spectator and spectacle. On the planes, he lay with his eyes closed most of the time, not able to sleep. He had no appetite for the food they offered and felt a stifling weight over him, like a draped thick cloak that pressed him against his seat.

When he emerged from the airport terminal in Bengaluru, the pre-dawn twilight had crept over the horizon, and the humid breeze caught hold. As it left, he felt the dense air, and the sound of nightingales could be heard nearby and off in the distance. After a short walk, he spotted his wife and son in the small crowd who waited for the arrivals. Leela smiled at him, then looked down at his son. Seena ran toward him, laughing. Krish knelt to greet Seena and grabbed him as he ran up.

Krish held him close, then brought his head up and looked into his son's large, smiling eyes. At that moment, those pristine portals revealed to Krish's soul his own being and becoming. He had flashbacks of conversations and images from the not-too-distant past, and misty visions of a not-too-distant future. He was spellbound in humility and shame for that momentary eternity, confronted by the sanctity of humanity he no longer felt worthy of beholding. The captive moment held him paralyzed and awestruck, and he felt hot to his core, as if his heart was bleeding out inside his chest. As he held his son close again, Arya Krish rested his head on that little shoulder, and as he looked up at his smiling wife as she approached, he wept.

PART TWO
THE BAD BLOOD

CHAPTER NINE

He didn't feel like a killer at that moment as Arya Krish looked out the tall, slim, rectangular window at whatever was outside. The only remorse that gnawed at him was the dissatisfaction with the means he'd used to attain his vengeance against the man he held responsible for his father's death so many years ago. He remembered the first time he felt it, even before he pushed that button outside the airport. The exhilaration, giddiness, and anticipation during the premeditations that led to the final action were left unwrought somehow. His nemesis never saw it coming and would never know it was *he* who dispensed Steinhart's fate and justice.

Krish had imagined the scene again many times — the moment of Steinhart's death in his absence. He relished the details that morphed with each iteration and were vicarious, at best. He wasn't there to look Steinhart in the eyes and watch the life leave him. His retribution felt unconsummated and, in retrospect, left his revenge irrevocably unfulfilled. All the while, the bad blood that emerged went septic from the sediment of irredeemable past deeds and perfused his thoughts. He felt it in his limbs and in his breath. Giddiness was replaced with heavy apathy, and the exhilaration was followed up with weary fatigue.

"Feels like it's going to be an unusually hot summer," Krish said with a distant look.

Krish didn't see it, but the man in the black suit standing behind him in front of the desk nodded. The man continued his Secret Service stance.

Krish continued to look out the window, and his mind

went in and out of thoughts and reflections of recent dramatic events. The sky was pale blue in the bright sunshine, and after a few days of scattered showers, the bucolic splendor below appeared exceptionally green and flourishing.

It had been almost three weeks since the death of Vladimir Steinhart of cardiac arrest. As the other co-director of Alpha Corp and Beacon Medical Institute, Arya Krish was summoned back home from India to the Washington, DC, area. He needed to lead the transition of leadership and power. Krish had returned to DC earlier that day. Jason Rook picked him up at the airport, loaded his luggage in the back of the limousine, and opened the back door for him. Krish looked out at the scenery through the slightly tinted windows. As was often the case when he returned from India, he noticed how quiet and cold it was in the car. The divider between them was down, but neither spoke through the entire drive.

Krish turned and glanced at Rook, then walked over to the large wooden desk and sat in the leather chair. He gestured to Rook to take a seat across from him, and Rook did so. Krish looked down at the desk drawers speculatively. Curious, he arbitrarily opened the top one on his right.

"Here we are, Mr. Rook, along the lines of my prediction during our conversation that early morning at the Alpha Corp campus. Remember? The morning after the run-in — so to speak — with Marcus Knight." He paused to look up at Rook. "Tides have shifted swiftly." He looked back down at the drawer's contents with an approving nod. "To be frank, I find Steinhart's death serendipitous." He pulled out a bottle of liquor and inspected it. "What can you tell me about it?"

"I don't have much to add to what's already known, Dr. Krish," Rook said. "He was found dead in this office from apparent cardiac arrest. The inquiry was brief, no compelling evidence of foul play was found, and the body has since been cremated, per his wishes."

Krish wondered if the pacemaker was removed before the body was cremated or was burned to ash along with the rest. And if it was removed, what happened to it? He nodded and remained silent.

What he didn't know was that Rook was being discreet. In fact, Rook had been there, in that office, when Steinhart died. It was as Krish had imagined that night outside the airport as he held the device that deactivated Steinhart's pacemaker in his hand. Rook watched Steinhart clutch his chest mid-sentence and collapse near the rectangular window and remained silent. He'd walked up to Steinhart's body and knelt down, confirmed he was dead, paused for a moment, then left the office. His presence there was unknown to anyone.

As they sat across from each other in these current moments of silence, Krish and Rook were cognizant of what was not said between them. Skepticism, speculation, and suspicion were thick in the air, mutually recognized and shared.

Arya Krish spoke first. "Mr. Rook, I once told you I hadn't made up my mind about you. I also remember you telling me I didn't know anything about you, which honestly, remains quite true also. So you may find it odd to hear me say that I've somehow come to trust you. And as you've said to me on prior occasions, I am not trying to flatter you by saying so."

"I wouldn't insult you by presuming so, Dr. Krish," Rook answered. "But yes, I do find it odd that you trust me. By any measure, we have been adversaries up 'til this point."

Krish nodded thoughtfully and leaned back in his chair. "I wouldn't put it quite like that, Mr. Rook. Rivals, perhaps, though even that sounds a bit strong. You were an agent and still are, except you were working for the wrong cause up 'til now. Yes, it seems like you chose to do so to suspend your conscience. I hope either willingly or by coercion. But what's the point in discussing this further? The truth is, now we're unwittingly on the same side. I will rely on you heavily to help me see this enterprise through. I'm chasing a vast and ambitious vision for Alpha Corp, Beacon Medical Institute, modern medicine, and society at large. I won't be able to achieve much of it on my own."

Jason Rook shrugged. "As you said, Dr. Krish, I am an agent, and you are in command now. I think we can move forward from here without further speculative dialogue."

Arya Krish eyed him in an appraising manner. He was particularly curious about Rook's background and origins. But for the time being, he would leave it be. They were at a critical point in the tide of affairs, and Krish agreed it was crucial to move forward swiftly. "So be it," he said, and they got to work.

Krish began his orientation to the Alpha Corp conglomerate's machinery, and Rook's knowledge of its vast operations was impressive and critical. Krish had begun to scratch the service over the past year or so while he faced off with Steinhart. He learned about the slush funds, narcotic distribution, and, of course, the massive lobbying used to gain and maintain political influence. These were in addition to the slow but steady absorption of healthcare entities in the mid-Atlantic and Northeast regions of the US. While other facets of Alpha Corp's international operations were important and expanded beyond the healthcare and political realm, Krish remained focused on the most relevant means to his end. If anything, the rest of it would feed into his cause, and he didn't think much of their particulars.

They spent hours going over account information, personnel, administrative structure, and more. Steinhart had maintained secretive sovereignty and exclusive authority, in a legal corporate manner, as well as a Mafioso-like power pyramid that controlled off-the-books resources and assets under the Alpha Corp shell. But ultimate authority had been solely with Steinhart. Their mutually all-in partnership agreement now gave that authority and access to Arya Krish and made the transition admittedly daunting. Most of the executives in the upper hierarchy would remain clueless and compliant. Their day-to-day lives were unchanged as they continued to serve their mundane purpose, including the board of directors. However, Steinhart kept a few closer under his wing. He'd relied on them to conduct the more nefarious business that gave Alpha Corp its power. These individuals were the topic of conversation at the moment.

"As far as the others like me on the Alpha Corp payroll, they'll all fall in line. Based on my assessment, one of the threats with a special loyalty to Steinhart was Marcus Knight," Rook said. "He's no longer a factor, obviously."

"Why was Knight so loyal to Steinhart?" Krish asked.

"I don't know the details, but apparently Steinhart rescued Marcus from very dire straits, which resulted in a type of obligatory kinship. Knight was very duty-bound, I'll give him that, and loyal, as a result. We came from a similar background."

They had moved to the other end of the office and sat near the computers, away from the desk and single, thin, rectangular window. Krish rubbed his eyes, stood, and paced across the room.

Krish went back to the window again, remained standing, and looked out. "Who's this other guy? What do we know about him?" Krish projected his voice across the room.

"Ryan Pratt," Rook said with a natural resentment in his tone. "He kind of acted as Steinhart's proxy in many high-level business dealings, particularly with recruitment, as well as with politicians and executives. They knew each other for a long time, it seemed. Cut from the same cloth, you could say. Except Pratt was a subordinate and spineless if you ask me, unlike Steinhart. That made him a very effective Number Two. Pratt is as greedy as he is ugly, and he's equally shrewd. He's wasted his substance in riotous living. Likes his drugs and hookers, that sort of thing. Now, the only thing he's any good for is self-defilement. No family, as far as I know, and he doesn't care for much else other than the gratuitous indulgence of his wealth and power. A lot of it is within Alpha Corp's sphere of influence. He likes to travel a lot, as a result."

Arya Krish listened quietly, taking in every word. Despite only knowing what he was just told about Pratt, Rook's words infused immediate contempt that quickly seeded itself deep in his psyche. "How do we handle him?" he asked.

"What would you want done?"

Krish paused. "I want him out of the way. Can he be controlled with the usual bribery or blackmail? Keep him happy and out of the way?"

Rook shook his head. "Despite his greed, he covets the power he wields, like I said. And he knows he has leverage over us now with his knowledge, experience, and influence within Alpha Corp. Plus, he was personally close to Steinhart. He'll want to exploit it and preserve the old order. In my opinion, blackmail won't be all that effective against him, either. I'm not sure we can find anything substantial to hold over his head that may not somehow be tied back to Alpha Corp. It's not going to get rid of him for good."

Krish turned and looked back at Rook. The look on Rook's face completed the thought. Krish looked back out of the window. Before he started overthinking it, he said, "We haven't come this far only to be obstructed by this man."

"I'll take care of it," Rook said, and Krish perceived the eagerness in the reply. He felt Rook was egging him on with an ulterior motive.

"How?"

"Does it matter, Dr. Krish? The bottom line is neutralizing this liability so we can advance our objective, correct? That is the pragmatic approach you need to operate with now from the command position. It's not necessary, or wise, to be involved further beyond that."

Rook's words felt both cold and precise to Krish, and he brooded silently for a moment. He debated once again how much he could trust Rook. The implications were clear. Pratt was likely to be killed if needed to get him out of the way, and Krish was complicit by leaving it up to Rook. Was it necessary? Is this how it would be from this point forward?

"I have to meet him." Krish felt he was coming out of a trance. "I need to try to negotiate something with him, maybe pay him off to relinquish his Alpha Corp holdings. Based on what you're telling me, he seems like the type who would take the right offer if his vices are more important than Alpha Corp stock."

"With all due respect, Dr. Krish, based on what I know, it would be a waste of time. Like I said, he and Steinhart go all the way back to the beginning. However, if that's how you wish to proceed, I'll arrange it. Where and when?"

Rook's reminder of Pratt's loyalty to Steinhart weighed on Krish and feeling as if it pushed him into a corner. "First thing tomorrow morning, bring him here," Krish said.

He sat alone in the office afterward and ruminated, then turned his attention to the laptop on the desk. Krish accessed the personnel files and ultimately pulled up Jason Rook's record. It was disappointingly abbreviated. The scant facts available, however, were compelling enough and piqued Krish's interest. Rook's military service spanned several years in the early course of the first Middle East War, though the record was not detailed. He had a wife, labeled deceased, at age 32. Again, the lack of information in the file left Krish's curiosity unquenched, but whatever there was on Rook added some dimension to the man.

The next day, Krish stood for a while and looked out

toward the morning sun, which had started to clear the tree line below, then walked over and sat at the desk. He rested his arms with folded hands on the desk and watched the door calmly. Within moments, Jason Rook opened it and made way for his visitor. Ryan Pratt entered with a pre-ordered look of prissy annoyance that irritated Krish instantly. He didn't say anything as Pratt stood near the door. After a moment, Krish gestured with his hand toward the seat in front of the desk.

Pratt smirked condescendingly and walked slowly toward the chair with his hands in his pockets. "Dr. Arya Krish. I suppose it was due time for us to meet."

Krish observed Pratt as he slowly made his way to the chair and sat down. Pratt had the remnants of good looks despite Rook's description but was aged beyond his years. He wore the irrevocable leathery tarnish of gratuitous self-defilement on his skin and features, like the picture of Dorian Gray. His eyes were sunken in but still retained the glint of intelligence. His speech had a shrill, prickly sound to it, as if he was scolding a child.

At least it felt that way to Krish. "Although Vladimir Steinhart never mentioned you, it made sense, having learned of your position in Alpha Corp," Krish said.

Pratt shrugged dismissively as he reached into his suit jacket pocket and took out his cigarettes. "And now Steinhart is dead. That pacemaker manufacturer is going to have to answer for that. I'll make sure of it." He eyed Krish as he lit his cigarette.

Krish did not attempt to mask his contempt as he remained silent and stared back. Any reflexive fear of discovery Krish felt from Pratt's words blinked away as it remained clear that Pratt had no clue what had actually happened to Steinhart. Pratt's comment didn't linger in his thoughts. Rather, he remembered Rook describing Pratt as spineless, and that was plainly obvious to Krish from the beginning. The longer he interacted with Pratt, the more tired he felt of this pest.

"I suppose that makes us near partners, Dr. Krish," Pratt said.

"I'm not sure how your math adds up in that regard, Mr. Pratt. You must expect me to know your arrangement with Steinhart. Yes, he shared much of his resources and rewards, but he made sure to retain all the authority and power over operational decision-making. What he probably didn't explicitly share with you were the details of our mutual power-sharing agreement, which included shared executive decision-making power over Beacon Medical Institute's main operations, as well as those of Alpha Corp. After his passing, that makes me more or less the sole director and CEO. You do not even have a seat on the board anymore since Steinhart's passing as part of your contract." Krish leaned back. "So this meeting was not intended to be a debriefing or negotiation. It is your resignation. With a generous severance package, I might add."

Krish waited for Pratt's reply. Pratt shifted uneasily with a searching look in his eyes, and Krish relished Pratt's lack of response.

"Well, be that as it may." Pratt stopped and took a drag from his cigarette. "I intend to stick around and put up a fight."

Krish was almost glad to hear him say so.

As Pratt stood and buttoned his suit jacket, he peered down his sharp nose at Krish, who remained seated. "Steinhart told me about your condescending air of moral superiority. He wasn't all that impressed, either. I find it a bit hypocritical if you ask me. I know quite well what it really takes to make the big things happen, the things that really matter to you. I can surmise what you've had to do, the minefield you've had to navigate as your ambitions became more demanding." Pratt walked slowly toward the other end of the office and looked around as if re-familiarizing himself with the room. "The only way to navigate a minefield is to know the field. Know where the mines are. That kind of knowledge only comes with direct experience, getting your hands dirty."

"If an apparent hypocrisy is as far as your dim-witted analysis got you, then I'm not sure we can communicate on the same level at all," Krish said.

Pratt turned back with a petulant glance in response to the brisk insult.

Krish recognized it and paused to dwell on the moment. "True, I am fundamentally a pragmatist," he said. "I do not claim any moral superiority for myself. Perhaps more so for the ends that I aspire to. I'm also aware some of my methods have left me divorced from those lofty principles and I am prepared to live with that, I suppose. But at least I strive for a higher purpose, something more than self-gratification."

Krish became silent as if he had said too much. He felt it odd that he had somehow confided that much to this man. Pratt looked at him without responding as if he expected him to go on. "Along those lines, Mr. Pratt, my offer to you should be appealing. We're forfeiting some of our auxiliary assets, which would give you independence to pursue whatever ends you desire in those arenas. Doesn't that give you what you want, which is basically to continue doing whatever you do? And I get what I want as well, which is you out of Alpha Corp."

"I helped Steinhart take Alpha Corp to the next level, Dr. Krish. It's not something I would walk away from so easily. I've invested time and labor that you would not be able to compensate for so easily," Pratt said with ill-concealed exasperation as he walked back toward Krish's desk. "And I know where the skeletons are. No, I'm not going anywhere, regardless of if you somehow fire me. You'll have to accept that."

"I'm taking things in a different direction here, and there's no room for you any longer."

Pratt smiled and shook his head in disapproval. "I'll see

you around, Dr. Krish. You can count on it." He turned and walked out.

Krish sat alone and brooded until Jason Rook opened the door as quietly as he closed it, then walked over and sat down.

"Well, Dr. Krish, that pretty much went as I would have expected."

Arya Krish shook his head. "Doesn't look like he's going to go away quietly, does it?"

"I've known him for many years. This encounter was nothing, in fact. He'll make it a hobby to obstruct you any way he can. I'm not trying to lay it on too thick, Dr. Krish, but I can tell you from experience that what you want to accomplish with Beacon and Alpha Corp, your vision for the Panacea Project, from what I have been able to tell so far, will be in jeopardy with Ryan Pratt in the mix. With everything you've done up 'til this point, whatever means you've had to employ, you have to remain just as decisive."

Rook paused and eyed Krish curiously. He was quite sure what he was implying was clear, but he deliberately waited on Krish's response to his words. Krish's expression remained unchanged, as he knew Rook indulged in his own speculations. Krish sat silently and looked at Rook, but his thoughts remained on his encounter with Ryan Pratt. Perhaps Rook had ulterior, personal motives for nudging him toward this decision, but it didn't seem to bother him much. Krish saw an unacceptable obstacle in Ryan Pratt, and he saw sitting in front of him a means to an end. A calm, cold look came over Krish's face, and he sighed softly as if in resignation.

"Ryan Pratt cannot be a part of this any longer." He shook his head and was going to continue, but it was all Rook needed to hear.

"I'll handle it," Rook replied quickly, and before Krish said or asked anything more, he got up, nodded at Krish respectfully, and left. Krish watched him leave without trying to stop him.

***

It was a moonless night, and the misty drizzle was seen only under the yellow streetlights. Jason Rook sat in a car across the street from the multi-story condominium building where Pratt kept a discreet residence. Pratt was expected to be there that night, sleeping off one of his binges. It was past midnight, and other than a few other parked cars on the curb, the street was empty. Rook occasionally glanced down the street and checked his mirrors. Otherwise, he sat and watched the building. The faint patter of rain on the car was the only sound. He was not waiting for anything in particular, and no hesitation held him back. It was a moment of reflection that gave Rook pause as memories of the past ebbed forth and led to an anticipation of what would be his final encounter with Pratt. And while he indulged in the prospects, there was no visceral reaction. His hardened nerves maintained their reserve while his mind threw itself back to the distant past, well over a decade ago. That was shortly after he'd returned home from his final deployment. It was the first time he'd met Ryan Pratt and Vladimir Steinhart.

***

About a Decade Ago:

One of the first bitterly cold days in early December ushered in winter in New York City. Jason Rook sat on a bench in Washington Park and looked at the passers-by. The gray sky cast down an oppressive pall, perhaps only perceivable to Rook in his state of mind. It seemed everyone else was oblivious. A crisp breeze cut through the layers of his thick, utilitarian fleece sweatshirt and winter cap, and felt as if it was biting his skin, but it didn't cause him much discomfort. He didn't take notice of it, in fact, because his destitution and despair numbed such sensations. Rook's light blue eyes were alert and strained as he looked out at the bustling scene. His thoughts were preoccupied, but he took notice of a man who approached from a distance. The man walked with his hands in his pockets as he crossed the street. He wore a thick overcoat and a blood-red tie, had slick brown hair, and an expressionless face. The man walked toward the bench where Rook sat alone. Rook continued to stare ahead as the man stood next to him.

"Hello, Mr. Rook," he said. He smiled.

Rook glanced up quickly at him, then looked straight ahead again. From that glance, he noted the man's dark, alert eyes looking at him in an appraising manner. The man was clean-shaven. While he seemed young, fine creases lined his sharp features. He turned and faced the same direction Rook was looking but remained standing with his hands in his pockets. Their breath clouded in the cold air as they spoke without making much eye contact.

"Do I know you?" Rook asked.

"Well, I'm sure you would remember if you did, Mr. Rook. That sort of thing wouldn't lapse your memory now, would it?"

"OK. Who the hell are you, and what do you want?"

"My name is Ryan Pratt. I represent Alpha Corp. Perhaps you've heard of it?"

Rook frowned and shrugged his shoulders dismissively.

"We'd like to think we're emerging as the leader in the healthcare industry, at least regionally, for now. Of course, we have ambitions of achieving much more. Our operations are expanding rapidly, and our recruitment has become vigorous to keep up."

"So you're a recruiter? How'd you find me? I don't see what I would have to offer a healthcare company."

"As I mentioned, we're expanding our horizons. We're looking to become something more, as it were. It's a multi-billion-dollar industry, Mr. Rook, and in that world, so much is possible and needs protected. The nature of the position we're looking to fill calls for someone with strategic and operational training and experience. Military training helps. As to how we found you?" Pratt finally sat next to Rook and looked straight ahead. "Admittedly, that wasn't easy. But once we knew you were local, we felt you would fit in quite nicely."

"Frankly, it all sounds rather vague and unappealing." Rook sighed as he stood. "Not interested."

Pratt watched him walk away without saying anything for a moment, then called out to him. "I suggest you at least hear us out, Mr. Rook. After all, you really have nothing left to lose at this point, do you?"

Rook stopped and turned around. "What would you know about what I have and don't have?"

"Let's face it, Mr. Rook. You have nothing. You've been discharged from the military, your wife left you before you returned, you're broke, and you're obviously unemployed." Pratt gave a condescending smile as he stood and walked slowly over to Rook. He sensed that he was getting under Rook's skin from the irritated look on his face. "Listen," he continued, softening his tone deliberately. "You could either continue circling the drain, you know, chase odd jobs or scrape a living in some demeaning rent-a-cop uniform. Or you can come with me and be part of something greater. At least hear our offer. I'll introduce you to Mr. Steinhart, the director of Alpha Corp, the top guy. He's asked to meet you in person and make our pitch. It's an opportunity that has presented itself, Mr. Rook, one that someone with your capabilities, and in your circumstances should not dismiss thoughtlessly. It may give you an out. I think your survival instincts are telling you the same."

Rook remained silent for a moment. He looked away from Pratt at the bustling scene around him. Pratt stood still and watched him, waiting patiently.

"Fine. I'll go meet this Steinhart," Rook said.

He sat silently in the back of the car as they drove outside the city. The windows were blacked out, and the divider isolated him. While his instincts and training had him initially keep track of the turns and the time elapsed, he eventually let it go. His thoughts turned over Pratt's words as he recognized the calculated effect they had. It was no coincidence that Pratt found him at that moment. Rook had exhausted what little resources he had in reserve upon his return from duty. He'd slipped through the cracks of the inadequate VA system. He'd sat on that park bench and contemplated his very survival when seemingly out of nowhere came a foothold, something he could not allow himself to discard.

Rook's meditations were interrupted by the sensation of the car turning a corner and coming to a stop. Soon, the door was opened for him, and he felt the burst of cold air as he exited. Rook looked around at the surrounding naked trees before he turned and faced the brick building. Pratt gestured toward the single door, then got back in the car and drove along the narrow driveway that disappeared down the hill. Rook turned toward the steel door, where another man in a black suit and tie stood with his hands folded in front of him. As Rook approached, the other man opened the door. Rook went inside and down the long hallway toward another set of double doors. As he approached and was about to reach for the handle, the heavy wooden door opened. A man in an expensive gray suit and dark blue tie held it open for him.

"Come in, Mr. Rook," the man said. He waited for Rook to grab the door before he turned and went back into the room.

Rook hesitated for a moment, then went inside and let the door close behind him. He turned and looked around the vast room that could have easily accommodated 50 people, then watched the man walk to the other end toward the large panoramic window. Steinhart went to the small bar near the window and poured bourbon into two glasses. Rook stayed near the door for a moment and observed his surroundings. The room was elegantly furnished in Victorian style, and the natural light shimmered off the ornate marble floors, illuminating the tall tray ceilings with decorative crown moldings that completed the regal façade. Steinhart signaled to Rook to come over to the window and held out one of the glasses. Rook walked over to him, took the glass, and looked out the window at the perfectly lined trees below.

"The view is even more impressive in the spring and summer, with all the greenery. It's admittedly a little bleak now." Steinhart took a sip of his drink. "My name is Vladimir Steinhart, Director here at Alpha Corp." He extended his hand.

"Jason Rook, as you know." Rook shook his hand.

"Yes, of course," Steinhart said. "You'll have to forgive us for the somewhat dramatic approach in bringing you here, Mr. Rook. You've chosen to remain off the grid, so to speak, so it seemed the most practical way to arrange for us to meet. I expect Mr. Pratt has explained why we've asked you here?"

"Not really. He made it sound like you guys are recruiting as part of some expansion efforts for the company at large. I'm still wondering how you found me and why you chose me, as Pratt suggested."

Steinhart nodded in acknowledgement as he took another sip, then walked past Rook a few steps, and stood near the window. Rook turned around and faced him. Steinhart had a contemplative look on his face, and his eyes were slightly squinted, which somehow conveyed a shrewd intelligence. He smiled occasionally while he spoke as if he was musing to himself.

"Well, that is somewhat arbitrary, admittedly. The position we're looking to fill favors some background in law enforcement or military. It would involve overseeing security and logistics, which in our enterprise is very complicated and often requires skill sets that such a training background provides. The industry can be quite cut-throat." Steinhart turned and looked at Rook. "I realize I'm being vague, and deliberately so, mainly because of the confidentiality that's required. Obviously, were you to come on board, there would be full disclosure."

"Kind of a tough bargain on my end, Mr. Steinhart. You're asking me to sign without knowing exactly what I'm signing up for. What makes you think I'd even be interested in a job like this?"

Steinhart didn't respond right away. He smiled subtly again as if he anticipated Rook's response. "Obviously, I don't know if you're interested or not, Mr. Rook. I suppose that is the entire purpose of this meeting, to ascertain exactly what it is you want. I think once we both agree on what you want, the rest becomes easy."

Steinhart turned and looked at Rook, then walked toward his desk and sat behind it. His back was slightly turned to Rook, who finished his drink, went back to the bar, and poured another before coming to the desk. Steinhart gestured toward the chair in front of him and continued.

"Let me begin by admitting we've looked into you, Mr. Rook. Investigated you, in fact. Here is my take on it," he said with a whimsical look. "You're a military veteran past the end of a career that started at age 18 and culminated in the Special Forces, with all the cryptic and glorious implication that carries. I say so with all sincere respect, believe me. I wouldn't presume to imagine what you've experienced and seen in this world, and your service to our country is worthy of honoring. I can't help but reflect on your plight now, and I do know quite a bit. I know that your estranged ex-wife, who left you a few years ago while you were deployed, has cancer and is fighting the odds. Your sustenance from the odd jobs you've been through up until this point has not even come close to what she needs."

Rook observed Steinhart quietly as he spoke and occasionally took a sip from his drink. Steinhart continued with escalating enthusiasm. His inscrutable dark brown eyes darted around the room, and he occasionally locked eyes with Rook. He had a cadence that made everything he said sound authoritative, like a preacher belting out the gospel.

"It's frustrating to think about it," Steinhart said. "You've been left in a position where in one way you are vastly overqualified for most meaningful work, and at the same time unfit for most mainstream work." He paused and looked at Rook. "But I'm describing more what you need rather than want. I realize that. What you want is purpose, Mr. Rook, something larger than yourself to serve and protect, as you did your whole adult life in military service. If I may say so, you are serving a higher cause in supporting her anonymously. But there is no way you can live out your days driving cabs or writing traffic tickets like normal people. You have been forged to function in a different capacity." Steinhart paused for a moment of reflection, then continued. "Well then. Coming to the point now, Mr. Rook. I believe you have a place in our corporation. More than that, I don't hesitate to say you would be playing a crucial role in our most ambitious visions for the future of not only this company but the industry and society at large."

He went on about his master plan for the healthcare industry and, subsequently, the political landscape that it influenced. In retrospect, it could not have been more obvious. Steinhart's ruthless selfishness and blind avarice for money and power were clear, just by the way he endlessly talked. Rook observed Steinhart's mannerisms as he went on. His chiseled stonewashed features smirked and twitched in escalating excitement as Steinhart articulated Alpha Corp's consolidation of insurance, pharmaceuticals, hospitals, and healthcare systems. This was a seemingly ludicrous proposition, given obvious monopoly infringements. But the political culture and climate were already changing, as decades of lobbying tightened the corporate juggernauts' stranglehold over government policy, basically by controlling the policy makers.

"So anyway," he said, "we are big players, Mr. Rook, playing a big game in a vast field. The name of the game? Conquer the field. The position I am offering you is essentially my chief of staff. You will be directly involved in executing the operations that accomplish our largest and most long-term goals. The rewards will be vast and extravagant, as will be the demands from us. What makes you so qualified for this job? Your training and experience, believe it or not, will be relevant along the way. But the qualities of a man trained as a specialized military and intelligence operative are invaluable in and of themselves."

Steinhart paused, stared at Rook for a moment, then reached into his drawer. He pulled out a bank check and slid it toward Rook face down. Rook picked it up and looked at it, then looked at Steinhart without much expression despite his undeniable shock.

"That is a check for $600,000, Mr. Rook. It would be your signing bonus if you accept my job offer before you leave. And don't worry about taxes. Your salary will be variable and most likely much higher, but no less than that. Also, we can and will help your ex-wife with her illness, independent of your salary and benefits. It has broken your bank up until this point, but it will no longer be a burden. In fact, Mr. Rook, under my employment, you won't have much burden at all in your life, I can assure you. I will reiterate, however, that I will demand a lot from you as well. Everything, in fact. This is the offer, Mr. Rook, and it is as specific as it gets. Be advised it expires at the end of this meeting. That's it." He waved a hand.

They remained silent as Rook glanced back and forth between the check in his hand and Steinhart.

***

Jason Rook sat in his car across the street from Pratt's building in the dark, reflecting for a moment on everything that had happened since then, over the years. It all started with the meeting with Steinhart and Pratt. If Rook was Steinhart's chief of staff, Pratt was vice president. He looked toward Pratt's building with a stern countenance, then got out of the car and walked across the street in the misty rain. He punched the security code and entered the building.

Pratt was in deep slumber. All the lights were off as his front door opened silently, and Rook entered. He walked toward Pratt's bedroom door, stood in front of it, and listened. Nothing stirred, and he knew Pratt was asleep.

The thundering sound of the door being kicked in did not quite startle Pratt awake since his slumber was largely drug-induced. But it did cause him to stir suddenly and sit up in a stupor. Rook walked up to him with his silenced pistol in hand at his side and stood at the bedside. He watched Pratt in the dim light that leaked in from the street through the blinds. Pratt turned his head as if looking around with his eyes closed for a second, then went to lie down again.

Rook swiftly slapped him across the face, finally startling him awake. Pratt's eyes opened and looked up. Rook waited as Pratt adjusted to the light. He wanted Pratt to look right at him and he knew when Pratt recognized him by his petrified eyes. Rook knew he was the last thing Pratt would see, and raised his gun.

CHAPTER TEN

As Jay Asher faced the new incoming physicians at the Institute, his eyes looked past them. His mind was somewhere else.

Arya Krish sat next to him and observed the preoccupied look that still never quite left Asher's face since that night on the road and the incident with Marcus Knight. Krish had recognized the mannerisms—the uneasy shuffling of the feet, the far-off look—that he'd noticed in himself for a while. He felt the weary weight of choices and actions much longer than the three months that had passed since that night on the country road and the death of Vladimir Steinhart that occurred shortly thereafter. Krish's eyes shifted from Asher to the physicians who faced him. He saw the eager, bright eyes that looked on in anticipation but felt far away from the whole scene as if it was a pretense.

The sky was thinly overcast, and silver daylight came in through the windows and glistened faintly off the polished oak floors. The dozen or so physicians all had on their white coats, which caught the natural light and almost glowed in the dim ambience. Krish wore a black suit, while Jay Asher had on his Class A military uniform. They sat in silence until Krish stood and stepped forward to address the physicians. They looked at him in anticipation.

"Welcome to Beacon Medical Institute," he said with conviction in his voice. "You have demonstrated yourselves as the cream of an elite crop, and we welcome you to join a pedigree that is few and proud. Beacon is dedicated with solemn resolve to the nurturing and advancement of humanity on an unprecedented scale."

Arya Krish scanned their faces with a searching look. He had experienced so many similar moments that the alienation and disconnect he felt now were obvious and undeniable. He strained to remember the galvanized feeling he shared with his new, handpicked colleagues when he addressed prior groups and searched for it in that moment with quiet desperation. The physicians continued to give him their undivided attention.

"You know." Krish paused and paced slowly in front of the group. He spoke in a distant manner while Jay Asher sat off to the right and watched him. "I've welcomed your prior counterparts with a similar speech. And despite the repetition, for my part, it was sincere and renewed each time. But, significant events have occurred recently, namely those leading to the merger of Beacon Medical Institute and Alpha Corp. These events have ushered in a period of transition and transformation."

Krish paused and glanced at Asher. Asher looked away from Krish toward the group, none of whom likely noticed the pensive look on his face.

"You may be called to rise to such an occasion, in a distinctly different manner than your predecessors, in this new period of being and becoming for Beacon." Krish stopped pacing and gave each of them a scrutinizing look. They were obviously captivated.

After Arya Krish finished addressing them, he introduced Dr. Jay Asher, veteran Lt. Colonel, United States Marines, as the co-director of Beacon Medical Institute. When the formal orientation concluded, the two of them stayed back after the new physicians were dismissed. The clouds outside had broken slightly, allowing periods of sunshine to flood the large room. They sat and talked of various things.

After a while, Asher stood during a silence, walked toward the panoramic windows, and looked out one of them. His arms were folded behind him. They were far enough from each other that their voices echoed as they spoke. Asher said. "Vincent Halliday was in touch with me a few times these past weeks."

Krish remained seated and silent for a moment as he watched Asher. "Oh yeah? What did he want?"

"He wondered what was going on since you haven't been in touch with him in a while."

"That's true. I've been a little busy."

Asher turned from the window and toward him with a puzzled look. "Yeah? Well, join the club. I'm a little curious myself. Where've you been?"

Krish leaned forward in his chair. "Well, we've had to consolidate the merger of Alpha and Beacon. I've had to spend time over there at Alpha Corp and establish our presence. We had to comb through the corporate hierarchy and clear the weeds." He nodded casually.

"Yeah? Anything else I should know?" Asher asked. He shrugged.

"Look, I had to go at that one alone," Krish said. "I had to confront some of the remaining minions of Steinhart one way or another. Clean house, as it were. It was also a test for Jason Rook and his role in our new venture. He may turn out to be a valuable and effective resource. At this point, I can say I'm glad Rook's on our side."

"Kind of risky keeping him in the fold." Asher smiled and shook his head in disapproval. "Cynical, ex-military, soldier without a cause. Could be unpredictable."

"Now he has our cause, our vision. I told him once his moral compass was rusted over, but could be restored. Hopefully, that'll be the case." Krish stood, walked up to the window, and positioned himself next to Asher. They looked out at the view of Washington, DC, as they spoke.

"So, now that the dust seems to have settled, what comes next?" Asher asked.

"The Alpha Beacon machine will be directed toward our most important projects. We'll expand healthcare systems in the whole metropolitan area," Arya Krish said, as if thinking out loud. "The Veterans Administration—I know how much you want to get involved with that, and we want to make a move quickly like we talked about before. It'll start with our own models in the private sector that demonstrate how elite American healthcare should look for the soldiers and the public at large. The VA will be in our sights as a political endgame. Right off the bat, we'll expand our PR campaign and advance our R&D projects—neuro-AI interface, next generation organ synthesis. And obviously, the Panacea Project as it enters its next phase with the new protocols going live. That's the next milestone for us, getting the protocols going. I'm going to meet up with Halliday and Chowan later."

His voice trailed off before he mentioned the other local project initiatives, like the charter schools, free clinics, and neighborhood outreach programs. His thoughts also drifted toward his international interests that Praveen oversaw in India. Krish felt his mind fall back to the origins, to VC Farm and the orphanages. As a result, inevitably, he thought of Murthy. That encounter with a man all those years ago continued to haunt him.

Asher looked at Krish during the prolonged silence and saw he was daydreaming again. "You might want to meet with Jason Rook, too, while you're at it. It seemed like he had matters of importance to discuss."

Krish snapped out of his ruminations and nodded. "Yeah, I plan to," he said distantly.

Asher nodded and observed Krish with narrow, scrutinizing eyes. "Do you remember that conversation when you asked for my help, when you first described your ultimate plan, your vision for Beacon, and for yourself? You know I mean it when I say you can and will achieve anything you put your mind to. I've known that as long as I've known you. But I don't know how else to say this. I'm not sure you've thought this one all the way through," Asher said.

"I think that's pretty much what you told me in that conversation."

"So, what direction are the tides of fortune taking us?" Asher asked a little flippantly.

"Look, I know I went off the grid there for a bit," Krish said as he acknowledged Asher's frustration. "I was incommunicado, a bit abruptly. But like I said, I've had to bring some closure to several matters. At first, it felt like I was lost in a large field, and I don't know what to expect next. And I won't lie to you. This new position I'm in is daunting and menacing to the conscience. I get what you were referring to before. But I'm going to keep my eyes on the prize and take refuge in the prospects of the Panacea Project and the amazing changes it will bring. And now, I'm realizing the new power, we must exert our influence in the social and political realms at the highest level. Whatever means the corrupt use to keep their power, now we can wield them, too. Steinhart operated in this secret world where others just like him, ruthless, greedy, and amoral, had power beyond the public's knowledge and imagination. We'll have to play their game better than they do. That's the endgame, the way I see it."

Asher remained silent as they stood with their hands in their pockets and looked out the large window.

"I understand all of that. All I'm saying is we're here now. We've slain the monster and taken its place. We are going to have to be ready for other monsters. There are more, for certain," Asher said.

"Yes." Krish paused. "Do you remember when I asked if we had to become a monster to slay a monster?"

"Yeah, I remember. You indicated it was already too late." Asher looked at Krish. He noticed the subtle, strained look come over his face as Krish remained silent. It was quite a while before either spoke, as both had retreated into their own reverie.

"Things have changed and have changed me," Krish said. "Nowadays, I have recurring dreams or versions of the same dream. Not nightmares, really, but strange, unsettling dreams of either being chased by someone or I'm the one chasing. Toward the end of the dream, it always winds up with me in a car and driving off a cliff-side road. I fall for a while and realize that I'm dreaming and wait to wake up." Krish looked at Asher. "What is that a symptom of?"

Asher shrugged. "Guilty conscience, maybe?"

Krish shook his head without answering, as if it was more complicated than that.

"I also have unsettling dreams, if that helps," Asher said. "But it's not from a guilty conscience. Mine are mundane, in fact. Maybe it's partly post-traumatic stress. Who knows? It's basically a version of an incident, as you said. Anyway, I'll say this. Back when you justified your plans for Steinhart by calling it a combat scenario, I was disappointed at the comparison. But that night on the road, our encounter with Marcus Knight? I've been near enough combat situations to know what it feels like, and that was it. No question. They tried to take us out first. I couldn't have imagined something like that happening. No doubt that had a profound impact on you as well."

"So your conscience is clear?"

"Not as simple as that, no." Asher nodded. "Maybe I don't think about it as much as you, though." Krish nodded, and the conversation drifted to R&D and lighter topics as they talked before parting ways.

The imminent herald of the genetic revolution, as substantial as the industrial, nuclear, and computer revolutions, had Krish animated with exhilarating anticipation. Optimism prevailed in Krish's spirit as he walked to the R&D lab to meet with Vincent Halliday and Kai Chowan and begin rolling out the treatment protocols for the clinical trials of Alpha Corp and the Panacea Project at Beacon. At that moment, he gave little thought to the tainted history that was dragged in as well. He thought more of the vast possibilities as he entered the lab and looked toward the far back corner of the warehouse-size underground facility. A single station was lit by a bright white light above, and he heard the faint echoes of Halliday and Chowan talking grow louder as he walked toward them. As he approached, he saw them sitting on work stools in front of a computer. They saw him and stood, smiling. He smiled back, and everyone shook hands.

"Gentlemen, good to see you," Krish said. "It's been a while. Hope everyone's well."

The three of them convened over the early logistics of the Panacea protocols, the actual clinical application of the R&D from the better part of the past decade. Those protocols would be accelerated since the merger with Alpha Corp. The glaring imminent prospects obscured Krish's troubled ruminations again as he listened and enthusiastically discussed the various algorithms that comprised the different treatment protocols targeting various medical conditions. Their attention eventually drifted toward the gene augmentation protocols, by far the largest and most advanced.

"We're combining our next-generation CRISPR-based gene primers with their nanotech delivery system," Halliday said. They all leaned forward and stared at the computer screen. "Alpha Corp invested most of their resources toward developing synthetic carbon nano-filament molecules for a delivery system based on adeno-associated viral models. They were ahead of us on that front." Halliday looked over at Chowan, "Of course, their human HLA compatibility data gave them what was needed to achieve immune inertia with both the delivery system and the genetic inserts. We had the gene primer insert tech already, and now we see what it can do." Halliday gestured at the screen.

Krish nodded with excitement in his eyes. "That is excellent, Dr. Halliday. I think we should have a formal conference with some of the others and finalize the first batch of treatment protocols that will go live. I've already been assessing the assets we have in the FDA and other government and academic agencies to expedite certifications and approvals." He looked up at Chowan, who nodded attentively as he watched the computer screen.

Krish paused as a somber look came over his face. "Listen, Dr. Chowan," he said. "We've only spoken briefly since you joined us from Alpha Corp. I want to hear what you think about all this, using the data from Alpha Corp's human trials. While the study design and results were scientifically sound—obviously, since the trials were designed by people like you—what you've told me about how Alpha Corp went about recruitment exposes clear ethical violations. And yet here we are, using it for our purpose now, to complete the Panacea Project."

The three men stepped back from the computer station and stood in a circle facing each other. Krish and Halliday waited respectfully as they watched Chowan nod as he marshaled his thoughts.

"I've reflected on it quite a bit since joining here," he said with his thick, fluent accent. "For the first time since leaving home, I've felt like I'm doing something truly worthwhile, and I feel free again. It's odd to think back to the circumstances I had backed myself into in the name of fulfilling my duty toward my family, supposedly lifting them out of some perceived disadvantaged life back home. It made me compliant with the home surveillance, implanted monitoring devices, restricted communication and travel access, and all the dehumanization that was masked and embellished with lavish amenities and consolation creature comforts. I came to accept the cage I built for myself." He paused and observed the look of empathy and intrigue on their faces. "There is no doubt in my mind that in the hands of Vladimir Steinhart and the old order at Alpha Corp, the technology we were trying to develop before anyone else would have been used for nothing more than unscrupulous profit, with complete disregard to any ethical or humanitarian implications. Seeing where the future is headed now, I am content and relieved, Dr. Krish. I feel like a normal person again."

"We're honored to have you on our team now, Dr. Chowan. Truly," Krish said, and Halliday nodded in agreement. As they shook hands, Krish put his hand on Chowan's shoulder. He caught a look on his face that made him think Chowan was holding something back, but it passed quickly. Krish excused himself and signaled Halliday to accompany him while Chowan remained back and continued their work.

They left the R&D lab and were in the large hallway toward Administration when Krish looked back toward the lab. "So, what do you think of Dr. Chowan, honestly?" he asked. He turned to Halliday with an intent look. "You might be the one working closest to him. How's he transitioned over, by your assessment? He's the only one this high up we didn't handpick."

"He seems to fit in well, Dr. Krish. I've enjoyed working with him. He's pretty much all business, though. Doesn't seek out much interaction beyond that, you know?"

"Yeah, I got that sense of him early on," Krish said. He nodded as they walked side by side. "Can you believe it? We're finally reaching the end of the Panacea Project. Regardless of when you start counting, it's been a long and, at times, rough road. I can't help getting excited by the imminent culmination of it all. You've been there from the beginning. I can imagine you share the same rush."

"Absolutely, Dr. Krish. It's been a long time coming."

"Between me and you, it's obvious how much the Alpha Corp's human trials help fill in the gaps and catapult us to a point that otherwise was still years away," Krish said with a somber look. "Just as obvious as the ethical breach. I confess I continue to struggle with it, as do you, I'm sure. We don't need to get into it now, but it made me wonder how Chowan sees it all, having been through what he's been through, and to see it play out this way now."

"He seemed sincere just now, with the way he expressed his perspective," Halliday said. He paused. "Having said that, when you spend enough time with him, you start feeling like he's always preoccupied. And this is strictly a hunch, but he seems to be hiding something. I certainly don't think he's told anyone his whole story. I haven't gotten much out of him. Frankly, there may not be much relevant there."

Krish nodded without answering and brooded silently as they walked.

***

It was several weeks later. The late afternoon daylight was diminished by dense storm clouds and lit Arya Krish's office at Beacon Medical Institute just enough to cast long gothic shadows that obscured Krish's face somewhat. He sat behind his desk with his back to the large panoramic windows and listened to Jason Rook. The clouds had rolled in only in the last half hour; before that, it was mostly sunny and bright. The contrast in ambience had not escaped Krish's observation, or Rook's, for that matter. While Krish was fully concentrated on their conversation, he thought, *The clouds will likely pass shortly.* The Administrative Wing would be sparsely staffed on the holiday, and their conversation was certain to be uninterrupted. Krish reached out slowly and took the bottle of fine bourbon in his hand. He poured two glasses and passed one to Rook while he finished making his point.

"So, that's the big three at the special interest lobbying level." Rook leaned for his glass and sat back, "Alpha Corp in the Northeast, Esper Enterprises in the South, and Silo in the West.

As far as Big Pharma and the federal government go, those other two are your rivals. There's a pecking order below of the dozens of smaller health systems geographically that play out in the regional turf wars."

Krish leaned back with his glass and remained silent for a moment. He looked down at his drink with a thoughtful countenance. Then he nodded to himself in understanding, looked up at Rook, and held up his glass.

"Well, now we're at the top of that order," Krish said casually. Rook reciprocated, and they took a sip in silence. "Uncharted territory, for me at least. Looks like Steinhart made a committed play for it over several years. The roster of politicians on his payroll spans through all three branches of government. Impressive and disturbing all at once."

"It is a constant grind, Dr. Krish. That kind of power and influence becomes the ultimate endgame, and it consumes your resources with its demanding upkeep."

Krish nodded again in a preoccupied manner, turned his chair toward the window, and looked up at the sky. He watched the fast-moving dark clouds pass in front of the sun, making it briefly visible as a glowing disc behind them, which allowed Krish to gaze directly at it. He scanned the horizon and looked for the cloud line and the direction it moved, then paused. The gravity of the conversation invariably led Krish to ruminate, as he often did, about the sinister path to get here and the irredeemable choices made. But despite the inevitable confrontation of conscience, Arya Krish always regained his calm, and his breathing relaxed, along with the tense muscles, as he felt the weight lift momentarily. His thoughts would then converge again, completely attached to the task at hand.

"It's a lot to process, Mr. Rook, I'll admit," Krish said. "I've taken the time to review and learn as much as I can about all the operations, but I still rely heavily on your knowledge and advice, not to mention your direct efforts in facilitating our endeavors. It looks like I'm putting you in a new position compared to your primary role with Steinhart." Krish turned and faced Rook, who remained silent and looked down at his glass. "You were with him going on ten years, it looked."

Jason Rook nodded. He still looked down with a thoughtful expression. "I'm sure my record has the exact date." He looked up as he took a sip.

Arya Krish nodded back. "Yes, it does. But it's not as detailed as you think. I was able to surmise the circumstances that led you to join Alpha Corp. But beyond that, your tenure is vague and nondescript, on paper anyway. I can't help but inquire, Mr. Rook, what made you stay all that time?"

"What makes you think I would've wanted to get out, Dr. Krish? Have I given that impression somehow? Or is there something in the file that piqued the thought?"

"Not particularly. I'd say it's more so my personal impression from our prior meetings. I suppose that engendered some trust, in part. I did presume your military background. That played a part. And now knowing more, I'm certain that your moral constitution would find a man like Vladimir Steinhart repelling. He seems to have either coerced you or taken advantage of some vulnerability, possibly in regards to your wife." Krish paused. Rook remained silent as he looked at him and waited for him to continue. "After she died, did you remain with Alpha Corp by choice?" Krish waited for Rook to answer and recognized the appraising look on his face, which now seemed more defensive than commanding.

"I suppose I try to convince myself I had a choice," Rook replied dryly. "Though I don't think Steinhart would've stopped me if I left. Despite his resources, he wouldn't have found me if I didn't want him to. Fact is, I had no reason to leave. I was very well off. And Steinhart lived up to his end and more, as far as I was concerned. I owed him my allegiance. Besides, as you probably know as well, nothing else was out there for me to do. No other family, just my ex-wife while she was alive. No kids." Rook finished his drink and leaned forward to pour himself another. "Ultimately, I became comfortable in my circumstances and confined by them."

Krish sat silently for a moment and watched him, then turned toward the window. He was surprised by Rook's candor. Krish watched the cloud line approach and watched the sun break through until it was too bright, then turned back toward Rook. Sunshine flooded the room through the large, tall windows. Their conversation continued and slowly drifted back to corporate operations.

"Those are the means used in the political field, the tiers of influence that we use. The most common and effective example is bribery in its various forms. It strokes the asset's power while keeping it under control. It usually takes care of much of our business goals. Other more ambitious ends may require higher-tier means, such as the threat of loss, in its various forms." Rook paused. "That's how the game is played. Keep in mind, Dr. Krish, the same applies to you. Your rivals will have similar means at their disposal and a track record of using them. It's the grander scope of the new field you're operating in, stuff that masses, so to speak, either don't know or don't care about."

"I understand what we're up against, I think. We have to be able and willing to fight fire with fire," Krish said. He stared distantly at Rook for a moment, then stood and paced behind the desk along the large window. He looked down and retreated into his thoughts. Rook waited for him to speak and watched Krish's alert, dark eyes dart back and forth out the window toward the view.

"I am keenly aware of all that will be required of us." Krish stopped and leaned against the front of the large desk.

"And now, all the resources at our disposal must be directed toward the ultimate ends. Having said that, some of Alpha Corp's operations are going to be contracted or be eliminated. Offhand, the compromised foreign production and black marketing of narcotics, the price gouging in vulnerable markets abroad of all those second-class chemo drugs that didn't meet our FDA standards. We will withdraw from all of that." Arya Krish paused for a moment, then added, "Those medicines are on their way to obsolescence anyhow, with the emergence of the Panacea technology now imminent."

"The Panacea Project will demand so much of your resources as it stands, without trying to budget in the independent social and humanitarian aid programs already in conception. Contracting those other operations in such a significant manner will shrink our resources considerably." Rook paused. "With all due respect, Dr. Krish, there is no way you are aware of all that will be required of us. You do not have the experience. And there is knowledge that can only be gained from the field, from experience."

"It's an obscene enterprise, Mr. Rook. It exploits the desperation of vulnerable poor people, and it looks like Vladimir and that Ryan Pratt guy profited individually by actively participating in the black markets. Drug lords, essentially. You must have known of this," Krish said tersely.

"Knew about it early on and obstructed it within my capabilities, for what it's worth. But they got wind of some of my meddling eventually and walled me off. Ryan Pratt was more involved with that than Steinhart. That much I know for a fact."

Krish neither believed him nor doubted him. "So now we focus our attention on getting FDA approval for our Panacea protocols as an experimental treatment to start, at least, if that goes faster. You mentioned the FDA commissioner's affiliations with Alpha Corp previously?"

"Yes. He'll cooperate without much further coercion. By my estimate, we should be able to push through FDA approval within weeks, with his support. There's been a good bit of red tape he can push us through, but this guy needs to be encouraged along the way. Let's just say his star rose despite his efforts to blunder it, so he was a targeted asset in the DHHS. There is a chance for you to meet with him coming up soon, at the anniversary gala. Some personal face-to-face time would go a long way with him."

Krish nodded. "That sounds fine. Anything to facilitate the progress."

The gala was already on the calendar, planned before Arya Krish met Vladimir Steinhart for the first time. Krish had decided at some point to keep the event. It wasn't the first time he had attended an occasion of such sorts, but never on this scale and never as the host. Now, he was the Director of Alpha Corp, and the gala celebrated the markedly advanced anniversary of its existence. The power and influence attained lent to a strangely daunting crowd of physicians, top-level business administrators, industry moguls, relevant government officials, and politicians. The crowd would take it as a fundraising opportunity, along with other prominent players in the vast healthcare and pharmaceutical industrial complex, and Alpha Corp was king of the hill. The newly acquired status was on full display, and Krish brought to it the favorable reputation of Beacon Medical Institute.

Everyone was dressed in similar formal dark, evening colors for the black-tie event, and a large crowd mingled in the large ballroom, socializing before the dinner and entertainment. Krish walked slowly with his drink, frequently shaking hands with people who approached him. He quickly learned not to stand in one place, as the inevitable consequence of a gathering crowd led to quick adaptation. He walked casually, and when someone came his way, he smiled and nodded, sometimes shaking hands, then a quick verbal exchange before the 'I'll catch up with you again soon' or another such comment while breaking away. In between such encounters, Krish looked around like it was the first time he walked into the most opulent Las Vegas casino, taking in the sights and sounds with scrutinizing curiosity. But always on his mind was the inevitable encounter with the commissioner of the Food and Drug Administration, part of the Department of Health and Human Services: Richard Filmore. Filmore was Krish's path of least resistance to going live with the Panacea protocols. Filmore's star was indisputably on the rise in that realm, as Rook had mentioned, with a cabinet position as Secretary of Health and Human Services the next rung above him. Alpha Corp and Beacon Medical's backing was certainly worth his while and was coveted, in fact. But as Rook had mentioned, he needed stroking. So when Krish caught Filmore's glance, he made his way steadily in Filmore's direction with an intent smile.

"Dr. Filmore? Or do you prefer Commissioner Filmore?" Krish said as they shook hands. Prior to being appointed, Filmore was head of several health systems in upstate New York.

"Haven't been able to get anyone to call me Commish so far! Of course, I won't hide my aspirations. Secretary Filmore would be the preferred title, no doubt." Filmore grinned from ear to ear. It looked like he had too many teeth when he did so. And when he talked, his lips moved rather unnaturally. It was like watching a bad ventriloquist. "It's nice to finally meet you, Dr. Krish. It's an honor, in fact," Filmore added respectfully.

Krish's pre-eminence in the health care and humanitarian realm was in full bloom, with international recognition making recent news. His personable interaction only enhanced that stature, which he deliberately took advantage of under the circumstances. His disdain, however, made it an effort not to come off pretentious.

"I'm glad as well, Dr. Filmore. I've followed your research and career with admiration, even prior to your appointment in the

FDA. I admit at the time Beacon Medical Institute wasn't robust enough to spar with Alpha Corp in the regional acquisition of the health systems you were heading. But now I'm obviously pleased with how things went, as you should be. Congratulations on your success."

"Thank you very much, Dr. Krish! This is amazing." Filmore gestured grandly at the crowd. "Quite a congregation of wealth and power. I've been at similar events, though I mean it when I say this truly stands apart. I have always marveled at how vast the field of health and humanitarian service is in our society. It is such a substantial sector, with one of the largest lobbying forces. And what such an occasion does best, and why they're so important, is they bring these forces together and allow them to interact and transact. It's one of those rare occasions when things actually get done, you know what I mean? I mean, despite the festive and luxuriously recreational atmosphere, a lot of business is going down. You can bet on it."

Krish's already furrowed brow progressively deepened as Filmore spoke, and his large, dark, scrutinizing eyes were narrow and fixed on the spectacle. Filmore gesticulated restlessly while he spoke, plainly intoxicated by his own exuberant verbosity, while his parted hair bounced up and down like a flailing toupee. Arya Krish watched his cartoonish behavior, amused and revolted all at once. He imagined a bucking horse he had to ride to get to his goal as Filmore went on, but his voice had started fading away, when suddenly Filmore snared Krish's attention again.

"I mentioned the Cabinet position," Filmore said. "That is the next stop on the career track I've chosen. All connections matter for those eyeing a future like that. Frankly, that's what draws me to these events. Of course, the current Secretary and I have had a dicey relationship up 'til this point. But anyway, my compliments again, Dr. Krish, on the gala. Truly stands out as the highlight for all those who've attended."

"I'm impressed by it myself. I admit all of it was set in place before Steinhart passed away, before the merger of Alpha Corp and Beacon Medical Institute, in fact."

"Makes sense. Ah yes, Vladimir Steinhart. I met him two or three times, at most. I did not find him amicable, but he was intelligent, shrewd, and had an earned reputation for keeping up his end of the bargain. He kind of forced you to like him."

"Did you deal much with him after leaving New York?"

"No, not directly, anyway. Alpha Corp, as you well know, is a big pharma marquee name, so there's a history there. Definitely helped him politically. The fact that Alpha Corp is local and has always been near DC. And I don't mind being candid, Dr. Krish," Filmore said, with the widest smile and the most teeth yet. Arya Krish could not help but be amused. "I think most everyone who matters in the healthcare industrial complex is happy and optimistic with the emergence of new leadership in the private sector."

"Thank you, Dr. Filmore. Well, good luck, and let me know if I can be of any help to you." Krish smiled back. They wished each other a pleasant evening and shook hands firmly. It was obvious nothing more had to be said, and Rook was right. Filmore was an established asset. He just needed a personal show of respect. As Filmore walked away, Krish had an urgent compulsion to wash his hands. He turned away as he watched Filmore for a moment before scanning the room again, observing the crowd. His eyes searched for the one other person he would be interested in meeting, the guy above Filmore.

The Secretary of Health and Human Services was gracious enough to make an appearance, which was expected, given Alpha Corp's contribution to his boss in the White House. Arya Krish spotted him and slowly made his way in that direction. As Filmore had said, Alpha Corp was perhaps the biggest lobbyer in the Big Pharma, and their influence on the current administration and current majority party at large had a direct impact on legislative outcomes for many years. Krish felt a vaguely familiar rush and giddiness as he approached the Secretary, flush with the power his position in Alpha Corp wielded. He remembered Jason Rook describing how Steinhart would be directly involved in drafting and writing legislation. He literally wrote the laws that the lawmakers would vote on. So there was no doubt that Krish would command the Secretary's attention, and the prospects of Krish's influence on him were so keenly felt it gave Krish butterflies in his stomach for a moment. But it had passed by the time the Secretary noticed Krish's approach and turned toward him. Krish stood tall and confident, and he had a pleasant, natural smile on his face as he scrutinized the Secretary intently when they shook hands. The man was older and only a little shorter, with well-groomed gray hair that was left over on his male pattern balding head. His eyes were sharp and appraising as well, Krish thought.

"Dr. Arya Krish, I hoped I'd have the chance to meet you on this occasion."

"It's an honor to finally get the chance to meet you, Secretary Templeton."

Templeton signaled Krish to follow and made his way to the nearest end of the ballroom, where it was relatively less crowded. They spoke uninterrupted while some staff kept their distance and deflected the passers-by.

"I won't be able to stay much longer, Dr. Krish. You'll have to forgive me. But I did want to congratulate you on your personal success over there at Beacon Medical Institute and now with your new position with Alpha Corp."

"Thank you, sir, I'm glad you came, and we got to speak to each other for the first time. I was a supporter of many of your colleagues in the administration and on Capitol Hill. In fact, I was just talking to someone under your wing. Richard Filmore."

Krish paused and observed Templeton's face. There may have been a wince or a grimace, almost imperceptible, but Krish was struck by a subtle negative reaction on Templeton's part.

"Sure, recent replacement for commissioner of the FDA. I don't know him well, but between you and me, I wasn't overly impressed by the few encounters I've had with him. But overall, I'm quite optimistic about the direction we're going. I anticipate we will be in future collaboration, you and I, that is," Templeton said. He changed the topic. "The anticipation of the results of the Panacea Project clinical trials hasn't escaped me. It's already proving to be the blockbuster it was built up to be."

"It is exciting, for sure. I've been waiting for this for a long time. Between you and me." Krish paused, then continued. "We're ready for the Panacea protocols to go live, and it's going to be a blockbuster. All the models and testing have been unequivocally positive. I'm hoping patient recruitment can start within the next few weeks."

"Well, I look forward to our collaboration in providing the best healthcare in the world to the American people," Templeton said and nodded. Krish looked at him and tried to decipher how genuine the smiling look of admiration was. Templeton suddenly seemed like such a politician, and it felt like something else was communicated between them in that silent exchange of looks.

"I think our collaboration will be very important, especially in light of recent developments at the VA. It seems there will be a new Secretary appointment."

"Yes," Templeton said. He smiled. "I'm glad you're keeping up with that, Dr. Krish."

"More than just keeping up, sir, as you may know. I've been endorsing our own Dr. Jay Asher publicly while waiting on his decision, of course, whether he goes for the position." Krish gave a confident smile back. Templeton nodded in acknowledgement. *Of course, he knew.* "I hope to continue advocating for him at this important crossroads. With the arrival of the future, everything is about to change, and we will need good leadership to find our way to success. Of course, the President would be the one to nominate him."

"He's caught a lot of attention, if that helps. Jay Asher is in the conversation, that I know. You guys have my vote of confidence, for what it's worth," Templeton said, and they shook hands cordially. Again, Krish didn't know how seriously to take him. They spoke for a bit longer, then parted ways soon after. To Krish, the brief encounter was productive. At that moment, he couldn't deny the flushed feeling of the newfound access and exposure his operation had gained. The fact that they had exchanged contact information meant he could maintain correspondence and build a rapport at the highest levels. Krish was charged with the intoxicating energy in the room as he mingled and watched with sinister pride as others ingratiated themselves to him. He found he enjoyed the company more and more, amused by the dissent toward them that accompanied it. Krish recognized with every encounter that the ingratiating started with themselves first and foremost. It was the means to the end and grandly effective. The media hype that erupted spontaneously at the anticipated revolution that was about to arrive was widespread in both social and conventional media outlets, with special attention drawn toward some high-profile patients who were among the first to be treated by the new Panacea protocols. They were quickly dubbed Patient Zeros.

CHAPTER ELEVEN

Arya Krish opened the door quietly. As he discreetly entered, he looked at Senator John Bringer. They exchanged a quick acknowledging nod, the kind shared by two people with over a seven-year doctor-patient history and friendship prior to that. The room was more than a generic patient room. It didn't have the typical utilitarian, sterile look. It was more like a Victorian apartment and was outfitted with the most modern medical technology. As Krish walked toward the center of the room, he saw the oncology physician at the side of the large recliner where Bringer sat. Krish waved as she looked up and said hi. She finished her sentence and shook Bringer's hand before she walked out, nodding again to Krish as she passed by. Krish continued to the chair and smiled as he extended his hand toward Bringer.

"How are you, young man?" Bringer asked. He smiled back as they shook hands. "It's been a long time."

"Yes, sir. Too long, I would say. In fact, I'm sure I don't qualify as a young man anymore." Krish sat across from Bringer in a similar chair.

"This is some setup you've created here," Bringer said. He looked around and pointed at the fireplace. "Looks like you've gone to great lengths to make the patient feel at home."

Krish nodded cordially. "It's the least I could do. I'm honored you trust me enough to volunteer as a Patient Zero, as we've come to call them here. And I'm glad you've agreed to spend the trial duration here at the Institute."

"The honor is mine, Mr. Krish," Bringer said. "I am becoming very familiar with the early success you've had in the other Panacea protocols."

"These first months since going live with these protocols have been some of the most difficult in recent memory, sir. I won't lie to you. But at the same time, it has been the most exciting and has exceeded my expectations."

Bringer leaned forward with a raised hand pointing up. "And as a result, your expectations and ambitions will be that much higher!" He had the look of a wise, grayed professor. Overall, he appeared to be fit for a man who had undergone multiple cycles of conventional chemotherapy for refractory leukemia.

"Not necessarily a bad thing, though. Right, sir?" Krish smiled. Before Bringer replied, the door opened again. They turned their heads and watched the oncologist come back inside. She looked down and tapped away on the paper-thin tablet she held. She walked up to Bringer and handed it to him.

"Bet you never imagined your fellowship training would be anything like this," he said as he took the tablet. "Ushering in a new era in medicine, right?" He barely glanced at the screen before he quickly signed with his index finger. Then he handed it back with a smile. The oncologist paused and looked over at Arya Krish quizzically.

"Dr. Bringer, we want you to look over the protocol that you'll be participating in. I'd love to hear your thoughts, sir." Krish gestured at the device.

Bringer waved a dismissive hand. "No need, Mr. Krish. I'm sure you all know what you're doing better than I." He looked up at the young oncology fellow. "You know, I can't help but get a little kick out of being called Dr. Bringer instead of Senator by your boss here." He pointed at Krish. "We go way back, you know. I had the pleasure of being close friends with his parents and knew him when he was a teenager. He was so polite and respectful, always addressed me as 'sir', and 'Dr. Bringer'. And so, to reciprocate genuinely, I would address him as Mr. Krish. This was long before he had accomplished what he has since. But it's nice some things haven't changed." Bringer winked.

Krish nodded slowly. "Dr. Bringer was more than a friend to my family," he said. The young physician fellow listened with interest in her eyes. "He was a great mentor to my father, in particular. You may be too young to remember Arnold Technologies. It was essentially the premier research institution of its day, started by Dr. Arnold and Dr. Bringer here."

The physician fellow smiled and nodded at Bringer, who continued to watch Krish quietly while he listened.

"Dr. Arnold tried to recruit my father in person, I understand. He passed up that opportunity for the A1 Group, which ultimately absorbed Arnold Technologies. It was a decision my dad regretted for the rest of his life." Krish looked at Bringer solemnly.

Bringer remained silent with a thoughtful countenance. During that dense silence, the young oncology physician glanced back and forth at the two men before she excused herself and left quietly.

"It was my personal honor to mentor your father, as you put it," Bringer said. "In fact, I've come to regret losing touch with you since his passing. I want you to know I've followed your ascension with proud interest all along. I know your parents would be extremely proud as well."

"Thank you, sir. That means a lot." Krish said. He smiled.

"And your wife and son, how are they? Leela is her name, right? And your son, remind me?"

"Seena."

"Ah, of course." Bringer nodded with acknowledgement. "Named after your uncle, I remember now. I met your father's younger brother once. Forgive me again, Mr. Krish, for not remembering right away."

"No need to apologize, sir. As you said, we haven't been in touch lately, and you've been a very busy man!"

"I've been blessed with a productive life so far, Mr. Krish." Bringer paused. "And now, in my 70s, I have to deal with this."

"I believe we can help you. We can do precisely what has not been possible up 'til this point with your disease and so much more. You'll see." Krish gave a nod of resolve.

Bringer looked up and nodded back with reverence and assurance in his eyes. "There's no question you are ushering in a new era, as I said before, beyond modern medicine," he said, and adjusted himself in his seat. A distant, thoughtful look came over his countenance once again, and observing it, Krish remained silent in anticipation. "You will, as a result, be charged with being a steward of it all you know," Bringer continued and looked around the room thoughtfully. "I'm sure by now your mind has boggled contemplating the depths of the implications this breakthrough will have on society. The age of genetic engineering demonstrates incredible power over the very stuff that makes up all of us, the building blocks. And while the guiding light should always redirect us to the altruistic applications — curing illness, preventing or reversing so many genetic diseases that modern medicine has been completely helpless against till now — I've been a politician long enough to know the social dialogue will quickly turn to notions of designer babies, eugenics, and super soldiers. Consequently, the imperative to apply some sort of moral and lawful regulation to this new capability will ultimately be taken up by the government, and they'll come knocking on your door. Dealing with that will become as much of a challenge as the actual ethical implications of what has been attained by your accomplishment."

Krish sighed and looked up toward the ceiling. "I've already had to deal with government bureaucracy a good bit to get things this far, this fast. As you're well aware, Alpha Corp has a lot of friends there on Capitol Hill, politicians and officials on our side now, so to speak—not that they particularly care much for what we're trying to do here, more so for their own benefit from arrangements with them that go back before the merger. The old order, so to speak."

"Ah, yes. Beware of entangled alliances," Bringer said, nodding. "It's the nature of the field you're operating in, and only with experience comes the knowledge of how to be most effective in attaining your goal. Of course, you will be repulsed along the way, then you justify it, then you accept it, and perhaps even indulge in the power you attain as a result of it. But make no mistake, you are waging a battle here over this new technology and what it will wind up doing to our lives, which is why I say you are the steward of it all, and you'll need to continue to use whatever means at your disposal to see it through. If millions— eventually billions—of people are to benefit from it, then it's worth whatever it takes, isn't it?"

Krish remained silent, glancing up at Bringer with dull eyes. He wouldn't expect Bringer to justify so easily all that was done to get to that point if he knew everything. Perhaps Bringer lacked the perspective, the vision, the resolve, and the unflinching dedication to the ultimate cause. Krish strained to remind himself. Steward of it all? More like the monster outside the gates to the inner sanctum, created to protect from the outside. The familiar weight again settled in his arms and shoulder as if he was sinking into the chair. He drew a sharp, deep breath and sat up deliberately.

"Well." Krish paused and forced himself out of his seat. "I'll be looking in on you frequently, Dr. Bringer."

Bringer remained seated and nodded with a smile. "I'm glad you stopped in, young man. I have a feeling I will be very grateful for what you have accomplished." They shook hands, and Krish left.

John Bringer would be dead in six months from his refractory cancer that resisted all available measures so far if not for the Panacea protocols. The cancer succumbed immediately to the new superior capability, and Bringer would instead be blessed with longevity and remain an active force of good, and a valuable advocate to Krish's cause. His unequivocal success story made him the poster child of the overall positive outcomes across the board, as the Panacea protocols smashed through previously insurmountable barriers and limitations of medical science.

But it wasn't always the case. The success of the Panacea protocols across various platforms was of blockbuster proportions, but there were failures in certain protocols that ventured into the realms of the implausible. Spinal cord injury and nerve and muscle regeneration were one such frontier. While some case-specific success stories were already demonstrating possibilities, there was still much that was proving to be just beyond reach.

The patient was 19 years old when he had a traumatic cervical spine injury that rendered him quadriplegic. It resulted from an altercation, incidental as circumstances could have been when he was pushed off a balcony and struck a fire hydrant. He was 26 now, and Arya Krish had known him as a patient for a few years already, going back to initial consultations as an ID specialist, though the encounters were much more infrequent as of late since Krish had stepped back from direct patient care. At this point, the years of being a bedbound quadriplegic relentlessly took its toll on mind and flesh and may have passed a threshold that prevented the young new medical technology from making any gains in his case.

When Krish approached the large sliding door to the ICU room, he paused before entering. For some reason, at that moment, the dormant memory fired a remote synapse, and he remembered the patient was an All-American high school running back before his injury. As he entered, he saw the patient lying flat on the bed.

Only his head was visible. The rest of his thin body was covered by white hospital blankets. His eyes looked at the ceiling, and as Krish approached, he turned his head and looked over. He was a short black man with short hair and a handsome, clean-shaven face. His large dark eyes seemed to exhibit both sadness and determination, and his voice had a lilting sternness as he spoke softly.

"How you doing, sir?" Krish asked. He went to the bedside and looked down at the patient.

"I don't know why I'm still in the ICU, doc, or why I was even brought here."

"You feeling any better?"

"I feel better, but still having trouble with my catheter," he said and shook his head submissively. Krish nodded, took the isolation stethoscope off the IV pole, and examined the patient. He pulled the blankets down and exposed the thin chest with a visible rib cage under the vastly tattooed skin. The ritual of the physician examining the patient played out in silence, as Krish glanced at the patient's deep tracheostomy scar on the middle of the neck. He placed the stethoscope over the left chest and listened while he glanced at the percutaneous gastrostomy feeding tube that was in position, palpated the soft, thin abdomen, and inspected the cystostomy catheter site. The patient didn't really have much sensation below the nipple line and stared straight up at the ceiling without reacting to the exam. Krish covered him up again, then took the other end of the blankets and uncovered his bony legs. The pressure wounds were bandaged, covering the exposed muscles and tendons that Krish had examined previously, and were left undisturbed. When he was done, Krish paused and stood silently, looking at the patient.

"Well, sir, I don't have anything new since I saw you last. We're using the data from our efforts this far into the protocol to see what we can learn and apply it in the next version.

Tomorrow, we'll sample the cervical spine and see what, if any, cellular changes have occurred. Maybe the next round will yield more results." Krish paused and waited to see if the patient would reply, but he remained silent for a while as he kept his gaze slightly away, up toward the ceiling. When he spoke, it was in a testimonial manner, and he would occasionally glance over at Krish with a strained, tired look.

"I need to get this catheter fixed and get out of here, man. It's not working out. There's no point in being here. But I don't want to go and then come back to the hospital sick again because it's leaking or blocked. I'm worried about that more than the protocol not working honestly, doc. No offense, but I didn't expect it to work anyway. I thank you guys for trying. Like I said before, you're one of the only ones who don't rush in and out. You stand there and listen and pretend to care, at least."

Tears welled up in his eyes and streamed down his face. His countenance was unchanged, but he was forced to twist his cheeks and turn to wipe his face on the pillow. Arya Krish watched him try to get comfortable for a moment, then reached for a tissue and helped him. The patient took an effortful deep breath and sighed. Krish felt he was looking down at some mystical oracle; the white blankets that covered the man's body glowed in the overhead light, and only his head and face were visible.

"We're going to keep trying, sir. I can promise you that much, at least."

The patient shook his head as he continued to look away. "You can't fix everything, doc. My body is too far gone," he said.

Krish fought off the flash of irritability. "Just because we're not there yet does not mean we can't get there soon. You're young. You can still benefit from the next breakthrough."

"The next breakthrough, doc? Am I really supposed to hope that after you find a way to reconnect the nerves in my neck, my body will magically spring to life? Look at me. You've seen it. The dead weight is skin and bones, slowly being eaten away by pressure sores and infections." He paused to catch his breath. Krish watched his upper chest heave for air before calming down again. "And I'm not young, not really, right," he continued. "I'm 187 years old, man. Might as well be. A 26- year-old quadriplegic—dead weight from the shoulders down. You ever imagine that doc, having dead weight dragging you down constantly? That's not 26. It's a fate worse than death."

Krish remained silent while they looked at each other. He was right. Regenerating or repairing nerve damage at the cellular level, regenerating flesh and bone, was all still science fiction, despite what the Panacea technology was demonstrating and making a reality.

"I don't pretend to know everything you are going through, sir. I can only imagine," Krish said.

The young man pressed his lips together solemnly as he looked away and nodded politely. "Like I said, doc, I appreciate you and what you're trying to do."

The young man looked away and closed his eyes, and it was clear he wished to be left alone at that moment. Without saying more, Krish put his hand on the patient's upper shoulder, where he knew it could be felt, and turned and walked out.

***

The night talk show host, the one with the silver hair slicked back, enthusiastically introduced Arya Krish.

"So join me in welcoming back from *the* Beacon Medical Institute and now director of Alpha Corp, Dr. Arya Krish!" he said with an emphatic gesture toward the other side of the set. Krish waited until the staff member gave him the signal, then entered. He glanced out, smiling toward the applauding standing audience as he adjusted to the stage-like lighting. The host had come around his desk and met Krish almost halfway, extending his right hand out in genuine anticipation. He gestured back toward the set politely as they made their way and sat down casually while the audience continued to applaud. Krish smiled and waved while keenly observing the faces, taking in the reality of the moment as a vindicating culmination of a well-planned and well-executed media and PR campaign, riding the early success of the Panacea protocols.

As the applause died down, the host looked over at him with a smile. "Welcome back, Dr. Krish. Always a pleasure!"

"I'm happy to be here again."

"A lot has happened since your last appearance, the merger of Beacon Medical Institute with Alpha Corp being the big one, with you solely at the helm as Director, correct?"

"That's right."

"Director — is that like CEO? President?" asked the host in a playful manner.

"Maybe all that, a little bit," Krish replied, to the host's delight as the audience laughed. Quite a bit of compulsory banter followed, and Krish was seamless in his witty dialogue with the talk show host before the topic drifted more in-depth to the Panacea technology.

"Well, the keystone of this new technology is based on physiology that exists in nature in bacteria and some other micro-organisms," Krish explained at one point. "These organisms use segments of DNA called 'clustered regularly interspaced short palindromic repeats,' or CRISPR, to defend against foreign DNA being inserted, say from viruses. It is basically bacteria's virus protection software. Since the discovery of this physiology, one of science's pursuits has been to apply these mechanisms to human cells. Why? The CRISPR-type physiologies that exist in nature have long been shown to have potential effects on human genes and, as a result, have the potential to cure so many, if not most, human diseases. By manipulating that same physiology through new carbon-based nano-technology, we have revolutionized the way we manipulate genes and alter biochemical outcomes in cellular function and, thus, human physiology in so many aspects. So much of what makes and breaks us as human beings is affected by genetics and biochemistry that this new technology can now augment. It has already reached the level where we can basically write genetic code and direct cellular behavior through the interaction of our nanotechnology with living biological systems."

"It sounds like the stuff of science fiction is now—not just becoming a reality—but is already, in fact, reality. You've demonstrated it through the Panacea protocols. You've essentially perfected gene editing. Let me see," the host said and paused, referencing his cards, "if I can hit some of the highlights. So, eradication of HIV and other viral infections that were incurable, if treatable at all—Ebola and rabies, as examples. This is feasible now essentially by altering the functionality of immune system cells by gene editing. Correct me if I'm wrong," he said, glancing up at Krish, who nodded with approval. "And this can be cost-efficiently done with reproducible results now, and so the natural evolution would be including this sort of technology in the pre-natal realm. This, of course, I'm inferring from your most recent op-ed, Dr. Krish."

"Right." Krish nodded. "Sticking with the medical application of this technology, designer babies seems to be the popular term. That article you mention talks about the kinds of things that we are mapping in the genome that are becoming very nuanced. Traits such as intelligence, emotional stability, memories, creativity, and altruism are all increasingly being plucked from abstraction and being mapped out in our genetic code. So now with the technology to change that code, I think society will be wrestling with the sequelae for the foreseeable future. The frontier of genetics remains vast and largely uncharted, in my opinion, so yes, while what was science fiction not too long ago is now a fact of life, there is so much more yet to be conceived. But the more we can identify and modify the genes that make us, we will have to confront the basic notions of the very nature of humanity and conscience that may demand re-defining."

After the applause died down, the host remained thoughtfully silent for a moment and studied his index cards. "So many implications of this technology are already apparent," he said. "The ramifications will most certainly go beyond medical science, as you've mentioned. How will the genetic data and the profiling that result from this be handled as a privacy issue? So many such socio-ethical...humanitarian issues are bound to arise as we navigate this new field. I think it will take a degree of humility and restraint to wield this knowledge for the betterment of mankind. What do you see as the potential height of trajectory for this technology?"

"Probably it's application in a direct neuro-AI interface piques the imagination the most. The current neuro-AI technology seems to have leveled off. The potential biogenetic connection engenders ideas of direct knowledge acquisition, access to a collective conscience, the new 'hive cloud,' so to speak—that is the direction that my mind goes when contemplating it. We could optimize our genetic makeup with this technology to make ourselves most compatible with an AI interface."

"So what you're saying is, at some point, I actually will be able to know Kung Fu all of a sudden by downloading it into my brain?" the host asked with marked intrigue that drew laughter from the audience. "Well, I think I speak for many when I say the magnitude of what you're doing at Beacon Medical Institute is catching everyone's attention, and we are rooting for your success as the pioneer," he said, and the audience erupted. Arya Krish looked around and raised his folded hands, genuinely overwhelmed by the moment, then straightened up in his seat and looked over at the host as the audience became silent.

Krish nodded thoughtfully. "It has been a challenge, admittedly, to maintain perspective of the scale we are operating in. I think one navigates such a field only with the knowledge and experience he gains along the way. There's not much you can do to prepare yourself."

"And what are the challenges you are facing now, at this stage?" the host asked. "Or what are the challenges you anticipate down the road? I mean, the ethical ramifications we can continue to speculate about range from disease prevention to eugenics — the systematic genetic enhancement of a population. On top of that, the global scale this will all take on, once this technology becomes reproducible, means it will outgrow any single person's or agency's ability to control its long-term effects, which we can't even predict to a large extent."

"It'll certainly make us re-consider everything we think we know right now about life, death, what is considered normal, what are the boundaries and limitations in applying these new capabilities, who gets to decide — all of these and more are going to be major debates that likely will play out in the public and political arena as well. This new technological age will span beyond our brief role, and the Panacea protocols will fade into its place in history as the sentinel breakthrough. But at this time, *we* are the first ones doing it, here and now. No one else is doing what we're doing."

"Does being in that position at the moment bring about a sense of responsibility, of guardianship even, over what you've created?"

"Well, the idea of stewardship over technology has been around for a long time and has been administered in the past in various examples, and as you pointed out, it is often the pioneers that create the system in which the technology operates — at least in the beginning. We've seen this play out with artificial intelligence in recent years. I think that, in fact, will be the defining challenge in the near future — the administration of this technology in a way that will maximize the benefit for humanity with the least harm. Frankly, it's difficult to see further into the horizon than that. Right now, I find myself caught up in the moment."

The host smiled. "Now, you've mentioned already the inevitable part the government will play in this, if not take charge of it. It'll come down to the collaboration between government and the private sector then, as it always does. And those who follow politics, such as me, recognize the simple fact — that the private sector has a big part in the power that the government wields. Of course, we're talking about special interest groups, lobbyists, the conglomerates that bring the money to the table, like Big Energy, Big Tech, and Big Pharma, which now you, Dr. Krish, are the major player. You, sir, individually, will have a significant influence over actual law making. Let's be honest here. That is literally what happens, isn't it? Having the lobbyists participate in writing the laws that are put up for vote! How does that feel?"

The audience murmured softly while Arya Krish nodded and took a moment to answer. "Again, I would say that I'm caught up in the moment," he said. "But what you've described has not escaped me, and I see it as an opportunity, and perhaps a calling, to be able to do some real good from it. It will be by operating within the system you've described, yes, that is the reality of it. I don't think I'm capable of unmaking that, but playing the game for the right cause can still get us where we want to go."

"And tied into all this is your main purpose, as you've put it: the ongoing humanitarian enterprises here and abroad, with all the remarkable change that has resulted in so many people's lives. More recently, the charter school projects in the Washington DC area have been making headlines locally, and the recent op-eds you've written certainly have an emphatic voice when discussing philanthropy in America, especially toward children in need. You've expressed your personal vision and purpose as serving the sanctity of humanity."

"I appreciate the term 'emphatic voice' as the nice way of putting it. 'Preachy' and 'self-righteous,' it's been criticized as, by some," Krish said smiling, and the audience laughed softly in acknowledgement. "But yes, we've accumulated a lot of experience working on very large-scale projects over the years, like you mentioned, and I think it is important to escalate our ambitions given we have a glimpse of what is going to be possible in the near future. The influence we can have on government policy-making in all these regards can be directed toward that service, I believe."

"But you've made it clear many times you plan to remain in the private sector and not seek public office of any sort?"

Krish smiled. "That is correct."

The host smiled and nodded, looked down at the index card, then moved on to other lighter topics and scripted monologue. Krish dwelled on the matter longer in his mind, only distantly following the show, thereafter, engaging the more mundane topics on autopilot. He found himself shifting in his seat impatiently at one point after he was joined by other guests in a panel discussion. It became difficult to even focus on the debates, and he glanced back and forth with a preoccupied and pensive look that had settled in, which he made little effort to conceal. Quite exhausted by the end of it all, his shoulders drooped, and the fatigue had settled in his eyes as he drove home alone in a silent reverie.

***

He sat on the floor off to the side a little later that night and watched his son Seena playing with his toy trucks. Seena was on all-fours, his small hand holding the firetruck and his face right up next to it, with wild surmise in his wide eyes, as he softly narrated the dialogue and story that flowed out in his pretend play. Arya Krish watched him with tired and withdrawn eyes and a soft smile that would flash whenever Seena looked up at him. He couldn't help but remember that moment in the airport after he pushed the button when he looked into his son's eyes. Re-living that caused the tired and thoughtful expression to linger on his face as of late, and the strain in his almond-shaped eyes replaced the prior bright and alert look. From time to time, he unconsciously straightened his posture and took deep, purposeful breaths to ease the tension as he relaxed his muscles sequentially from head to toe to feel the weight lift momentarily.

Krish came downstairs after putting Seena to bed and sat next to Leela. Their shoulders pressed up against each other as they sat quietly and watched TV.

"It's amazing to see how his imagination has blossomed all of a sudden, isn't it?" Krish said.

"Yeah, it's a really nice phase for him now to see him get immersed in his own imagination."

"Nice phase. It'll be missed, I anticipate, when we reminisce in the future."

Leela glanced over at him, then back at the TV. "Probably. Best to savor the moment when it's around then, huh?"

Krish nodded and didn't respond right away. "Feels like the time's just slipping by, and I'm missing out on these things." He paused, and Leela remained silent, waiting for him to continue. "But our efforts are paying off more than could have been expected," he continued with a sigh as he slouched down and leaned back.

"Maybe you should take some time off, recharge a little, spend time at home. I'm sure things will sustain over at Beacon without you for a while. Because, at this point, we haven't seen you around much lately. You realize you've spent most nights at the Institute for the past month at least?"

"Well, I haven't exactly been lounging around playing poker with the guys, right? You know exactly what I've been straining every fiber of my being for. You've always encouraged me along the way. What's changed now?"

"What's changed? I'm watching it consume you, Arya. You…you've changed. And all the while, *we* are being gradually pushed further into the background," she said emphatically, gesturing to herself, and upstairs where Seena slept.

"That has not escaped me, OK? It's been part of the sacrifices that we've all made along the way. What we're trying to do is bigger, though, isn't it? It must be, to be worth the dedication and sacrifice. Sometimes it feels silly to say that sort of thing."

"Who's we and our?" Leela asked with new irritation in her voice. "It seems like you've put it all on your shoulders alone. You have so many resources and people at your disposal. Why haven't you delegated more? You have friends and colleagues that are so close to you and loyal. Are they working as hard?"

"Believe me, I've asked a lot of my friends, and they've come through. This has been a crucial time. I've had to see much of it through in person. There simply isn't another way. You don't think I've recognized what's been compromised here? I regret the cost of it all," he said, his voice trailing off a little toward the end. Frustration mounted on Arya's countenance, and his speech became increasingly pressured. Leela shifted uneasily.

"Then you recognize that you won't get this time back. It'll pass by before you know it."

"It is the price to pay to accomplish something great. The prospects are limited only by our effort I feel." Krish paused. "I must sound crazy every time I say something like that. Maybe it is crazy."

"Or maybe you have to be a little crazy to attain what you speak of."

Krish turned and smiled at her. "Well? What else can be

done then? Can't have it both ways. So either settle for less and savor the rest or give yourself completely to realize a vision."

There was a lull in the conversation, and they both sat quietly for a moment while the TV played on in the background during their individual reveries.

"A quiet and modest life brings more joy than a pursuit of success bound with constant unrest," Leela said.

"That sounds pretty unambitious."

"Albert Einstein said that."

Arya Krish gave a conceding shrug. "Well, it seems he chose the latter."

"I think the point was that you can get consumed in chasing the prize and lose sight of yourself and what is actually important in life, like family, and happiness."

"Do I seem unhappy?"

"Yes, as a matter of fact. Most of the time, when you're actually here, you pace around in your own world. You don't talk to me much, or listen for that matter, and seem irritated when we're around. And you're not engaged with Seena much anymore either."

"Well, like I said before, time doesn't allow for everything. Right now it must be given toward the work."

"I see, but you have made the time to go to galas and do TV interviews. My point is that you should give as much priority and time to your family."

His eyes rolled away from her, and she suddenly stopped speaking when she noticed. The scornful look she shot him was fortunately captured indirectly, only in his peripheral vision, diminishing the sting that would have otherwise unmanned him completely, and he sat silently after a soft, exasperating sigh. They sat with their shoulders apart and were quiet for the most part while they watched TV together.

CHAPTER TWELVE

The broken finger incident several months later was as incidental as it could be, and the arbitrary circumstances were mundane in their routine. Yet it would color Arya Krish's experiences for a long time after the injury healed. Krish was walking down the steps as he left Beacon late one night, as he always did. He looked down at his phone and was admittedly preoccupied. Nonetheless, his misstep was indeed an anomalous fluke. He pitched forward and fell awkwardly while he juggled his phone with his right hand on the way down. Krish extended his left arm, as he should, to break his fall. Unfortunately, his hand got jammed on the corner of the staircase.

The tell-tale sound, like a twig snapping, shot into his brain through his ears and rattled in every bone in his body as the proximal joint of his left ring finger bent 90 degrees in the wrong direction. He grabbed it immediately, scrambled to his feet quickly, and cradled it with his other hand as he leaned against the wall in the well-lit stairwell. Anger toward the cruel fates flashed initially, but Krish was quickly calm again as he raised his hand closer to his face to examine it while the throbbing pain intensified gradually. He slowly pressed on the bones of his finger and decided they were not likely broken. But the joint was. He looked at his wedding ring, and the thought of removing it before the finger swelled passed his mind, but as he stared at it, he decided not to for some reason. The ring was a replica of his father's wedding band—24-karat gold with a small embedded diamond and etched rays surrounding it, intended to resemble the sun. At that moment, when he held it, it fulfilled its purpose as a symbol of an ideal, something larger than itself and himself, and exerted the power bestowed by its owner from the meaning given by wearing it faithfully. Another invocation of the sanctity of humanity, like the look in his son's innocent eyes, and as Krish turned the ring around his increasingly swollen finger, in that moment, for whatever reason, he felt he had to leave it be.

When Jay Asher opened the door to Krish's office the next day, he saw the hand surgeon from behind in his scrubs and white coat in mid-sentence, facing Krish as he sat behind his desk, brooding over his left hand and turning his ring slowly at the base of the injured finger. Asher walked in, quietly closed the door, and stood in the background. The other two glanced over at him and nodded in acknowledgment, and he reciprocated.

"So anyway," the hand surgeon continued as he put the hand-held X-ray device in its case, "no bone fracture, but obviously, that proximal joint is broken. You likely ruptured the volar plate and hood, as we call it."

The surgeon was demonstrating the anatomy on his own hand, and Arya Krish averted his gaze from his finger to watch and listened attentively.

"We'll get a portable MR scanner up here later today, take a look at the tendons and connective tissues. If there are significant tears, microsurgery may be indicated. Might have to cut that ring off in that case. The swelling might cause it to choke the finger."

"The ring's not coming off," Krish said defensively as he turned it at the base of the finger. His brow furrowed at the mention of it. "I can turn it easily. It's fine for now. The swelling is mainly over the joint."

"Otherwise a splint for a few weeks usually suffices, but slightly different than the one you have now," the surgeon said. He gestured at the aluminum splint Krish had placed himself the night before. "This one allows you to flex the distal joint, which is important." He took out another plastic splint and handed it over to Krish. He paused and watched Krish exchange the splint, then continued. "Yeah, the flexor digitorum profundus passes through the superficialis tendon, so allowing it to flex strengthens that anatomy while it heals." The surgeon turned back and glanced at Asher again. Then he turned and stepped toward the door. "All right, Krish. Let me know how it goes."

"Thanks, doc. Appreciate your time and attention," Krish said earnestly. He waved back as the surgeon left and closed the door behind him. Asher walked across the large room toward Krish's desk.

"Well, in the end, it all resolves itself of its own volition," Krish said to himself, but loud enough to know Asher would hear it. He looked up at Asher and smiled with a resigned look on his face.

"What the hell does that mean?" Asher asked with a curious expression as he sat across from Krish. "While we're sharing, what's all this?" Asher gestured toward Krish's finger.

"Basically snapped this joint all the way back. Slipped and fell going down the stairs yesterday. Freak accident, what else can I say? I guess it can happen to anyone," Krish said, as if trying to convince himself.

"Yeah, it happens," Asher said with a conceding nod.

"I was looking down at my phone. Probably wasn't necessary."

"Well, you'll get it checked for any damage that needs surgical repair. Otherwise, it'll heal up. It just takes time. The art of medicine is distracting the patient while nature cures the disease, as Voltaire said."

"Exactly," Krish said, nodding as he looked down at his finger and turned his ring. "In the end, it all resolves itself of its own volition over time." Then, a puzzled look came over his face. "Maybe it wasn't just a freak accident, though. No question I find myself increasingly preoccupied, distracted by the circumstances

I've created for myself — surely that could have played a role."

Asher extended the paper-thin tablet he was holding toward Krish. "Well, there remain practical and urgent matters that need attention."

Krish reached out with a curious look and took the tablet in his hand. Asher sat back and folded his hands up near his serious face as he waited while Krish scrolled through the content. "This looks like assorted data from the last phase of the Panacea trials," he said.

"Our new R&D security caught this data transfer from Kai Chowan's computer and account onto a flash drive. It was flagged as an unauthorized transfer and caught Jason Rook's attention."

Krish looked up from the tablet at Asher for a moment with a puzzled frown, then continued reading the tablet. "What was Chowan up to?" he asked.

"Rook tracked him to a meeting in a satellite office of Esper Enterprises in Rockville."

"Esper? They're based down in Atlanta. I didn't even know they operated around here."

Asher shrugged. "Well, you're right. Their health systems are largely in the south, while Alpha Corp, up till this point, pretty much dominated the mid and northeast. But it shouldn't surprise us that they have some presence in this area, especially now with Panacea protocols in top gear. Anyway, looks like Chowan took a meeting with them and presumably passed along Beacon's secrets."

"Do we know for sure he gave this data to them?" Krish asked, leaning forward. His brow was furrowed, and his tired eyes were keen with interest and concern.

"Not explicitly. Rook is advising we put him on more surveillance. He brought up audio devices, bugging his house — you know, *a la* Alpha Corp's former policies," Asher said.

Krish shook his head dismissively. He remained silent as

he scrolled through the contents on the tablet again. "This data is actually fairly old, given we've rolled out our protocols across the board now for many months. It isn't all that compromising to us at this point. When did this happen?" he said, putting the device down.

"Just over the past few days."

Krish was silent for a moment, and a distant look came over his face as he sat and quietly brooded. Asher watched and waited reluctantly as exasperation slowly brewed.

"Why wasn't I informed immediately?" Krish asked.

Asher didn't answer right away and watched Krish turn his wedding ring around his injured finger. He waited for Krish to notice he hadn't answered yet and looked up at him.

"Well, you haven't exactly been plugged in the last few weeks," he said pointedly. "You barely reply to emails or texts, haven't held or attended meetings."

Krish nodded, then sat up straight and scooted his chair in close to his desk. "I know. I'm trying to manage my time between work and family somehow." He leaned in over the desk and looked down at the tablet thoughtfully. "OK, I get it," he said with a heavy sigh. "We need to get to the bottom of this. What have you guys come up with?"

"Well, like I just said, we're going to be watching Chowan a lot closer. Track his movements and get some more insight on the next meeting he has with our rivals."

"So we want to track him, listen in on him, watch him with cameras, all of it, huh? Now, we become the cage keepers. I remember talking with him a while ago. He spoke gratefully about how he was feeling like a normal person again since joining the Institute and coming out of Steinhart's Alpha Corp stranglehold."

Krish sighed again and shook his head as tangential memories of prior events ebbed forth, including their first meeting with Chowan that night they were attacked by Marcus Knight. His shoulders became heavy and his neck muscles tightened as he again recalled standing outside the airport and pressing that button. He pushed a button, a bad man died, and Krish conveniently didn't have to confront the heinous act directly. He took slow, deep breaths as his chest became heavy at the thought of the irony of that unfulfilled retribution.

"I happen to agree with Rook on this one. It's the best way to ascertain what is going on with Kai Chowan," Asher said.

Krish came out of his rumination. "Why don't we just confront him about it?" he asked.

"It makes sense to figure out what's motivating him before we reveal what we know. Rook is going to let us know when Chowan makes another move, and he'll be tracking him more directly."

"Let's set up a meeting and have Rook report to both of us directly," Krish said quickly. "No hasty decisions, otherwise, no escalating surveillance on Chowan until then."

***

Kai Chowan stared intently at the computer screen as he sat in the short, small chair in front of the large oak desk. Behind the desk, the man in the dark suit sat in a much larger and taller chair and watched Chowan silently, looking down at him from his perched seat behind the desk with an appraising and disappointed frown. Chowan was already a pawn going back to his Alpha Corp tenure, and unfortunately, it followed him to Beacon Medical Institute, as the tentacles of other corporate monsters in the healthcare and Big Pharma industrial complex continued to ruthlessly pursue the upper hand in the power struggle, and the metaphorical arms race of the new genetic age was well underway. Chowan was one of many cogs in the wheel, as was the man behind the desk, for that matter. He was no one important and didn't have any real power. He was an agent, a pawn, for his boss. But he postured well.

"So, as you can see, Dr. Chowan," the man said as he gestured at the display, "the data you supplied us did not turn out to be very useful. It didn't advance our progress much and was far less than what we expected from you, frankly."

"I'm not sure what more you want from me," Chowan said as sternly as he could muster, "I don't exactly have complete access to everything at Beacon Medical Institute. Maybe you overestimate my position there."

"You're one of the team leaders in the Panacea protocols. I think our speculations about your access and position are accurate enough. In fact, if I remember correctly, we had also requested security access information for the remotely stored data at Beacon, which you have yet to provide."

"I've already told you. They've moved much of their most sensitive data to stand-alone storage within the Institute. Access is only possible at the physical terminal."

"I realize that. You'll have to do it in person then."

Chowan shook his head with frustration and defiance and didn't reply.

The man behind the desk paused for a moment and glared at Chowan with obvious exasperation. "Look, Dr. Chowan, I don't like having to remind you what is at stake here for yourself and your family back home in China. Do I really need to reiterate our presence and influence in that country? The sway we have over your siblings' education and employment at the medical college and biotech companies? Not to mention the political pressure we can exert on your family's holdings there."

"You've made it all abundantly clear more than once. It's the only reason I'm cooperating, obviously," Chowan replied with ill-concealed disdain.

"And don't think your friends at Beacon can help you in that regard if you were to go to them with our arrangement here," the man added with menace in his voice. "Even with Alpha Corp's backing, they don't have the resources in that country that we do."

Chowan looked away from him and sighed as he closed his eyes, as if trying to tune him out. "I'm doing whatever I can here. I don't know what else to tell you."

"Fine, we'll carry on then and look to meet again in the coming weeks. Someone will be in touch with you and keeping tabs as well." The man stood and looked down at Chowan, an obvious indication that he was dismissed.

Chowan slowly rose and was escorted out of the building by security. When he got into his car parked across the street he sat alone in despair, occasionally looking up at the security guards at the entrance of the building peering at him. Languidly, he pushed the start button, put the car in gear, and drove off. He hadn't noticed the sedan parked a little farther up the road. Jason Rook sat and watched and monitored him remotely with the surveillance devices he had already planted in Chowan's vehicle and on his person.

***

For a long time, the medical attachment to the Marines had been part of the US Navy. With the advent of advanced surgical units that operated on or near the front lines side by side with them, the Marines eventually wound up absorbing that unit. Jay Asher, M.D. had operated, so to speak, and personally trained one of the first such units. As one of its creators, he ushered in the successful use of them and quickly demonstrated the life-saving potential.

So it was Lt. Colonel Jay Asher, not Commander, who stood inside the previously shot-up room that had since been converted to a temporary command post, inside a cleared building about half a mile from the front line within the urban desert terrain in the Middle East War. The surrounding blocks were post-apocalyptic after weeks of fierce fighting, strewn with rubble, and largely deserted, but not completely. The few remaining desperate civilians were caught in the crossfire between us and them, and the enemy shamelessly and deliberately hid within the civilian pockets as the final few made their last stand, making clearing each block building by building tedious and dangerous.

Asher listened with great concentration as the Marine on the other end of the radio gave his triage assessment. Wounded soldier shot in several places, including the upper leg, injuring the femoral artery. The tourniquet was tied, and the bleeding was partly controlled but not completely, and the limb was obviously threatened. Prompt surgical repair, at least as a temporary intervention, can save the limb and, for that matter, the soldier's life. It wasn't the most complicated injury scenario the unit had handled or was capable of handling. They can have up to three field trauma surgeons and two combat Marines in a mobile unit dispatch, though this run needed only two surgeons. They had to go through two other buildings, including the one the wounded soldier was in, both of which were still being cleared. Asher heard sporadic gunfire over the radio. The surgeons carried side arms along with surgical and tactical gear. The two combat soldiers escorted them through long hallways and collapsed stairways, and on more than one occasion, they scrambled to evade the enemy. To Asher, it all seemed vaguely familiar, as if he had done it before or seen it in some movie.

They had entered the other building and approached the wounded soldier and the two others who were with him. Asher took notice of the different attire of the unconscious wounded man and realized he wasn't a Marine. He was Special Forces. Asher knew it somehow, though there was no definitive way to tell otherwise. The sensation of déjà vu hit again, though previously, the wounded soldier was a Marine, he thought. The two surgeons quickly knelt and laid out their gear. Large bore IV access, morphine, concentrated blood products, and fluid bolus while Asher quickly cut down the bloody pant leg and lavaged the wound. He swiftly dissected away damaged and dead tissue and, within moments, had the damaged artery isolated and ligated when the other surgeon joined, and they quickly repaired it. They packed the wound carefully after achieving the best hemostasis they could and took the tourniquet off. They observed no bleeding.

At that instant, the startling sound of gunfire diverted Asher's attention away from the wounded soldier as his head snapped up toward the other end of the hallway. The others quickly gathered and moved around the corner. Gunfire came from the other direction now, and the Marines returned fire. The surgeons stayed near the wounded man, shielded by the others. The scene quickly became chaotic, and the unit wound up spread apart. As Asher watched one of them move farther away, someone ran past them at the other end and disappeared around the corner. Asher quickly moved and waited for him to appear around the bend from the flank position.

The others were conspicuously absent from the scene now, presumably caught up on the other side of the assault. Asher pulled out his pistol and aimed it calmly down the hall. He saw the man suddenly appear with a rifle, taking his own aim. Asher quickly shot several rounds, and the man went down. Asher suddenly took aim again, anticipating another person to appear. It was as if he remembered it was going to happen. The person appeared as expected, a much younger boy, a teenager maybe. Reflexively, Asher pulled the trigger, knowing he could not explicitly see a weapon on the boy. The sensation of pulling the trigger was dulled, and it felt as if he had to squeeze with all his might. No matter how hard he squeezed, however, he could not hear the gunshot, as all sensations dimmed. Asher suddenly moved the finger away from the trigger and saw the figure fall, and the impression that he had shot a teenage civilian made time stand still. It didn't matter anyway. The mission was to evacuate the wounded soldier back to the cleared building. Asher turned and looked around at the puzzling scene around him as the sights and sounds melted.

When Arya Krish opened the door, the sound of a truck downshifting on the highway that was heard behind it became loud and clear as he saw Asher lying back in his chair inside, snoring restlessly with his mouth open. Krish tried to close the door quietly when Asher suddenly startled himself awake with a snort and sat up. Krish shook his head and smiled as he walked over and sat in front of the desk.

"You OK, my friend?" he asked.

Asher nodded his head slowly and wiped his eyes. "Yeah." He got his bearing straight. "Right at the peak of it. One of those recurring dreams, like we talked about before. Yeah, you're not the only one with them." He stretched, reached across his desk for the bottle of water, and took a long sip.

Krish nodded empathetically. "Not a good one, huh?"

"Never heard of a good recurring dream, have you? Who complains about a good recurring dream?"

Krish nodded, acknowledging the silly comment and the irritability. "OK, fine, you wanna talk another time then? We can meet up later. I was thinking about joining some rounds today actually."

"No, don't be ridiculous. I'm good, just been traveling so much that the time zones start messing with your sleep. It's funny," Asher said with a musing look, "That dream I was having—there've been so many versions. I start remembering it while I'm in the dream, you know what I mean? Sometimes, I realize I'm dreaming, in fact, and try to control it. Has that ever happened to you?"

"Yeah, it has," Krish said. He nodded. "What's your dream

about?"

Asher shrugged. "It's basically some generic scene where I'm in the field fixing a wounded soldier when we start taking fire, and I wind up shooting a couple of them."

"Wow, you ever been in a firefight like that? You've never mentioned anything before," Krish said with wide-eyed fascination.

"Don't really talk about it much, but yeah, some of the units took our function to the limits. It put the extra field training to the test. Of course, it's all dramatized and distorted in dreams, like in movies — a contorted amalgam of memories and made-up stuff."

"Well, I don't mean to label it, but that does sound a little PTSD."

"Well, if you don't mean to label it, then don't label it. I guess you and your recurring dreams have PTSD, too, then."

"My dreams are more metaphorical, not reliving past experiences so much."

"Yeah I remember, with the running away from something and the driving off the cliff."

"Oh good, you *were* paying attention then."

Asher smiled, scoffed, and sat silent for a moment. "So." He took another sip of water. "What's this meeting going to be about? Who all are expected? Why unannounced?"

"I wanted Jason Rook to meet us here as soon as he sent me this," Krish said. He handed Asher the small tablet device.

Asher tapped the screen to play the audio recording, which was transcribed on the screen. After finishing, Asher put the tablet down on the desk and turned toward Krish. "So Rook did this on his own? Was he surveilling Chowan without your knowledge or authorization? That is not good," Asher said.

"Of course, it's not good. But the fact remains that Chowan is compromising our operations still, and not just minor stuff.

The Panacea protocols. This guy was supposed to be on our side. I could have sworn I had the right read on him." Krish shook his head in frustration.

"Why is that such a let-down? It's not like we hand-picked this guy. He came over from Alpha Corp. We don't know him. Never did."

"Yeah, I know. But still. Our first encounter with him was so compelling. And that's the problem. He knows a lot of things, Jay. The human trials at Alpha Corp, Marcus Knight, to say the least—he was around for all of that."

Asher nodded thoughtfully. The gravity of Krish's point did not escape him. A worried look came over his face as his piercing hazel eyes peered again at the tablet screen.

"Not to mention Esper Enterprises," Asher continued, "who have obviously entered the technological arms race. Make no mistake, we have a head start, but this is an industrial-scale competition, just like the one for the first lightbulb and electric grid, the first mass-production automobile, nuclear, space, and so on. If Beacon is to remain ahead and in control, you are going to have to deal with Esper as well and anyone else like them."

Krish listened attentively with a brooding countenance. "Well, we'll have to keep all of that in mind, won't we, as we deliberate how to proceed from here. I've summoned Rook here, and believe me, I am going to confront him about what he's done. But he will also be involved in our conference about Chowan. Him, and Vincent Halliday."

"Halliday?" Asher asked. "What's he got to do with this?"

"He's worked closest with him since Chowan joined us. He's trustworthy."

Krish watched the door while he turned the ring on his braced finger. They remained silent for a few minutes while Krish paced around, and Asher sat at his desk looking at his phone. Soon enough, Jason Rook arrived, followed by Vincent Halliday.

They sat around Asher's large desk in their individual seats, exchanged a few formalities, and then got down to business.

"So," Krish said during a pause, addressing everyone, "now to the main reason I've asked you here. We all know about Kai Chowan's interactions with Esper Enterprises. We here are the only ones at Beacon that do know, and it must stay that way." He paused and surveyed while the others remained silent. "There can be no denying it now, with the evidence I've shown you. So, I wanted to convene before deciding how we are to proceed from here."

"Is it any more complicated than firing him?" Asher asked, as if to facilitate discourse.

"Well, certainly, we'll have to remove him from this compromised position. If he were to leave Beacon, there's nothing stopping him from joining Esper anyway. They wouldn't be covered by our restrictive covenant agreements," Krish replied.

"We should also consider using our knowledge to our advantage and leaving him in play," Rook said.

"What if we showed him the proof we have," Vincent Halliday added, and there was a pause. "It would be leverage. Litigious threats alone could give us an advantage over him."

"Advantage to what end? Blackmail, coercion?" Asher replied.

"I don't think that would neutralize him as a threat to operations," Rook interjected. "He would still have the option and ability to do a lot of damage if he wanted. Remember, he was there at the beginning, going back to Alpha Corp." Rook glanced over at Krish and met his attentive gaze.

"By your reasoning, there aren't many options for us. None worthy of consideration, in fact. I mean, you can't seriously be suggesting what I think you are," Asher said.

"I don't recall suggesting anything in particular, Dr. Asher," Rook said politely.

"Maybe he's playing them, staying loyal to us while protecting himself," Halliday said.

"You mean he's a double agent, running his own operation," Asher said with an amused look.

"I'm not saying he's running an operation. He definitely seems to be under the influence of Esper Enterprises, for whatever reason."

"I think that reason will be important to discern. I do not see any personal grudge toward us that would motivate him."

"He has a bad history with Alpha Corp, which is now inextricably part of our history," Krish said quietly.

"I think the prospect of Dr. Chowan having the guts to try to manipulate the situation as you seem to be hoping Dr. Halliday," Asher said, looking over at him, "is slim, to say the least. He's not that kind of guy."

Krish rocked back and forth in his chair and listened quietly, unknowingly turning the ring on his healing finger. The conversation faded in his ears as his mind retreated to its own private rumination of the points that were being debated. Each had raised an important issue, and it became frustratingly clear Kai Chowan was a grave liability, and he was easily keen to the notion that he had to be eliminated as a threat to Krish's mission.

"In the end, I'm going to need to look him in the eye and hear what he has to say. I'm going to speak to him myself, alone." He said suddenly at one point. The room went silent, and the others watched him stand and slowly make his way toward the door. Some puzzlement was in the air, but it was clear Arya Krish had made his decision, and further conference was unnecessary. The others rose to their feet, except Jay Asher, who remained seated behind his desk, watching Krish mainly while occasionally scanning the others' faces. Krish stood near the door, turning his ring, and nodded at Vincent Halliday. When Jason Rook approached, Krish turned to him and said, "Walk with me, Mr.

Rook."

Rook stopped outside the door and stood waiting. Krish turned back to Asher, nodded and waved, and closed the door behind him. He walked with Rook in silence for some distance.

"I'll get straight to the point," Krish said tersely. "You went behind my back with your unilateral actions on Chowan. I had not sanctioned any of it."

"That's true, Dr. Krish," Rook replied briskly. "But you did not explicitly forbid it, either. Dr. Asher said you did not want escalation. This was part of the existing surveillance after Chowan's data transfer was flagged."

"Sounds like excuses, Mr. Rook, and beneath you, if I may say so. I expect more transparency between us when it comes to you taking initiative. You have yourself clearly said I am in command. Have I made myself clear?" They had reached the door to Krish's office and stopped and turned to each other. Krish saw the appraising look in Rook's eyes as they stood silently. Rook's scrutinizing stare seemed to be trying to discern something about Krish, gauging him somehow. At least, that was Krish's impression at that moment.

"That is clear, Dr. Krish. As you point out, I have already acknowledged it. I was following through on something with good intentions in my defense. My position is to facilitate and act in the interests of the company. The way I see it, that's why you've kept me around. I have valuable experience, and there's no substitute for direct experience, no matter how smart you are. Field knowledge can't come by any other means."

"I agree, Mr. Rook, no better way to learn a lesson. That's why I never make the same mistake twice."

They stopped at the door to Krish's office, and he turned and stared at Rook. Both remained silent while the testosterone swirled, and both remained professional. "That'll be all for now, Mr. Rook," Krish added and went inside. Rook stood still while the door closed, then turned and walked away.

Arya Krish thought it fitting to confront Chowan in a similar fashion as the first time they met, which he thought back to as he made his way across the clearing toward the French door around the back of the house, unannounced. It wasn't quite the same menacing circumstances, however. He was alone this time, and it was broad daylight. He knew Chowan would be home and alone as well. Krish approached the door and knocked three times, then stood patiently with his arms at his side for over a minute and locked eyes with Kai Chowan when he finally opened the door.

"Dr. Krish?" Chowan said with a puzzled look. He had a certain display of concern that Krish found pretentious at that instant. "I'm surprised to see you here like this. Is everything all right? Come in, please," Chowan stepped back and opened the door for him. Krish walked into the familiar house, reliving the first time and only other time he was there, and walked slowly inside toward the same chair he had sat before. Chowan sat across from him, visibly anxious. Krish had a calm countenance as they spoke, his gaze fixed on Chowan with scrutinizing eyes.

"Can I get you anything, Dr. Krish?" Chowan asked. He gestured toward the kitchen.

"No thank you, Dr. Chowan," Krish said. Chowan nodded and remained silent, anticipating Dr. Krish to continue and reveal why he was there so unexpectedly. Krish looked at Chowan intently, then scanned around the room from where he sat. "Honestly, since our last encounter down in R&D, I've been meaning to spend some time with you. I remain haunted by the circumstances of our first meeting, and it seems to linger without closure in my mind, including other things."

Krish paused deliberately and stared. Chowan stared back with a curious, wide-eyed look. A subtle smile may have crept up on the corner of Krish's lip, but the nerves were leaden, and it didn't stay. Krish remained silent until it was obvious he was waiting for Chowan to speak.

"Yes," Chowan said distantly and leaned back. His eyes diverted as if he were recalling. "That's something I'll never forget."

"To me, it has since been regarded as a distinct tie that binds us, if you know what I mean. You're one of the few scientists we kept from Alpha Corp and the only one working that high up with the Panacea protocols."

Chowan sat back and remained silent, waiting for Krish to continue.

"Yet it struck me recently," Krish said, "that I've barely gotten to know you after all this time. Somehow, it seemed strange to me that it hadn't occurred to me up till recently." Krish paused and shifted in his seat. "Actually, I'll trouble you for a glass of water, please."

"Of course." Chowan quickly got up and headed to the kitchen. Neither spoke as Chowan went to the fridge, took out a bottle of sparkling water, fetched a glass from the cupboard, and poured Krish's drink. He brought it over and handed it to Krish, who smiled in acknowledgement, then sat down again. Krish took a sip and looked up at Chowan as if waiting for a response.

"I understand what you mean, Dr. Krish. I admit, though, that while I agree our shared experience is a tie that binds, I've largely considered myself an employee, a foot soldier, that kind of thing—and you, Dr. Halliday, Dr. Asher, are the bosses, so to speak."

"That's interesting. Somehow, I presumed there was more than that. What I mean is, I figured with all you went through, you stuck around because there was something here you believed in and wanted to remain a part of." Krish paused and took a sip while Chowan remained silent, watching him.

"I've been frank and honest about how I came to be here,

and the reason remains the same as to why I continue to do so. It all started with wanting to provide for my family back home," Chowan said with his articulate, thick accent.

"Yes, I remember. But there can be more to your life than that, right?" Chowan didn't answer. "Let me ask you," Krish said. "What do you see the future looking like for the nanotechnology. What will be its ultimate application? Conceptually, not getting too technical here."

"I tend to agree with what you've expressed in the past. Beyond medical application, the neuro-AI interface will be the next paradigm shift in humanity."

"Yeah, that's not far off. Amazing, isn't it?" Krish paused as they nodded at each other. "I'm looking ahead, and I have been contemplating your future role in all this. Having heard what you said about being a foot soldier, essentially just an employee, makes me wonder if you have that thread of dedication and service to something bigger than personal goals."

A puzzled look came over Chowan's face. "I'm not sure what you're trying to tell me, Dr. Krish. Is my job being called into question?"

Krish smiled and finished his drink. It seemed he had made up his mind. Chowan continued to conceal what he was doing in a private encounter where Krish, for some reason, had expected him to come clean. Misplaced faith, Krish thought as he stood and looked down at Chowan, who hesitated a moment before standing up as well. Krish paused as if giving him one last chance to say something before walking toward the front door. Chowan hustled ahead and stood at the door, waiting to open it as Krish approached.

"Dr. Krish, I did mean what I said before at the lab. I have felt a new sense of belonging since joining Beacon Medical Institute. I've learned that circumstances can be largely out of our control and seems to sweep us along despite any resistance."

Krish looked at him, smiled slightly, and nodded. Chowan opened the door, and Krish left.

As he approached the door to Krish's office at Beacon Medical Institute some weeks later, Vincent Halliday paused before knocking and listened to the muffled, angry voice inside. He couldn't make out what was being said, but it seemed he was hearing one side of a heated argument. Halliday checked his watch and decided to risk interrupting and knocked on the door, since he was keeping his appointment with Arya Krish.

"Yeah, I know how long it's been, OK? I'm not making excuses not to come home," He heard Krish yell on the phone as he opened the door and walked in. Halliday stood by the door for a moment, and when Krish saw him, he waved Halliday in. "I promise I'm going to come home as soon as I can, but I have a few more important things to do here. Tell Seena," Krish paused abruptly. With a long sigh, he slowly moved the phone away from his ear and glanced at the screen before putting it away in his pocket. He didn't acknowledge Halliday again, even after he sat down and waited quietly. Krish closed and rubbed his eyes, took a slow, deep breath, and swiveled his chair around toward Halliday.

"Sorry about that, Dr. Halliday. The missus isn't too happy at the moment." He gave a half-hearted laugh and smile. "Thanks for taking this meeting on short notice. I know how busy you are."

"Not at all, Dr. Krish. What can I do for you?"

"It's got to do with Chowan. Surveillance seems to indicate he's compiling another batch of IP data based on his activity, which he's been trying to cover up. But it definitely looks like he's going to meet with Esper Enterprises for another exchange. I've been thinking of a way to undermine Esper. Maybe we could corrupt the data they receive from Chowan somehow?"

"What did you have in mind?"

"Something that would cripple their tech infrastructure permanently," Krish said and paused deliberately, observing Halliday's reaction, and waited for his response.

"Like a worm or virus," Halliday said, nodding speculatively.

Krish smiled. "Precisely. I imagine it won't be so straightforward, though. They have state-of-the-art protection. We won't know what he's talking to them until he transfers it to his device. The virus would have to be included before or after the transfer and go undetected by Esper when they analyze it."

"The latter is certainly feasible. But you're right. To plant the bug we'd have to know exactly what files are being transferred and modify them in time."

There was a pause as Halliday leaned back and seemed to take a moment to think to himself. "It'd be helpful to know Chowan's actions in the system. It'll clue us in as to what and when he's planning to take the data."

"I'll have Mr. Rook plug you into all that. We anticipate Chowan will meet in-person again with Esper Enterprises. He's avoided remote or online interactions, knowing they can be flagged much easier."

"He'll have to transfer the data on-site since all the Panacea Project information is stored offline. So we'll have to somehow plant the bug on his device."

"Which means you're the one that will need to do it," Krish said.

"Yes, I should be able to manage that. Actually, if I can access his session from another station, I can add our bug to the transfer while it's happening."

"OK, consider yourself on call till the time comes. As always, I'm grateful for your efforts and discretion."

"Don't mention it, Dr. Krish. So, what are you going to do about Chowan afterwards? He can't continue to do this, right?"

Krish swiveled away toward the panoramic windows and didn't answer right away. "I haven't made a final decision, but I have narrowed the options down. What would you do, Dr. Halliday?"

"I think you should confront him, Dr. Krish, and cut off his access. Remove him from the protocols."

"So fire him basically?"

"No, not necessarily. We can keep an eye on him if he stays with Beacon. Keep your enemies closer, that sort of thing. His legal status in this country is dependent on us. I think that's strong leverage."

"What if he decides to quit and join Esper Enterprises or somewhere else? They can endorse his stay the same as us. Would anything prevent Chowan from doing that if he felt any heat from us?"

Halliday paused and went into a thoughtful silence. "I see what you mean, Dr. Krish. I guess I'm glad I'm not the one to make the call."

Krish looked over at him, then turned back toward the window. "Well, let's get started on this right away, Dr. Halliday. We'll meet again soon. Thanks again."

"Any time, Dr. Krish. I'll get to it immediately."

CHAPTER THIRTEEN

The dawn's early light poured over the clear eastern sky in Washington, DC, like a steady stream of oil. A low, dense fog lingered through the night on the National Mall as Arya Krish sat on the steps of the Lincoln Memorial and looked out at the Reflecting Pool and the World War II memorial beyond it. The Washington Monument was barely visible in the background. The scene was quiet, serene, and largely empty. Most passers-by were joggers, security, or police, some of whom recognized Krish and vice versa. He sat looking out, thinking of the historical moments when the entire area was packed with people, and shook his head in wonderment—that this was the very same place where it all happened. He struggled to comprehend what comprises such great moments—the kind of personality, the kind of faith, the kind of vision it must take for a person to create it. Was it a delusion of grandeur to even aspire for something like that? How does one summon and maintain the conviction and strength it must take? It all seemed just beyond his mind's grasp and left him brooding pensively as he spent the next few hours walking or sitting alone at various nearby spots that he had come to prefer over the years, to retreat for a moment from it all, on that crisp late-autumn morning.

The sun had risen beyond the horizon considerably as Krish sat languidly on a bench closer to the Capitol Building when he took vague notice of Jay Asher, nodding distantly as he approached. Asher looked around and took a deep breath as he stood next to Krish for a moment.

"The sun's still warm, even though the air is rather crisp," he said, nodding in self-agreement as if completing an inner dialogue. Krish glanced up at him, then closed his eyes and felt the warmth of the sun on his face, and took in a deep breath of the cool late-morning air.

"Yeah, still nice enough to enjoy outdoor DC," Krish said, also nodding.

"Absolutely, a suit jacket is more than comfortable. We may salvage some old-fashioned autumn weather yet," Asher said as he sat down. "Seems to be one thing I've noticed about the seasons in recent years. It's become drawn out extremes of winter and summer, while spring and fall have shrunk or sometimes skipped."

Krish looked at Asher for a moment, then leaned forward and rested his arms on his legs, and looked out at the view without replying. Asher was silent for a moment as well, then glanced over at Krish speculatively.

"Well then," he said, "stimulating banter aside, I reckon it was you that called this meeting. I assume this is business, not a social call."

"We'll get right down to it then. How'd it go on the Hill today?"

Asher shrugged. "Sit-downs with congressmen, committee heads. Feels like I'm being vetted alright. They made it seem like they were trying to keep it informal." He paused and looked down at Krish sitting on the bench. "Nothing really matters until the President makes a nomination. I'm not sure he even knows who I am."

Krish remained silent as he looked out at the scenery with concentration in his eyes. "I happen to have direct information that confirms your name is already in the conversation at that level."

Asher nodded sarcastically. "Oh, well, that's a relief."

"You're still mad about not including you in on the plan

from the beginning? As I said, this is the beginning. I saw the opportunity as it arose and acted on it when it was available — all very recently. We still have a ways to go to Secretary of Veteran Affairs, my friend. These were just the first maneuvers."

"Be that as it may, I'll raise the point again. What makes you think I want it?"

"It's not always about wanting it, is it? Like I said, it's an opportunity, that's all. An opportunity to put yourself in a position where a capable and dutiful person can do real good. We've talked about fixing the VA for a long time, haven't we?"

Asher nodded distantly and slowly sat next to Krish. "I'm completely earnest when I say that is a high compliment, implying I am capable and dutiful. Either one of those alone would be a superlative. And you're not one to patronize."

"Your military record alone stacks your qualifications. I'm sure you can appreciate the potential path to a real position of power."

"So that's what we're after in the end, after all. Power. That's something you can get consumed in the chase for; that's the problem. That's why I say I'm not sure I want it."

Krish shook his head thoughtfully. "Power does not have to always corrupt. What it always does is reveal what you really are. If you want to know what a person truly is, give them power. There have been great people with great power in history. Besides, anything is better than what's going on now. I'm sure we can do much better, and I see us in a position to do that."

"So this is our calling then? I'm summoned by the moment to go with the tide in the affairs of men that leads to fortune?"

"Yeah, something like that," Krish said, with an acknowledging smile. "This enterprise continues to evolve, and so do we. Like I said, Jay, this is just the beginning of this story. Look at what's happened in the past year! The Panacea protocols stand on their own results and merit, and around the DC area, we've already had an effect within widespread communities with the projects we're involved with."

"The charter schools," Asher said with an acknowledging nod. "That did come up, in fact. I admit having Beacon's resume attached to mine cast a much brighter light on us."

"The lobbying of Alpha Corp, staking a claim in the Executive hierarchy, it's just the next level, the next rung on the ladder to the top."

"And what is the top? Then what? We use the power toward the greater good — it's that simple? Are we the exception to the corruption and intoxication that accompanies all of it? We'll somehow be detached from all of that. And why, because we're noble and dutiful? The purity of our self-proclaimed altruism absolves us?"

"That sounds a bit crazy, hearing you say it," Krish said glibly.

Asher smiled and nodded. "Well, you know what all the great people in history have in common? They're all crazy and just right. Not too much, and not too little. Your ambition is industrious, my friend, to say the least. Is this the direction you really want to go? Is this the direction you want to take Beacon? Politics, lobbying, the jockeying for power in government positions…this was never the intention when you started this thing, right?"

Krish didn't answer right away and stared into the distance, pondering Asher's questions. "It was, and still is, about the Panacea Project. But as things evolved, the field we operate in gets bigger and bigger, and the possibilities reveal themselves only at the moment, so there's no way of anticipating what direction it all goes. But this is the path to ultimate success, and if the new technology is meant to truly advance humanity, it will need to be protected. The government is going to be a big player, and we need our seat at the table. But apart from all that, this campaign has been directly about the Veterans Administration right? It needs to, and can be, made right. We've demonstrated our model works within our own health system with Beacon's veterans' program."

Asher nodded slightly, and they remained silent again. He was obviously all-in with Krish from the beginning on this, so there was no need to express his agreement. But it was a piece of the puzzle, and the operation at large that it was entangled with brought about a certain angst that Asher shared with Krish. He glanced over at Krish and observed him turning his ring easily on the healed finger.

"You know who's becoming a real pain in the ass? Richard Filmore. That guy is looking for the next rung even if it isn't the ladder he's on."

"Filmore? Secretary of the VA? How does that fit? He's not even military, is he?"

"Of course he is, Naval Academy alumnus. Strong track record in the private sector before becoming Commissioner of the FDA, as you know."

"Even still," Krish said, shaking his head, "he can't compete with you."

"I wouldn't be so dismissive. He's got a lot of friends."

"Well, we prefer him exactly where he is. He's still a help to us while advancing the newer protocols."

"It looks like he'll need his ambitions swayed back in our favor."

"We'll make sure we remain in control. He's an asset."

Asher's eyes narrowed skeptically. "Not sure what exactly you mean by that. Is that CIA or Special Forces lingo?"

Krish sighed and remained silent, staring off at the view. "Whatever it takes, that seems to be the motto that gets us the furthest. The most effective battle cry, isn't it?"

Asher's countenance became thoughtful as he considered

the question. "By whatever means necessary. Yes that has been an effective *modus operandi* now and in the past. Tried and true."

"Still," Krish said, "you're the only person I can ask this question," he paused. "Will whatever we wind up accomplishing justify what we've done? All of it?"

"Too early to tell. I think it's possible, yes. But time will tell. Meanwhile, we must keep chasing it at this point, don't we? Because otherwise," Asher said and paused, "it won't justify what we've done, and we won't be able to live with that. But there's no question we are living in extraordinary times. This is going to be like discovering electricity, as far as I'm concerned, in terms of what it's going to do to the way people live. Actually, seeing this nanotechnology and genetic engineering in action, the capability is undeniable now. So yes, if that is the legacy, then it is justifiable. But that's just my opinion. Other than the not being able to live with ourselves part, it may not matter much."

"Well, that's all that does matter to us then. Looks like we keep chasing," Krish said. "Power, primary objectives, assets, liabilities, collateral damage...the entire lingo."

Asher remained thoughtfully silent for a moment. "On another matter: what was your final decision on Kai Chowan?"

Krish sighed. "Kai Chowan, just like Richard Filmore, has undergone threat and utility assessment and will be dealt with accordingly."

"Sounds again like you've been conferring with Jason Rook."

"Jason Rook has undergone his own threat and utility assessment as well. I'm not certain, but I am confident that I did right in trusting him. I admit though, I was wrong about Kai Chowan. Carelessly gave him the benefit of the doubt from the get-go for some reason."

Asher shrugged. "He's looking out for number one, just like everybody else. Shouldn't surprise you. He's a stranger otherwise."

Krish shook his head incredulously. "Can't argue with that. I think I connected his circumstances with things my father used to tell me about his experiences when he was young. Oh well, here we are now. This is just another obstacle to overcome. Is it worth it all, I ask again? I would say at the moment, yes, it is because we're about to bring about a paradigm shift that'll ripple through society at large, and we're the leader of the pack. And I'll tell you what, my friend, it is fitting—it should be us, and it should be here," Krish said, gesturing at the iconic surroundings. "Where else in the world can this great time in history play out?"

Asher smiled. "Amen to that. But I will say this—I don't think politics is for me."

They spoke of other things for a while before parting ways. Afterwards, Krish would spend most of the day meeting with lawmakers and others before making his way back to Beacon later that night. Slumped in his chair in the largely empty Administration building, he had sat alone in his office for who knows how long, in a ruminative daze, when the door knocked softly, and he looked up to see Jason Rook enter quietly and walk over to the desk. He looked the same every time, no matter what time of day or night, with the trim black suit and tie, slicked-back silver hair, and attentive pale blue eyes, without a hint of complacency.

"Come in, Mr. Rook," Krish said languidly and straightened up in his chair.

"Thank you, Dr. Krish. I'm glad we were able to meet on short notice."

Krish shrugged. "I was here anyhow. So, Chowan made his move?"

Rook handed him the small paper tablet. "See for yourself. That is the data he transferred offline, in person, in R&D."

"And Halliday?"

"He was successful."

"Is Chowan trying to hide his transactions somehow? I find it hard to believe this guy has the guts to make blatantly unauthorized data transfers without some countermeasure."

"He did try to mask his trail. It looks like the device he downloaded it to was outfitted with some protection, too, probably provided by Esper Enterprises. But we have our own countermeasures."

Krish nodded. "Good. That should keep Esper preoccupied for the foreseeable future."

Rook's eyes narrowed as he observed Krish's distracted demeanor. "There is still the matter of dealing with Kai Chowan himself."

Krish glanced over at Rook, searching those keen, narrow eyes for that distinct glint, the patina of the hunter's instinct, an attribute Krish sought out in himself as a perceived asset, if not virtue, that would give him the critical edge. It inevitably made him relive certain past moments — pushing that button that ended a life, looking into the house of a man whose family he destroyed for building permits all those years ago. But this was a fleeting thought; the distracted demeanor was due to something else as Krish waited to broach another subject.

"Yes, I've made a decision on Kai Chowan. But another reason I wanted to meet you in person was DARPA. You've heard of it, I'm sure."

"Defense Advanced Research Projects Agency. They've contacted you?"

"Yes, they did, in their own style. The man I met, our conversation, everything about it was intriguing and esoteric," Krish said. Rook leaned forward intently.

"Dr. Krish, Kai Chowan knows things that only very few other people know and is nowhere near as trustworthy. He was in the car that night with the Marcus Knight incident."

"I know, Mr. Rook. I was there, too."

"Then you must share my concern."

"I have planned my action on Chowan."

Rook shook his head and leaned back. "He will remain a liability as long as he's alive," he said bluntly. "He can go to the authorities, go to the media, blow us up on social media by himself. He's a walking disaster. Everything you have worked for is in jeopardy, and I am not exaggerating, Dr. Krish."

"So be it. I refuse to consider killing someone an option on the table in every contingency. That is what you've been implying, isn't it, as the only solution?"

"You've kept me in the inner circle because of my experience, and I am offering you my insight now. How can you trust Chowan again after he already betrayed you?" Rook's display of baffled frustration caught Krish's attention. He hadn't seen Rook show much emotion at all before. Krish sensed the doubt simmering in him. "Beware, that is what you are doing, Dr. Krish. You are trusting him to stay quiet and out of the way. He can cause plenty of trouble wherever he is if he wanted to. How do you know he won't do anything?"

"Because I've spoken to him since and looked him in the eye. And while I did project the notion that there is only one other option, I feel like part of me understands him, for what it's worth, at least enough to give him the benefit of the doubt. After all," Krish said and paused, "people can deserve a second chance, don't you think, Mr. Rook?"

"Some people."

Krish nodded solemnly. "We agree on something then. Besides, I say again emphatically — I am not considering murder an option." He paused and glanced at Rook, who seemed to have an almost accusatory, skeptical look. "For what it's worth, we're going to keep tabs on him. But I've made my read on Chowan, and my decision. I value your advice, but I'm not vacillating. We need to shift our attention to the next moves. The government tentacles are tightening, between this new DARPA collaboration that is kind of being imposed on us, and the Senate committee hearings, and on and on."

"As our field of operation expands, such obstacles and encounters are to be expected. But I wouldn't consider DARPA an adversary, though they will exert their government influence on you, a private sector operator, in the name of national security and whatnot. But remember, a lot of major advances—nuclear, air and space, GPS, and the internet—have been spawned by military projects by them. The way I see it, you would be serving the country yet again by working with them."

"Be that as it may, the field of operation, as you put it, seems to be expanding inexorably. I've been feeling more and more like we're losing control or falling behind."

"We're big players, playing a big game in a vast field. The name of the game? Conquer the field," Jason Rook said as if remembering a prior conversation.

Krish looked at him curiously for a moment. "Knowing is becoming," he said languidly as if remembering a prior conversation himself. "You're right. Our entanglement with the government will not be entirely adversarial."

There wasn't much said thereafter, and while Jason Rook left with a conspicuously frustrated look, Arya Krish may not have noticed. He sat alone quietly, recollecting the recent meeting with DARPA management. Nothing was clandestine about the meeting. It happened in Krish's office in the Admin Building at Beacon Medical Institute. Still, when he was contacted and made the arrangements, privacy and security were formally assessed.

Naturally, Krish had done some background research on the Defense Advanced Research Projects Agency, and as a result, there was considerable anticipation and even cautious optimism that immersed Krish in the moment. Krish observed the man from the Department of Defense (DoD), who was the guy that the head of DARPA would report to, as he opened the door and entered. It seemed unusual to Krish that while it was DARPA that first contacted him, it was quickly kicked up and taken over by DoD management. The circumstances seemed to heighten Krish's awareness, and he sensed a vaguely familiar exhilaration in the moment as he stood from behind his desk and watched the man while bright sunshine flooded through the panoramic windows. The man appeared to have a military background even though he wore an ordinary dark suit; his gait and posture were formal and disciplined, his dark eyes alert and observant, and his speech measured.

It was a business meeting from the start, and the expected matters came up in sequence, such as genetic database security, privacy rights, pandemic control measures, and bioterrorism. The proposed collaboration between Beacon and DARPA invoked history, as the man cited prior examples at one point in the conversation. It didn't seem like a sales pitch at all, more like a well-packaged, articulate agenda. He paced slowly in front of Krish's desk while he spoke in a pedantic cadence. At least, it seemed that way to Krish as he sat listening intently with narrow, attentive eyes, observing the man as he spoke. It was an occasion to contemplate the vast ramifications that were being presented to Krish with vivid clarity like no prior moment. The trajectory of the Panacea technology's legacy was being revealed in glimmers of official-sounding speculation and imagination, and Krish was in the moment with every fiber of his being.

The man said, "My point is, it was, in fact, a collaboration between military and private enterprises that led to all these life-changing developments of the modern age and will be part of the pantheon that we are about to join as history is again unfolding before us."

He paused for a second as if he finally felt he had said

enough. Krish continued to eye him quietly and suspiciously. The man seems so much like a politician at that moment. There was no denying the legacy of Beacon Medical Institute and the foundation of this technology that was being built. But there was already the impending loss of control, if Krish had any to begin with, that brought a rush of angst and even resentment from the depths. It gave rise to a cold, calculated determination, seeking an increasingly anguished vindication, with ruthless altruism as the only means to attain it. Arya Krish felt the pangs of the voracious appetite for power that power itself begets. He had made leaps in the power grab to maintain control over the Panacea technologies, and the more attained, the more desired.

"I will say this, Dr. Krish," the man said almost on cue, re-directing Krish's thoughts, "we've played a part in the pursuit of the genetic age for decades, and watching the last few years play out has been extraordinary. The rise of Beacon Medical Institute, followed by the merger with Alpha Corp, has made it a reality. It is frankly remarkable."

Krish recognized some sincerity but, at the same time, was skeptical of the pandering. His field of vision broadened once again as he saw another asset, another means, another compromise. The political successes were playing out in real-time, and his thoughts swarmed between cabinet positions, FDA fast-tracks, and his vision of social reformation it all facilitated. The meeting concluded shortly after, as the fatigue had settled in, and his limbs became heavy. Krish spent the rest of the day sitting alone in his office. Over and over again, he reviewed the surveillance and data compromised by Kai Chowan.

***

A single bright white light was overhead where Krish sat in the far corner of R&D while the rest of the lab was dark. He saw the doorway light up far off on the other side of the vast lab. The door opened, and Kai Chowan's silhouette entered. He became visible under the white light when he approached the station and stood at the side of the table across from Krish.

"Dr. Krish," Chowan said with apprehension. "What's happening? I was surprised to be summoned so urgently in the middle of the night.

Krish said nothing as he swiveled the computer screen and observed Chowan's expression as he scanned the transcripts and other evidence detailing the subterfuge he was engaged in with Esper Enterprises.

"Dr. Chowan," Krish said, "you're leaving Beacon Medical Institute. Your visa is being revoked, and you'll be returning to China as soon as we arrange it."

Chowan nodded speculatively as if expecting it. There was no shock, no denial. "I suppose I could stay in the US and work somewhere else," he said and glanced at Krish with a curious look, as if attempting defiant confidence.

Krish shrugged dismissively, though he was surprised by Chowan's hasty and audacious response. "You can try. But you'll have a target on your back. Guys like Esper Enterprises won't relent just because you left here to join them."

"And Beacon? Are you trained on that target as well?"

"Yes, if necessary. You've stolen company IP, Dr. Chowan, and compromised the Panacea Project at large. There are obvious liabilities."

"IP I helped create. And given the conditions and circumstances under which that all transpired, even though it was before you came into the picture, I feel I have some leverage here."

Krish's eyes were dull, and his face was cold and expressionless. Chowan must have seen it plainly on Krish's face, but just in case he missed it, Krish turned and nodded behind him toward the dark corner of the lab, causing Chowan to look in that direction as Jason Rook walked into the light and stood quietly behind Krish. Chowan couldn't hold back the concerned, thoughtful frown that fell over his face. No doubt he recalled the incident with Marcus Knight in that moment. He looked back at the computer screen and remained silent.

"I don't suppose you remember at this point," Chowan said with a sigh of resignation, "or have you ever experienced a time when you did not have the extraordinary power and wealth that you've attained. But for the rest of us caught in the current, you realize that the more you resist, the worse it gets, so you relent, go limp, and let it sweep you away." He paused and shook his head as if in disapproval. "I think I've always been that way. Despite being told I'm brilliant along the way... I've always lacked that singular quality that allows true greatness, and as a result, I have been content being carried with the tide, accepting wherever it takes me. Unlike others who have it in them, who are able to shift the very tides themselves. Like you, Dr. Krish. And like Mr. Steinhart. Though, don't take me wrong, you two are nothing alike otherwise. But that part of your nature is something you and him share I think. It's necessary to do spectacular things, good or bad. Me? I'm left at the mercy of the likes of you, and Esper Enterprises. But believe me when I say, Dr. Krish," he said, and paused deliberately. "I hope you beat everyone at their own game. I can't help but root for you to accomplish everything you have imagined because it is a vision so ambitious that even if you are partially successful, I can remain proud of the humble role I played in it all."

Rook was still dimly visible in the background, but Chowan spoke as if he was the only person in the room like he dictated a letter. He did not look at Krish even once and was not at all interested in his surroundings. Krish listened intently and scrutinized Chowan while he spoke. Conflicting currents were in his own mind as Krish wrestled with resentment toward Chowan for speculating on things he obviously didn't understand, as if trying to conjure notions of guilt or empathy from Krish—yet at the same time agreed with what Chowan said, and recoiled from it even though it was something he had recognized long before. The muscles in his neck tightened again, and he took a compulsory deep breath as he suppressed the creeping chill. Krish shifted uneasily in his seat before he spoke.

"I feel I've always been sincere toward you, Dr. Chowan. I don't want to see you get hurt; quite the contrary, I somehow felt a kinship since the first time we met, oddly enough, given we never got to know each other thereafter. But I think I've made it a point to look out for you since our paths have converged. So, truth be told, this was quite a betrayal on your part. I am sorry for that, and you should be as well. Having said that, I can tell you we won't cause you any trouble as long as you agree to leave and stay out of the way."

"It seems I don't have much choice left, Dr. Krish. I hope that means you can also protect me from others," Chowan said, glancing at Rook again.

Krish paused as if considering what to say next. There didn't seem to be much left to discuss. "We'll be speaking again soon, Dr. Chowan. You'll be placed on administrative leave in the meantime. I'll summon you again when ready. Make sure you are available."

Chowan nodded silently, then turned and walked into the darkness toward the exit at the other end of the lab. Krish and Rook watched him leave in silence before Rook walked into the light and came over to the table. Krish swiveled in his direction as he approached.

"Well, what do you think?" he asked.

"We'll have to keep him under close surveillance indefinitely," Rook said.

Krish nodded. He shifted uneasily as he felt the resentment toward Chowan for his betrayal fester within. He rolled his neck slowly, trying to shake the heavy feeling that settled on his shoulders, and a cold look came over his face.

"We have to make sure nothing compromises our efforts at this point. I think I'll have to rely more and more on you and trust you'll operate under mutually agreed protocols." He paused and locked eyes with Rook. "I'm not going to be watching over your shoulder all the time. Not possible anyhow. I'll be deferring to you on many operations. Despite what happened with Chowan, I trust my read on people, so I think, and hope, that I can rely on you."

"Absolutely."

It felt as if a significant weight had been lifted off after the Chowan situation was finally resolved, as far as Krish was concerned. So much energy and time had been diverted from the ever-expanding protocols, which had been implemented at tertiary centers in the Alpha Corp network. The geographic expansion and reproducible results hastened the government's tentacles while Krish continued to bask in the publicity and social popularity he and his movement had earned along the way. The announcement of Vincent Halliday's nomination for Nobel Prizes brightened the spotlight on Beacon Medical Institute, while on the other hand, its dubious fusion with Alpha Corp and the entanglement of all the vast operations between the two were equally under scrutiny, and Krish would find himself shaking off the daunting pressure of congressional review, political deal-making, lobbying transactions, all part of the amalgam of power, politics, and social reformation.

***

Arya Krish knocked quietly before opening the heavy wooden door to John Bringer's office. As he walked in, he saw Bringer standing near the fireplace at the far end of the large room. Bringer seemed absorbed in thought as he gazed at the fire, looking up only after Krish had entered and walked halfway across the room toward him. Bringer smiled and walked toward him, and they came to a set of large leather chairs in the center of the room. Bringer gestured at one of the chairs. They shook hands and sat down together.

"Thank you for seeing me on short notice, senator."

"Still sounds strange coming from you, young man. As I've mentioned before, I've preferred you calling me Dr. Bringer."

Krish smiled. "As you wish, sir, though your ascension to senate majority leader did seem to warrant due respect. I was very happy to hear the news. It's been a long time coming, if you ask me."

"Well, now that I've managed to linger around a bit longer," Bringer said, and smiled as he leaned forward and extended his hand. "And before we discuss anything else, I don't think I ever thanked you for saving my life, Dr. Krish."

Krish's eyes softened as he slowly shook Bringer's hand. "Don't mention it, Dr. Bringer," he said at length. "I consider myself the fortunate one. And I have to say, I've become accustomed to you calling me Mr. Krish."

Bringer smiled and nodded and unexpectedly rose from his chair, as if too restless to sit in it, and walked slowly toward the window. Krish remained sitting as he watched. It had been more than a year, which was more than his life expectancy at the time, since one of the first Panacea protocols healed John Bringer. Krish observed his slightly hunched, slightly shuffled gait as he made his way to the window and stood looking out as if trying to see past something in the distance. He tried to straighten up and took a deep breath before speaking.

"The affliction took its toll on me nonetheless," Bringer said, "and age itself has caught up, I think. My father used to say no one wants to get old, and no one wants to die young, so where does that leave us? Then again, sometimes I wonder what's there to be scared about; growing old and dying happens to everyone, right?"

Krish smiled. "I suppose being old and sick is what people fear more so than death itself sometimes."

"And this new genetic engineering technology will certainly change the way we're born, the way we age, and the way we die," John Bringer said, and scrutinized Krish's countenance for a moment before continuing. "I happen to be very proud of you son. You did it, and it makes you a great man," Bringer said with a contemplative look. Arya Krish did a double take and looked over at him with wide-eyed curiosity.

"What makes you say that?" he said with a smile.

"Why not? It should be said, if not for what has been achieved by you, then for what else? I'm nowhere near as proud as your parents would've been, of course."

Krish looked down solemnly. "That is kind of you to say, sir; it's the nicest thing anyone has said to me, in fact. But I think if you knew everything I know, you'd be inclined to think differently."

"Nonsense," Bringer said, smiling. "First of all, I'm not as naïve or unaware as you imply. Don't get me wrong, I believe you when you say you know certain things, I get it. But we are in a moment of history, and you're at the lead of it. A brave new era, a brave new technology. You might be a man for the ages!"

Bringer paused and sat back, taking a deep breath.

Krish remained speechless for a moment. "I'm very proud as well, Dr. Bringer, of what we've done at Beacon," Krish said. "But to be perfectly honest, I can claim no individual credit for it. It can be a great moral achievement, I hope."

"Who said anything about moral achievement? This technology will be applied for the good, the bad, and the ugly, son. It is inevitable. That doesn't mean nothing can or should be done about it. Great moments require great leaders. You've broken away from the pack and separated yourself from the common man."

"What was deemed necessary along the way has left a heavy weight to carry around everywhere I go. I've made terrible mistakes along the way in the name of the greater good."

Bringer leaned forward with an amused look. "Ah, flawed and self-aware; what a fate for us!" He laughed briefly as he sat back. "Remember, human greatness is flawed because it is human. So don't be too hard on yourself."

Krish glanced broodingly at Bringer, then looked down silently. He couldn't help but feel that Bringer didn't know what he was talking about because he had never made those choices, the ones that made Krish re-live the moments with Steinhart and the moment outside the airport, where he committed the remote act that brought all the consequences except the cold revenge that went woefully unwrought. Bringer's remarks did seem naïve in that moment, but at the same time, there was sanctity in the man's wisdom for that very reason, the innocence rather than naïveté. It was in those tense moments in conversations lately that Krish felt as if everyone around him knew exactly what he had done. His eyes narrowed unknowingly as he observed Bringer suspiciously.

"And now, it would seem that we have been chosen for this moment," Bringer continued. "As we've talked about before, the government has already started scrutinizing this new technology and looking to administrate over it. That is, of course, why you're here, isn't it?"

"Yes, it is, sir. You've been such an ally and advocate, now I feel our roles are all the more demanding, and critical now. Beacon Medical Institute is the vanguard of this new industry, for the foreseeable future. It will remain a collaboration between government and the private sector."

"Well, as I said, we have been chosen for this moment one way or another, and I can't think it fortunate that you are at the helm over there at Beacon. Whatever trajectory this new age takes, how this will become a part of everyone's everyday life, beyond genetic engineering, it will be shaped by what happens now. And remember what I told you before—" he said, pausing to lock eyes with Krish, "—beware of entangled alliances. You may regard the government as an adversary, but you're certainly displaying at least the promise of collaboration."

"While I'm optimistic, I'm wary of the government encroaching. I don't intend to wind up some private sector contractor in a system the government exclusively controls. There'll have to be checks and balances. I've been battling government overreach for a long time, long before the merger and the Panacea technology."

"This new age will certainly require the kind of oversight and regulation you are wary of, though. But now it's different, isn't it? Our society as a whole will have to decide how genetic engineering is going to be used and how to prevent its abuse. And as we've talked about, the trajectory of this technology only expands the prospects of its utility and abuse."

"Believe me, sir, I gained plenty of insight on its trajectory from my dealings with DARPA. We obviously talked about the neural AI interface, now possible with this nanotechnology. This new age, as you put it, culminates in that, I think, the direct interface between the human brain and artificial intelligence and all the possibilities of expanding human conscience. I've written about this recently," Krish said and smiled.

"I know, I've been an enthusiastic reader of your op-eds," Bringer said, smiling back. "But where your insight remains limited, young man," he continued and slowly walked back toward Krish with a far-off thoughtful look, "is in the global geopolitical scale that this will take on, and your ambition will expand along with it, most certainly," he said and paused in front of a chair. "Take it from a man who's been in politics half his life," Bringer added before sitting down again.

Krish couldn't help shifting in his chair restlessly."Well, I try to be a student of history, sir. I've studied the ways that the government has participated, intervened, and administered such technological paradigm shifts. This new age, as you put it, will demand a new order to preside over it. And it is us in this moment who will shape the foundation and precedence." Krish paused and observed Bringer as he sat silently, and detected fatigue in Bringer's slightly squinted pale blue eyes.

"As I've said," Bringer said with a sigh. "I will serve as long as I am able. But I'm sure you've noticed I'm burning out. I think my time is limited, but in the meanwhile, you have a well-wisher and advocate, in this office."

Krish smiled gratefully without speaking. They sat quietly in a comfortable silence, retreating to their own thoughts for a moment, occasionally turning and gazing at the fireplace.

"When, as a scientist, you lose the sense of wonderment that drew you in, to begin with, you might close many doors to the knowledge and innovation you reach for. Similarly, in the field of politics and power, if you lose sight of why you're doing all this, you'll dissolve in the current," Bringer said. Krish looked over at him as if not knowing how to reply to that. "That first part was from my mentor a long time ago—about being a scientist," Bringer continued. "It came to mind for some reason, and I added the last part." He smiled in a self-amused manner as he leaned back and folded his hands across his chest.

"Your mentor, Dr. Arnold. Correct?"

Bringer nodded. "Poor man got chewed up and spit out by the corporate big leagues. He had all the same ambition and aptitude, Mr. Krish." His tone was suddenly serious. "He made enemies he didn't even know about and got swept aside. Alpha Corp, ironically."

"Dr. Arnold seemed to have avoided the tiresome labor of

fighting that current, maybe saving himself in doing so. He got out of the game and salvaged his own peace of mind, I would say."

Bringer nodded. "It is tiresome, isn't it? New enemies blindside you, and your alliances become all the more nefarious."

Krish was silent for a moment. "I am humble to the fact that I could use all the help I can get."

"You've approached it the right way, I think," Bringer said, "Remaining in the private sector but directly engaged with the government's power dynamic."

"Like you've been saying, sir, the government has invariably intervened. Apparently, I am to expect more summonses from the sub-committees; at least, that's the word on the Hill. I suppose I'm fortunate to have enough support not to be blindsided by it."

"Well keep in mind a lot of it is procedural, and I think you'll do fine, but yes, I've felt that pressure of being put on display and scrutinized. Everything you say and do will be picked apart. You absolutely should play into all your favoring advantages — your social popularity, philanthropic record, etc. It'll add to your trust and popularity if you represent yourself and your vision properly and tactfully. It's all part of the maneuvering strategy in this political chess match."

"It's a battlefield, and only the pawns are the knowers of the field," Krish said, and Bringer smiled as he observed the familiar fading look on Krish's face.

"A new order, we were saying, right?" Bringer said, bringing Krish out of his brief trance. "There is nothing more difficult to carry out, nor more doubtful of success, nor more dangerous to handle than to initiate a new order of things."

Krish nodded and smiled. "Machiavelli. *The Prince*." Bringer's eyes widened with his smile. "The reformer has enemies in all who profit from the old order, it goes on," Krish added, and they both leaned back, having drifted toward each other unknowingly as they spoke. They sat silently for a while before moving on to lighter matters like literature and current events. In the coming days, things quieted down, and Arya Krish felt more languid at Beacon, where he continued to spend most of his time. The new order, if there was such a thing, was slow going. The Panacea technology was in full bloom, and the prospects kept expanding as the new industry had already spread its horizons beyond the medical protocols that demonstrated the future of human-technology interaction. But any attempt to bask in the glory was abated by pangs of the affliction, the result of ruthless and hypocritical altruism, and continued to weigh Krish down. It occurred to him after the meeting with Bringer and lingered in his thoughts since. He needed to plug back in with his ultimate purpose, the ends that had to justify the means—the various humanitarian projects both domestic and abroad.

CHAPTER FOURTEEN

Arya Krish ran frantically, panting and trying desperately to gulp in as much air as he could with each breath. It was pitch dark all around him. He barely made out the light-colored frock the little girl in front of him wore as she ran farther and farther away. He turned his head back and looked behind him. He expected to see someone chasing him as well, but nothing was in the dark void. Krish was dimly aware of what was happening but continued to exert himself with all he could muster as he tried to catch up with what he presumed was a little girl running away from him or from something else. His face contorted into a strained grimace as he concentrated on lifting his legs up faster and taking longer strides. But the more he exerted himself, the heavier his legs became and the slower he ran. All the while, he watched the girl ahead of him as she became nothing more than an indiscernible blur in the distance.

Suddenly he stopped and stood still, only for an instant, before he inexplicably found himself driving alone in a car. The headlights barely illuminated enough of the winding road in front of him to anticipate the sharp turns. The shine of the metal guard rail in the headlights came too late. He slammed the break and jolted the wheel to the left as he tried to take the sudden hairpin turn. The car skidded out of control. He knew he was going over the edge, and as he had done in the past, he remembered the final encounter with Marcus Knight in that moment. He remembered Asher's expression behind the wheel as he tried to keep control. The car crashed through the railing and tumbled over into the abyss, and Krish felt himself go weightless. For what seemed like an eternity, the familiar falling sensation brought about a sudden serenity as he closed his eyes and waited for the inevitable.

Krish woke up with a soft gasp, and his wide-open eyes adjusted to the familiar surroundings of his bedroom. The powerful Indian sun was already bearing down, and its bright morning daylight partially came through the drawn curtains. He felt the breeze of the fan overhead as he gazed up at it and lay still for a moment as if waiting for the rest of his body to come to life. Slowly, he swung his heavy legs over the side and sat up, pushing himself up with his arms. He sat slumped over the side of the bed, his outstretched arms at his side and his back hunched over as if it supported a weary weight. It felt like a heavy cloak was draped over him. Eventually, the feeling passed, and he sluggishly rose to his feet. In a daze, he brushed his teeth. At one point, his concentration was focused as he leaned in and examined his face in the mirror. Later, he drank his coffee alone, in silence, and pondered the tasks of the day to come.

In the city, it was intolerable to have the window down because of the noise and traffic pollution. Krish stared blankly through the tinted glass in the quiet car until the bustling city roads gave way to open highways. Then Krish eagerly put the window down and enjoyed the warm breeze. After all, the whole intent was to relish the fruits of his labors and recharge with the limited time he had. Despite the unexpected events, he felt compelled to salvage something from this trip. The multi-lane highways faded into single-lane roads as they made their way into one of the outskirt towns. The children's campus was located just beyond that, a bit removed from the town itself, with a spattering of residential areas in between. This wasn't the itinerary at all. Krish's visit was planned for as much time as possible at his original and close-to-heart enterprise at one of the major children's institutes that started off as an orphanage. However, he could not help but resent the fact that most of the time had been spent muddling through the corrupt bureaucracy for its upkeep. Krish thought about it as he sat alone in his ancestral home and drank coffee. It was the upkeep of all the means employed to realize the goal, the ripple effects and residue of the perpetual interaction with the deplorable. The corruption and collateral damage had to continue to maintain what was attained. It was weary from skin to bone, but Krish seemed to quickly shake it off as he shifted in his seat and held his hand out the window, feeling the force of the warm wind. He was eager in anticipation of finally being able to take sanctuary in the shrine he had ultimately built and get a glimpse of the sanctity of humanity in the children there.

His thoughts were abraded by the shrill ring of his cell phone, which slightly startled him. Krish took his phone out and glanced at the screen before answering. Praveen did not wait for a hello on the other end of the line.

"Dr. Krish, how far are you?"

"A few hours still. We just got past the city. She hasn't returned yet, huh? The rest of her group? Mm-hm, and what about our security team? OK, call me if anything changes." The sprawling campus was located in rural country, next to a single main street small town and community that had benefitted from the increasingly expansive operation of the campus over time. Krish disconnected and looked down at the phone. He hadn't spoken to Praveen since last night. Apparently, the situation hadn't changed. Krish's eyes narrowed with concern over the sound of Praveen's voice.

His mind went back to early memories of the young girl who had run off during a field trip the previous day, as she had done before in the past. But now she'd been gone over 24 hours, and Krish recalled with melancholy the first encounter several years earlier. Her story was tragic from the beginning. By the time she was rescued and their paths crossed, she was already beyond reach. She never smiled, ever, as a result of having her spirit crushed so early. This was something Krish observed that haunted him from time to time. She was relatively older when she was rescued, and the damage was done. That never changed over the years, and now, in her early teens, she was more withdrawn, detached, and insubordinate, per Praveen's recent accounts. Krish couldn't help but feel the frustration mixed with resentment and guilt. In retrospect, Praveen's call the night prior seemed to underplay the grave situation. The adjacent small town was still developing, and the burden of responsibility over this runaway child had obviously hit Praveen and now Arya Krish. His mind was wracked by helpless concern, as he had no choice but to wait out the drive alone with the warm wind in his face.

As they passed through the small town near the campus, the intermittent burst of exhaust from the traffic forced Krish to close the window and observe the muffled scene through the tinted window. It struck him how much busier and more commercial the town had become already. The late afternoon sun started to descend behind the distant hills as Krish arrived at the administration building on the campus. He squinted as he looked in that direction when he got out of the car and looked around for any staff or children. A couple of groups were seen in the distance as he walked toward the building and entered. He took the stairs two at a time swiftly and walked in broad strides toward the large double doors down the hall and opened them without knocking. Inside the large office, Praveen abruptly stopped pacing and walked toward him as he entered.

"What's the latest?" Krish asked immediately as they shook hands in the middle of the room.

"The other two girls who were with her are back, Dr. Krish. Apparently, they had gone to a friend's place in town. Teenagers, we must deal with these sorts of things. Our security is usually plugged in. But Amaya went off on her own at some point.

"She's done this sort of thing before, even when she was

younger, I remember. But this is different, obviously. Something is wrong, Praveen. I get that they should have a semblance of normal life for that age under the circumstances, but I'm still shocked this happened. Where's the head of campus security? What's his name again?" Krish asked nervously.

"Mehta. He's out with the others. In town, actually."

"Get him on the phone."

Praveen quickly got his phone out and dialed. They stood silently and waited for an answer before Praveen eventually hung up. "Voicemail."

Krish shook his head and walked toward the window. He glanced out it for a moment before turning back to Praveen. "Go meet up with the others, Praveen. Call me when you get there. I want to check in with administration and the staff here on campus."

Praveen nodded and left. Krish visited various parts of the campus, which had largely retired for the day, given the ongoing situation. In retrospect, he would agonize over his attitude and spirit at that time before Praveen returned. Krish fretted in self-pity over the failed and ultimately futile effort to reconnect with something that he still perceived to be good and pure. But he found himself straining to become attune with that perceived sanctity if such a thing existed as he walked around alone as dusk settled. He checked his phone more frequently and tried calling Praveen without success. Again, he had mixed frustration as he recalled all that he had planned to see and do with his time. Now, he'd lost a chance of some sort of absolution and relief from his penitence. This was only amplified in that moment by the unexpected situation. It made his hands feel heavy while he paced restlessly after he returned to the admin building.

Later that evening, Arya Krish sat alone in a dull reverie as he looked out the window into the darkness. His back was turned to the door as Praveen entered. "Any news?" Krish asked without turning around.

Praveen didn't answer right away. He quickly wiped the sweat from his brow. "They found her, Dr. Krish. She's been taken to the hospital."

Krish swiveled around quickly in his chair and stood. "Hospital? Is she OK? What happened?"

"They found her half-conscious in an alley," Praveen said with a broken voice.

Arya Krish quickly walked over to him, breathing heavily. His nostrils flared, and his eyes were wide with concern. He noticed the tears streaming down Praveen's face. "What happened to her?" he asked again in a pressured manner as he restrained the panic.

"I don't have all the information, Dr. Krish," Praveen said nervously. "She was observed coming out of the house. Some good Samaritans followed her and ultimately came to her aid. They called the ambulance and the police."

Krish shook his head. "Wait, what house? Was she hurt? Praveen, I demand you tell me everything right now!"

Praveen looked down at the ground. He couldn't look Krish in the eye when he answered. "If the witnesses are right, the house belongs to one of the local landlords. I've heard of him in passing, mainly for his involvement in recent corruption scandals." Praveen paused and took a step back. "All I know about Amaya's condition is what the hospital told me. They weren't going to disclose anything, but I made it clear she was staying at the children's institute under our guardianship up to this point. I came to pick up documentation and records." He hesitated and could not look Krish in the eye. "They told me she was drugged and assaulted." Praveen could barely get the last part out and almost mumbled it under his breath as he wiped the tears away again.

If he said anything more, Krish didn't hear it. The only

thing he was acutely aware of was the hot, burning sensation that coursed through every capillary. It felt as if it would burst through every pore on his skin. He brought his shaking, clenched fists up near his face and tried to focus. As his mind still swarmed, he turned and headed out the door. Praveen hustled to keep up behind him.

"We're going there now," Krish said.

"To the hospital?"

"No, to the house."

"Dr. Krish, we notified the police already."

"We're going to the house now."

Arya Krish sat in the back of the car alone, almost pressed up against the door. He stared out the tinted window in silence, though he couldn't see much outside in the night.

As they pulled up to the house, it started to drizzle. It was nearly pitch dark, with no streetlight on the dirt road. The rain could only be seen in the single porch light.

Krish opened the car door himself without waiting for Praveen as soon as the car came to a stop. He walked slowly in a trance toward the front door. Krish paused in front of it for a moment and looked at the ground as the light rain pelted down. Then he straightened up and knocked loudly. Immediately, a commotion was in the house, and a grumbling, husky voice scolded the unknown, unwelcome visitor.

Krish listened intently as the voice grew louder. He was puzzled with anticipation, not knowing at that moment what he would do when the door opened. The light from inside beamed through the doorway as the voice opened the door. When they locked eyes, Krish took in the dull, angry, confused look on the voice's ugly face. In that instant, the bad blood within rushed forth to the surface with righteous rage that spanned back long before this encounter back to Steinhart, the A1 Group, and Krish's father. It was so visceral that he felt his body lunge forward almost unexpectedly as he violently shoved the thing back and quickly followed it in.

Praveen stood frozen near the car as he watched Krish enter the house.

Krish rushed the stumbling thing and shoved him again, knocking him down. Krish almost leapt as he climbed on top and swatted the thing's arms before he firmly grasped the throat with both hands. A punch landed firmly on Krish's lip, and in a stunned reflex, he lifted his left fist and pounded down on the ugly face repeatedly. He stopped only after the shooting pain from re-injuring his ring finger alerted him back to the throat. Krish fought and forgot the pain as his hands again squeezed down with all his might. He felt the cartilage rings of the windpipe crunch under the pressure of his hands. He closed his eyes and yelled out as he resisted recoiling from the startling sensation, a reflexive moment that reminded him of the sound his finger made when it broke. The enemy fought less and less now as its arms slowly sank to the floor. As if remembering to do so, Krish suddenly opened his eyes wide and locked eyes again with the enemy. From the glazed look, he recognized that life had started to leave.

Krish's mind had nearly left his own body as if it witnessed the whole thing from a corner on the ceiling. He didn't realize right away he was being pulled off, and turned his head slowly as if he was in a dream. He saw Praveen drag and pull him farther from the thing that lay on the floor. Krish did not resist. Ultimately, he brushed Praveen away and sat back against the far wall with his legs outstretched. He watched the thing writhe more and more as it slowly came back to life, as it grunted and gasped in recovery. Arya Krish watched with a petulant disdain and panted heavily himself as he gulped in as much air as he could with each breath. Praveen stood off to the side a little and stared at him intently.

Eventually, Krish slowly pulled himself up the wall and stood, but he still looked at the writhing one. He walked slowly toward the door, and as he passed Praveen, he paused. "Make sure they lock him up, prosecute him to the fullest extent, and give him the severest sentence. And keep him quiet. Pay whomever whatever is needed."

Praveen nodded quietly, and Krish stumbled out into the rain toward the car.

***

The sun was already up several hours later, but the window shades were drawn, and the hospital room was dark and still. Krish sat near the hospital bed and watched Amaya as she lay sedated and intubated. He had long since tuned out the beeping monitors, and though he hadn't slept in almost two days, his tired eyes hardly blinked and remained in a fixed gaze toward the bed. His mind drowned in a viscous pool of muddled thoughts and memories. He had sat there for several hours alone with the little girl, oblivious to his surroundings otherwise, and was only dimly aware of the door opening.

His wife entered quietly and stood by the door for a moment without saying anything. Arya Krish did not turn to look at her. Leela watched him as she walked over and initially went to hold him but changed her mind. She put her hand on his shoulder and stood quietly for a moment before she walked over to the hospital bed. She looked down at the little girl, glanced at the monitors, then slowly sat down in the other chair and scooted over next to Krish. She turned, looked at him, and waited for a moment to see if he would speak.

"Are you OK, Arya?" she asked softly with a quivering voice of concern.

Krish stared ahead and nodded distantly. He ran the tip of his tongue over his swollen and bruised lower lip.

"What did they say about her?"

"She's stable, sedated. They're giving her supportive care, mainly. She'll be OK, relatively."

"Praveen told me everything. What happened to you, Arya? How could you attack another person like that?"

"That—that *thing* was no person! That was a monster! Look what he did. A *rakshasa* does this, a demon, not any normal person."

"Arya, you almost killed a man!"

"Yeah. I failed this time."

"This time? What, you're gonna try again at some point?"

Krish buried his face in his hands and shook his head in despair. Leela remained silent and waited.

"I don't feel like a killer," Krish said languidly, almost in disbelief. Leela looked at him curiously. It felt like the most sincere thing he'd said in recent memory. He had murdered a man—it seemed so long ago—but what that forged him into was left unquenched by the distant and cowardly means by which it was done. He'd had no visceral component, no look in the eye, to consummate the choice and action. Last night, the vitriolic surge of the accumulated bad blood compelled him to attack that monster in a desperate attempt to fill that void. But it remained unchanged, and he was again left neither here nor there. It was a maddening state of limbo where he felt trapped. When he finally turned and made eye contact with Leela, his countenance melted into an exhausted, despaired look. She slowly moved closer to Krish until their shoulders touched, then leaned in, pressed her face against his, and put her arm around him.

Hot tears poured out of his eyes as Krish stared blankly. In that moment, he made the decision and told her everything—his father and the A1 Group, the encounter with Marcus Knight on the ravine road, the murder of Vladimir Steinhart, the pacemaker device, everything. In the end, he fell silent and slumped in his chair when she finally spoke.

"Arya," she said softly, "you achieved so much these last few years. It's truly extraordinary, and it has catapulted you into a realm never anticipated. The way you have helped countless people with such selfless dedication, by whatever means, it seems to have isolated you somehow, and you've become truly lost. If what you do is in the name of an ultimate good, and you really consider yourself an agent for it and nothing more, then you have only the duty not to betray it. You are not entitled to the fruits of your actions, which belong to your cause. You remain detached from it all. The ends do not justify the means. You betray your own vision and ideal in that way. That's where you became lost, particularly to those nearest to you. From the outside looking in, to the rest of us, to me, who knows you best and loves you most — a large part of you now seems out of reach."

She spoke slowly, almost in a whisper, with a soothing cadence, and to Arya Krish, it was entrancing. The sound of her voice echoed in his mind and resonated in every bone in his body. Her words washed over him like a healing salve and dissipated, for the moment, the bad blood that was cold and heavy inside, like stone. He felt the weight of it ease off his hands, which dangled like medicine balls at his sides, and the muscles in his neck and face relaxed. His gaze remained transfixed on the girl in the hospital bed, and in the background, the monitors and ventilator droned monotonously as Leela continued to soothe and counsel him. Tired and bloodshot eyes shot a glance in her direction, though he couldn't see her with their faces pressed together, and he slipped deeper into his lonely, punitive despair. He took a deep breath and let out a cathartic sigh as her voice came through again.

"If you're going to find your way back," she said, "you'll have to navigate the same field that led you here, the valleys and mountains of your mind, the twists and turns of the choices you've made, and the things you've done. Be the knower of that field, Arya, and come back to us for your sake and for mine. For us and Seena." She was silent as she kissed him on the side of the forehead, stroked his hair, then sat back. She wiped Krish's tears off her face. "We're at least as important as the rest of the world you're willing to sacrifice yourself for," she said. She smiled softly with her lips and her round, dark eyes. Arya Krish remained expressionless, exhausted of all emotion, as the two of them sat quietly with the young girl for a while.

The days that followed were a foggy and dull daze as all planned activities came to a screeching halt. Krish languished during the rest of his stay. On the day he left, Krish took his time, alone in his large room, and savored the private moment with quiet thoughts as he paused while packing the last box. Praveen stood at the doorway on the other end of the large home office with the rest of the luggage and waited. Leela and Seena were already downstairs.

"Remember how we were before we got too big?" Krish asked. He broke the silence with a sad, searching look.

"Too big, Dr. Krish?"

"Yeah, too big for our own good, you know? All we've done to get this big. The fangs and claws we've had to grow. You know what I'm talking about, Praveen? You remember that conversation, right?" A soft desperation was in Krish's voice.

"Yes, Dr. Krish. I remember." Praveen nodded solemnly.

Krish seemed relieved to hear it. "We became monsters, and now the fatigue from swinging those fangs and claws at others for so long has turned them from weapons to just vestigial burdens we must continue to bear. Dead weight."

Praveen sighed and didn't answer right away.

Krish stood silently and looked down at the last item in his hand. "Maybe we should stop," Krish said. It seemed he was talking more to himself. Praveen remained silent and listened. "Renounce it all. Leave it to others to carry forward and surrender ourselves to answer for our crimes."

"I've often heard you say you are a man of action, Dr. Krish. A life of renunciation would not seem to suit you. I do not think that is your nature. Look at what you've accomplished and all the people you've affected. Who else belongs in this position? Everything you've created, it becomes a part of you. Something you are obliged to safeguard."

"Be a steward of it all, you mean?" Krish asked. He recalled his conversation with John Bringer and scoffed. "I'm past that, Praveen. I'm the monster outside the sanctum." Krish glanced at the picture of his parents in the photo frame he held before finally putting it in the box. "But nonetheless, like I was saying, I think back and try to remember how we were. Like the VC Farm days. Remember those times? Can't believe it's been so many years. Remember how we were back then, Praveen?" Krish picked up the box and looked at Praveen, waiting for him to answer.

Praveen nodded and smiled distantly as if lost in the recollection for a moment. "That was a long time ago, Dr. Krish. A lot has happened to us since then."

Krish nodded slowly and walked toward the door. Praveen came into the hallway and let him pass, then took the box from him.

"I think that's the last of it, Praveen. Our journey is about to begin," Krish said as they stood in the hallway and looked back inside the room. He turned to Praveen with a thoughtful look. "You know what happens when you get too big for your own good?"

"I think I understand the expression, Dr. Krish. But I am not sure what happens."

"You can't lose the weight you used to throw around to accomplish what you wanted. It wears you out, and eventually, your knees buckle. You know what I mean?"

"Yes, Dr. Krish. I wish that you will find some peace on

this journey at least and come back restored. Enjoy your time with your family, Dr. Krish, and Godspeed your safe trip and return home."

"Thank you, Praveen. I'm grateful for everything you've done. Be well until we meet again."

***

When he arrived at the campsite, it was already dark. Only the silhouettes of the surrounding foothills could be seen, while the mountains in the background were hidden in the night. Even though he was there in his youth and knew what to expect, the next morning, when the distant memory of the scenery came alive again before his eyes when he poked his head out of the large tent, he stood frozen and was instantly awestruck at the sight. The large round foothills surrounding him were flush and green. The camp was already at several thousand feet in elevation, but the surrounding hills were dwarfed by the majestic Himalayan mountains that towered massively above them in the background, seemingly merging with the sky, passing the thin, flat clouds that moved swiftly. He saw his breath in the crisp morning air, and at that moment, the sun's warmth on his face was rejuvenating.

Arya Krish peered down out his open window at the back bus tires as they hung half off the precarious winding mountainside road that led to the temple plateau, many thousands of feet up the massive mountain face. It was enough to make anyone religious in that moment. The hairpin turns were frequent and haphazard, with fallen vehicles as menacing reminders of the real danger of the pilgrimage. Beside the mountain was another massive mountain, followed by another, and the clouds they pierced hung low overhead.

After they finally reached the temple summit, Krish didn't join his wife and son when they went through the entrance into the inner sanctum. As they approached, something made him pause while he listened to the silver sound of rhythmic chanting that came from within. He signaled them to go ahead and walked off to the side and stood by the temple wall. He reached out, touched the stone, and ran his hand over the cold, smooth surface. Krish walked away and stood off to the side, in a spot where no one else was nearby. He looked up at the large dark stone that shimmered in the bright sunshine and the pale, thin, blue sky that gave way to the snow-capped mountain peaks in the background. It surrounded and embraced him. He took a deep breath and felt the cold, pure air in his chest. His neck muscles relaxed, his head felt lighter on his shoulders, and his senses were attuned to the natural beauty. The mind became quiet, and he let thoughts pass, slowly directing them toward that complete calm he had almost caught a glimpse of in past meditations — less than a glimpse, a flash in the pan, a flicker of a moment, where the melding of the conscience with the senses and surroundings almost reveals a vague notion of oneness.

While he tried to relax, he strained to direct his thoughts in that direction. It felt like the harder he exerted himself, the more difficult it became, as if he was in some bad dream. It was because, all the while, the incurable bad blood within was as viscous and turbid as ever with karma, like old motor oil. Again, he felt the burden of sharp pangs in his mind — and neck, arms, chest, legs — from the affliction that disallowed him from completely immersing in the unity he sought desperately in that moment. It resonated in his bones and brought a new clarity in his mind, different than what he was reaching for.

In that meditation, he imagined a field of dandelions. The vision was like a dream coming to life before his eyes, which stared far past the temple, mountains, and sky in front of them. In his mind, his outstretched arm strained to grasp a dandelion that was just beyond reach. His face was contorted and desperate. Suddenly, everything relaxed, and the tension slowly ebbed back, which allowed a new calmness to rise like the tide as he came back to his surroundings. Now, he knew his place in the field and what was out of reach. He accepted it once and for all. Every muscle in his body relaxed, and he continued to take slow, deep breaths. The monster would remain outside the gates, serving the sanctity of humanity, unequivocally irredeemable yet unrelentingly seeking atonement. He might be exiled from the inner sanctum, but he could still achieve greatness as a dutiful and loving husband, father, and friend. That was still within his reach.

And, of course, he would remain a man of action, operating in a vast field of possibilities and consequences. After all, we are the sum of our choices. It is the process of being and becoming. The sound of his wife and son talking and laughing came through and replaced everything. When he turned his head, he saw them emerge from the inner sanctum. Arya Krish ran toward them, a newly woken knower of the field!

Phalgun Prativadi grew up in Maryland outside Washington, D.C. He went to college at Penn State and lived up and down the East Coast in young adulthood during medical training. For over ten years, he lived in the Pittsburgh, PA area with his wife and 2 kids, working as an infectious diseases physician.